MIDNIGHT MADNESS

Jem January was the last person Claudia expected to encounter in the dead of night in the library of Ravencroft. Yet there he was—and there she was, alone in the night with him.

Facing him, she met his gaze. She found herself caught, helpless as a rabbit pinned beneath a predator, staring into eyes that held all the brightness and all the mesmerizing promise of morning starlight.

Slowly Jem lifted his hand to where her hair met her cheek. She was appalled at the shudder of response that shot through her at his touch, but she seemed incapable of withdrawing from him. His head bent to hers until his lips rested on her mouth with a softness that was at first tentative, but which flamed immediately into urgency.

What was happening was unthinkable, her melting in the arms of a man who was a lowly servant . . . as unthinkable as it was undeniable . . . as unthinkable as it was irresistible. . . .

Lord Glenraven's Return

Lord Glenraven's Return

by

Anne Barbour

A SIGNET BOOK

SIGNET
Published by the Penguin Group
Penguin Books USA Inc., 375 Hudson Street,
New York, New York 10014, U.S.A.
Penguin Books Ltd, 27 Wrights Lane,
London W8 5TZ, England
Penguin Books Australia Ltd, Ringwood,
Victoria, Australia
Penguin Books Canada Ltd, 10 Alcorn Avenue,
Toronto, Ontario, Canada M4V 3B2
Penguin Books (N.Z.) Ltd, 182–190 Wairau Road,
Auckland 10, New Zealand

Penguin Books Ltd, Registered Offices:
Harmondsworth, Middlesex, England

First published by Signet,
an imprint of Dutton Signet,
a division of Penguin Books USA Inc.

First Printing, June, 1994
10 9 8 7 6 5 4 3 2 1

Printed in the United States of America

To the Black Hills Writers Group,
a talented, witty, intelligent and
all-around terrific bunch of folks

Chapter One

"If it's true that troubles come in threes then I have almost filled my quota for the week." Claudia Carstairs contemplated the tranquil scene outside the window in gloomy silence. It was early morning, her favorite time of day, and the sun cast dappled, summer shapes over the shaggy lawn that stretched down to a glittering patch of ornamental water. She found herself, however, utterly incapable of appreciating the pastoral beauty of the scene.

She turned away and, drawing a pair of ancient breeches and an equally shabby shirt and coat from the wardrobe near her bed, began dressing. Mentally, she counted her difficulties on her fingers. Jenny should have foaled by now and was showing signs that it would be a difficult birth. Squire Foster had given notice that he would no longer abide by the agreement reached many months ago between them on grazing land for her sheep. And now there was word of a stranger in the village asking questions about Ravencroft and its dead master.

She shivered at the thought, and paused with one boot in her hand. A stranger. It could be nothing at all, of course. Little Marshdean was not so out of the way that transients did not occasionally drift through on their way to Gloucester or even Wales. But this one had been about for two days now—and why was he asking about Emanuel?

She remained thoughtful as she finished dressing, then shrugged. There was nothing she could do about it, she told herself briskly. She ran a comb through her tangled, taffy-colored hair and caught it up tightly with a ribbon before pulling on a large, nondescript cap. From force of habit, she cast a glance in the mirror before she left the room, and this caused her to sigh again. "Good Lord," she murmured in exasperation, her light brown eyes narrowing. "Just look at yourself." It was not at her appearance at which she caviled. It was her height. She was small—a dab of a woman, she called herself—and it seemed as though man's clothing—her work clothes—made her seem shorter and much less prepossessing than she would have liked. She shrugged again. There was nothing she could do about that, either.

Claudia strode through the stillness of the great house and, as so often happened nowadays, an unexpected sense of elation surged through her. She was free! She was skirting the edge of financial disaster, but she was no longer the wife of Emanuel Carstairs. She had survived him, and would never have to endure the touch of a man again, nor would she ever again have to endure a man's domination and repression. Best of all, Ravencroft was hers!

At least, she smiled ruefully, as long as she could keep it out of the hands of her creditors—and her brother-in-law. At this thought, the smile fell from her lips. She had almost forgotten. Only four more days before Thomas and Rose would descend on her. Good heavens, it looked as though her troubles were coming in fours this week.

She tiptoed down the length of the corridor, having no desire to encounter her Aunt Augusta at this hour of the morning. She loved Aunt Gussie dearly, but she had no time for the lecture that would surely ensue on the extreme undesirability of young ladies "prancing about in front of the world in male clothing." She reached the kitchen and sniffed at the savory odor of fresh coffee and baking bread.

"Mmm, that smells marvelous, Mrs. Skinner," she said to the gray-haired woman standing near the stove who stopped what she was doing and brought a steaming cup to the table.

"I hope you're goin' t' sit down for a proper breakfast, Miz Claudia," said the woman. "It won't take a minute to fry some eggs, and the ham's all sliced."

Claudia embraced the woman's small, plump form.

"No time this morning, but I will have some of that bread." Reaching for a knife, she sliced a generous chunk and liberally applied butter and jam. She took a few sips of coffee. Then, still munching, she waved jauntily to the disapproving woman and headed for the stables.

She reached the yard just as Jonah Gibbs, her head stable man was leading Jenny from her stall. He touched the brim of his cap.

"Morning, ma'am." He gestured balefully at the mare. "Looks t'me as though she might be thinkin' about bringin' down her foal today. She's started spillin' her milk."

Claudia glanced at Jenny's dripping teats and then looked with fondness on the grizzled old horseman. He was her mainstay and her rock. What small success she had achieved as a breeder of horses could not have been accomplished without his advice and counsel. He was a crotchety old devil, she reflected amusedly, but he had been at Ravencroft all his life and his affection for her and for the estate was as abiding as the ancient Cotswold hills surrounding them.

"It's about time," she said, stroking the mare's nose. "Do you think there will be trouble?"

"Aye, she ain't let down one yet that she didn't fratch about. Thought she'd never take. The other colts was born months ago, and here she is, dropping hers in July. Silly daft beast," he said to the mare, who thrust her nose affectionately into his shirt front.

"With Warlock as the sire," Claudia replied, "the baby will probably be huge. And black as night," she added thinking of the raven's wing sheen of her prize stallion's coat. She uttered a silent prayer, for the long awaited colt, sired by their one and only stallion and dammed by their most promising mare, was expected to grow into the hope of the stable.

Jonah walked the mare up and down the yard, accommodating himself to the plodding motion of her heavy body and carefully inspecting her for further signs of incipient labor, and after watching for a moment, Claudia turned for a cursory glance at the stable yard. As always, the sight brought a flutter of pleasure. Ravencroft might yet be a small horse-breeding operation, but its stables, she was sure, could match the finest in England. They had been built in the time of what Claudia had come to think of as "the other family," the Standishes of Ravencroft, headed since the time of the eighth Henry Tudor by generations of Lords Glenraven. Until, that is, their home had been acquired by Emanuel Carstairs.

The buildings were finely crafted of brick and the same

Portland stone of which the main house was built. They were made to last, though they had been sadly neglected during the years of Emanuel's tenure, and the yard had been reduced to an unkempt clutter of household refuse. During the year since her husband's death, however, she and Jonah and Lucas, the young man whom she laughingly called her staff, had restored it to its former air of solid prosperity.

Claudia made her way to one of the stables. She paused for one last, appreciative glance at the morning, shimmering in warm radiance about her, before entering the building's dark interior. After making her rounds, assuring herself that the occupant of each stall had survived the night in good case, she reached for a pitchfork to begin the daily mucking-out chore.

She had been engaged in this, her least favorite activity of the day, for some minutes when she suddenly became aware that she was no longer alone. Whirling, she observed a man standing just inside the doorway, leaning against the jamb and appearing very much at his ease.

Without understanding how, she knew instantly that this was the stranger described to her by Lucas. "Hangin' around the Three Feathers, he was, like he hadn't another blessed thing t' do in the world except lounge about in the middle of the day soakin' up a pint o' heavy wet."

She stared assessingly at the stranger, taking in the dark coat and breeches fashioned of some cheap material. He was tall, and his slender form was silhouetted against the daylight. His hair was dark—black as Warlock's silky mane, Claudia thought irrelevantly. But his eyes were a surprising light gray. They seemed to blaze in the dimness of the stable.

"Who are ye, and what d' ye want?" she asked briskly, speaking deliberately in a rough country accent. She was not afraid of this man, of course. Jonah was right outside, and Lucas was probably about somewhere by now as well. Still, he made her uneasy, creeping up on her like a jungle predator.

He moved toward her with a casual grace that Claudia found unsettling.

"Excuse me, lad," he said in a tone of quiet authority at odd variance with the shabbiness of his dress. "I'm looking for the stable master." The smile that spread across his angular features added a surprising warmth to what was otherwise a rather forbidding countenance. He was younger than she had originally surmised—probably in his early twenties.

The stranger stopped abruptly, gazing at her in some surprise.

"I'm sorry." He spoke in the familiar soft accents of the Cotswold. He was from the area then? Not a transient? "I should have said—lass?"

"That's right," she replied, a certain belligerence in her tone. She had more than once been the recipient of unpleasant, if not overtly contemptuous familiarity from men beholding her in her work clothes. Not that her breeches and shirt could be called immodest, for they were shapeless and baggy and enveloping. It was just a peculiarity in the male nature, Claudia considered, that led them to believe a woman in man's clothes was ripe for any sort of coarse advance.

However, nothing beyond an expression of polite inquiry showed on the stranger's face.

"What d' ye want with the stable master, then?" Claudia asked, pitchfork still in hand.

"I'm lookin' fer work, miss. I was told in the village that the owner of this place raises horses. I've worked with horses before, and mayhap I could be of use here."

She gazed at him for a moment with narrowed eyes. He had been asking questions about Ravencroft, and now he was here asking for a position? Who was this man, and where was he from? And most important of all, what was he doing here? True, he did not look threatening, but to Claudia there seemed a tension about him, a look of coiled steel in that slender frame, now leaning negligently against a stall door. She watched as he turned to stroke the nose of the stall's occupant with long, gentle fingers.

"What's your name?" Claudia asked sharply, forgetting to maintain her country speech.

"Jem," replied the stranger, his brows lifting. "Jem January. Now, lass," he continued, "it's been pleasant talkin' with you, but would you please direct me to the stable master?"

Claudia read in his tone a certain disdain. Probably, she thought in rising indignation, he considered her a daughter of the soil, so unattractive that she had been unable to find a husband and was thus fit only for mucking out the stables, smelling of horse and garbed in disreputable clothing.

Jem January thought nothing of the sort. He had first thought her a stable lad, but his view had changed rapidly as he took note of the curve beneath the shirt of thick homespun and the musical voice that spoke to him so unpleasantly. His always lively curiosity was immediately captured, and when the malodorous apparition began to speak in the cultured accents of a gently bred female, it was further piqued.

Hc would have liked to have probed the little mystery further, but he had not, he reflected, come all this way to be sidetracked. He must gain access to Ravencroft, and since the current owner of the place was, from the reports he had gleaned in the village, attempting to revive the reputation of the estate as a source of prime horseflesh, a job in the stables seemed the best bet. Why, he wondered impatiently, was the wench so reluctant to let him see the man in charge?

"I doubt," she said, flushing, "that . . . "

She stopped abruptly, and Jem followed her gaze to discover the appearance in the doorway of a stooped old man. Behind him trooped a younger man, stalwart of build and pugnacious of expression.

"What is it, ma'am?" asked the older man. "We heard voices. Is everything all right?"

Ma'am? thought Jem. What was going on here?

"Yes, Jonah, everything is fine. This—young man has come looking for work."

Jonah! Jem looked closely at the face beneath the shock of white hair. Good God, it *was* Jonah. Jonah Gibbs! Lord, he hadn't reckoned on there being someone about the place who had been here before . . . Well, he'd just have to hope that the old man would not recognize him. After all, it had been twelve years. He smiled benignly into the seamed face.

Jonah snorted. "Lookin' for work, is he? And what will we pay him with, good wishes?" He turned to Jem and would have said more, but he halted abruptly and peered questioningly into the stranger's face. Before he could say more, the young man behind him stepped forward.

"That's him, Miz Carstairs. That's the feller I was tellin' you about—snoopin' in the village—about Ravencroft."

Mrs. Carstairs! Jem's brows lifted again in silent surprise. He seemed to be coming in for one shock after another this morning. Was this really the widow of Emanuel Carstairs? He had somehow expected someone more—well, more prepossessing. He turned a guileless gaze on her.

"Snooping?" he asked, his face a study in unsullied innocence. "Why, I suppose you could say I was. I'm pretty desperate for work, mum. As for—Ravencroft, is it? I figured I'd best discover which place would be the most likely in need of a good man, and this here's where I was directed." He removed his cap and stood holding it with both hands. "Are you Mrs. Carstairs, then? The lady what owns the place?"

His air of submissive respect seemed to Claudia wholly spurious, and she bestowed on him what she hoped was a regal nod, wishing she did not look so awful—or smell quite so bad. "Yes, I am," she replied. "And Jonah is right, I'm afraid. We are not hiring just now."

Jem's eyes grew wide. "But a lady like you—mucking out the stables. It ain't fit, mum. You need another hand, sure."

"That may be." Claudia spoke harshly. "However, we maintain a very small operation here, and to be very frank, young man, we cannot afford to hire any more help—at the moment."

"I'd work for board and a place to sleep, mum." Jem allowed a hint of desperation to creep into his voice. "And I could double as a footman, or valet—or even a butler."

Claudia had begun to turn away, but at these words, she spun about again.

"Butler?" She stared at him dubiously. "You don't look like a butler."

As she looked, a startling transformation came over the stranger. He drew himself up as though someone had thrust a poker up the back of his coat, and he swept his disordered hair into a semblance of smoothness. Making a bow that nicely combined a certain degree of subservience with the disdainful arrogance of a gentleman's servant, he spoke in accents utterly unlike those Claudia had just heard him use.

"Quite so, madam. However, it has been my experience that looks can be deceiving."

"Apparently so," Claudia said with some asperity. She chewed her lip and glanced at Jonah.

"Thomas and Rose will be here in a few days, and I have done nothing about a replacement for Morgan. Aunt Gussie is becoming most agitated."

Morgan. Jem wrinkled his forehead at the sound of the name. What had happened to Morgan? Passed away? He had been getting on in years when Jem had seen him last. He shook himself slightly and listened to Mrs. Carstairs's next words.

"Thomas will be highly affronted if he is greeted at the door by one of the maids. We don't even have anyone who can stand in as a footman."

"I'm your man, then," interposed Jem bestowing on her the most charming smile at his disposal. He became the immediate target of three suspicious pairs of eyes. The young widow stood for several moments in frowning abstraction.

Claudia did not trust this personable stranger any farther than she could throw the horse that stood behind him in its stall. Despite his air of candor, he had been asking questions. On the other hand, perhaps it would be better to keep him nearby, where she could monitor his curiosity.

"If you are indeed willing to work for board and a place to sleep, we will take you on. Jonah will show you where you will stay." She handed him her pitchfork. "After you've finished here, Jonah will give you additional duties."

Jem knew a tinge of disappointment and some apprehension. He hoped he would not be called on to perform any tasks calling for any actual knowledge of horsemanship. For, despite his claim to expertise, he doubted that the position he had held for a few weeks several years ago as sweeping boy in a livery stable would qualify him for anything more complicated than wielding that pitchfork or carrying water. Well, he would just have to trust in Providence to wangle him into the butler's job. Too bad about Morgan—although it wouldn't have done, he supposed, to have yet another old retainer about the place to recognize him.

The rest of the day passed uneventfully. Changing into the only other pair of breeches he had brought with him, and donning a shirt donated by young Lucas, who still hovered suspiciously, Jem wielded his pitchfork to good effect. After that, he carried water and distributed feed. His other chores proved no more difficult than currying and brushing and oiling leather. He began to think that he might be able to carry off his little charade without incident, after all.

His composure nearly deserted him, however, when he entered the tack room for the first time. Dear God, it was as though he had stepped out of it only yesterday. There, in one corner was the big, scarred desk used for the business of the stable operation. Next to it were the cabinets, dark with age, where generations of records had been kept. Against another wall, row upon row of ribbons and trophies rested in glass cases, and even—yes! There was the sketch he had made of Trusty, his first pony. It had been framed, and still hung between the portraits of two of the stable's most notable mares.

An unfamiliar pricking sensation stung between his eyes, and he gripped the back of a chair. A sound behind him made him whirl.

"Are ye in need of rest already, then, Mr. January?" asked Jonah in a caustic voice. He did not wait for a reply, but continued brusquely. "Ye'll find the gear that needs mendin' in the next room."

Wordlessly, Jem turned and fled from the little chamber.

He knew another bad moment when the supper hour approached. As he followed Jonah and Lucas into the main house, past the kitchen, he was again almost overwhelmed with memory. True, he had not spent much time in the nether regions of Ravencroft, but visions of gingerbread eaten in the warmth of a bustling kitchen rose up before him. Just there, he had sat nursing a scraped knee one December afternoon, while Cook plied him with salve and damson tarts.

Supper was taken in the lower-servants' hall, and Jem sat quietly, absorbing the chatter that flowed about him. It was apparent that the house was understaffed, too. He wondered how many tenants worked the fields. From what he'd heard in the village, the widow Carstairs kept sheep, though not nearly as large a flock as had roamed the Ravencroft pastures in years past.

At least she set a good table, he reflected appreciatively as he swallowed a succulent morsel of chicken, and she didn't skimp on the under servants. She seemed to be well-liked among her staff. He heard only fondness in the voices that spoke her name. He found his thoughts dwelling on the diminutive figure in outsize shirt and breeches. How in God's name had she come to marry Carstairs? he wondered. It had been hard to tell what she looked like with that equally oversized hat pulled about her ears, but she seemed a decent enough sort.

He shook himself. He did not want to think about the possible decency of Mrs. Emanuel Carstairs. One of his purposes in coming to Ravencroft had been for revenge. He had thirsted so badly for it for so long. He recalled his unbelieving rage when he discovered that the new owner of Ravencroft had been in the earth for nearly a year. He relaxed the fists that had clenched involuntarily. Retribution may have been denied him, but he would still accomplish his other goal. And when he had, the young widow would have to find somebody else's stables to muck out.

Slightly ashamed of his rancor, he finished his meal and hurried out to the stable to take care of the first of the evening chores allotted to him by Jonah.

It was some hours later when he was dismissed. After washing up at the pump in one corner of the stable yard, he strolled around to the front of the house and for many minutes simply stared at the facade of weathered, local stone, glowing in the late afternoon sun. It was a beautiful old manor, he thought affectionately, looking rather as if it had grown from the gently rolling landscape of the Cotswolds. The original building had formed a modest square, but subsequent generations, rejoicing in a fairly consistent prosperity, had added to the structure. Now a long, curving pair of wings embraced a sweeping drive and behind them, unseen, were other enlargements and additions. How was the widow managing to keep it all up, he wondered, turning to cast a sweeping glance about the now unkempt lawns surrounding him. It seemed to him that every tree, every shrub, and every crevice of the place held a special memory for him.

Soon, now, he thought exultantly. Soon . . .

He returned to the stable yard, and in the gathering darkness he perched on a railing in front of one of the buildings. He breathed in the scents of summer. *I am home*. The words formed themselves contentedly in his mind.

He became aware of Jonah's rangy form approaching, and made leaning room on the rail for the old man.

"Ye done pretty good t'day, laddy," Jonah said grudgingly. "Fer somebody new t' the job, that is." He stared off into the distance for several minutes, chewing ruminatively on a straw. Without looking at Jem, he continued. "And how does it feel t' be back home, Lord Glenraven?"

Chapter Two

Jem swiveled to face Jonah, his face a mask of blank surprise. "I beg your pardon?"

Jonah answered with a derisive bark of laughter. "Nay, don't be playing off yer tricks on me, me lord. I suspicioned it was you when I first clapped eyes on ye this morning. An' it weren't long before I was sure."

Jem studied the old man for a long moment before replying. "What was it that gave me away?" he asked finally.

"Oh, ye have the family look about ye. And there's the way ye carries yerself. Y' always did act more the lord than the lord hisself. Then, when I told you to fetch a new harness, you knew right where to go without bein' told."

Jem grinned sheepishly. "I should have known better than to try to fool you, you crafty old devil."

The creases in Jonah's face deepened. "Aye," he chuckled.

Jem's expression grew serious. "Can I trust you to keep my secret—for a little while?"

Jonah's smile faded. "That depends. I don't like the idea of keeping secrets from Miz Carstairs. Have you come to cause her hurt?" he asked suddenly.

"No!" exclaimed Jem. "Of course not. Well—at any rate . . . "

Jonah grunted. "If it ain't too much t' ask, just why have you come back? T' make trouble?"

Jem studied the old man, wondering how much to tell him. If he confided in Jonah, and Jonah went right to Mrs. Carstairs, to whom the stable man evidently felt he owed some allegiance, everything would be ruined. On the other hand, an ally somewhere on the estate would be of great help to him—someone who was familiar with the workings of the house under its new management. He knew Jonah to be an honest man who had always been devoted to the master and the master's family in the old days.

He drew a deep breath. "Jonah, how much do you know of what happened—when Father . . . ?"

"The day the old lord died and the place fell to Emanuel Carstairs was the blackest day ever t' befall Ravencroft and them whose lives are bound here." Jonah's expression was bitter. "Meanin' no disrespect, but none of us could ever understand how yer pa could have let it happen."

"But you seem to favor Carstairs's widow."

"Ah, there's another story. Word was she was well-nigh forced t' marry the old bastid. Her pa owed Carstairs money —just like your pa did—and bein' the randy old goat he was, he'd had his eye on Miss Claudia for a while. He always liked the pretty 'uns."

Jem shot him a startled glance. The pretty 'uns? A vision flitted through his mind of a shapeless figure, swathed in an unattractive assortment of rank male garments.

"I give 'er this, though," Jonah continued. "She didn't put up with much from 'im."

"Oh? Under the circumstances you've described, I would have thought her completely under his thumb."

Jonah's rough cackle sounded softly in the night. "Aye, that's what ye'd think, but the missus ain't one fer stayin' under anybody's thumb fer long. Oh, he tried his tricks with her, just like he done with his two wives afore her. Yup," he said in response to Jem's look of startled inquiry "Two. He took a wife within two weeks of his comin' to Ravencroft. She died a year later, and he took another within six months. She lasted a little longer—hung on for three years."

"How did they . . . "

"Oh, there was talk, of course. It's my belief Carstairs killed 'em both," he said baldly. "Oh, not apurpose, exactly—but I saw him hit Mrs. Julia, his first wife. Well, he hit her lots of times, but this one day—they was right out here in the stable yard. She was a little thing, and I guess she done somethin' t' rile him. Anyway, he lashed out at her with his fist, and she went down like a felled sapling. Hit her head on the corner of that water trough."

"My God," breathed Jem. "And there was no one by to help her?"

Jonah uttered a short, mirthless laugh. "There wan't anybody who could do that, don't ye know. It'd be worth a man's livelihood—and mebbe his life—to have stepped in. After a few minutes, she got up of herself and she seemed all right, but about a week later she took to her bed. Doctor called it a brain fever, and not three days after that, she died. I've always thought—well, I guess it don't matter what I thought."

"And his second wife?" Jem whispered the words.

"She ran out o' the house one night. He'd been at her, we heard. Her maid said you could hear the blows land. It was a cold night, and pourin' rain. She ran and ran. Carstairs went after her with some of the house servants, and it was hours before they found her, soaked and shiverin' in the churchyard. She went into an inflammation of the lungs, and was cold in the earth inside of a week."

"I knew the man was a monster." Jem's voice was choked. "But it appears I didn't know the half. To look at him, you'd never know what evil lurked below the surface."

"Yup," replied Jonah musingly. "Big feller, he was, bluff and hearty." Jem nodded, remembering. "always had a laugh and a clap on the back for them he considered important. The neighborhood nobs thought he was grand—they never saw the kicks and the curses for them that served him."

"But," continued Jem, "you say he was different with the present Mrs. Carstairs?"

"Aye. Oh, he started off just like with the others. I understand he thrashed her bloody one night. But," Jonah scratched his grizzled pate. "It never happened again. I dunno—he acted almost scairt of her after that, he did. Treated her with—well, I guess you could call it respect. Leastways, he took more back talk offa her than anybody else I ever saw. And—"

"But how did Carstairs die? I heard in the village he simply fell off his horse."

"Um—well, I guess that's about the right of it. He came home drunk one night, it seems. He was with another feller, and they were roisterin' along, singin' songs an' all. The other feller, Minchin, his name is, says all of a sudden Carstairs's horse took fright at somethin' and shied and took off runnin'.

Next thing Minchin knew, Carstairs was dead in the ditch, that thick neck o' his broke like kindlin'. Twere'nt no one sorry to see him gone, neither. Leastways nobody that knew him very good."

"Yes, I should imagine he was as bad a master as he was a husband."

"Worse. Flew into a rage over trifles—I remember him flyin' out to the stables—always one of his lists in his hand. He was a great one for makin' lists—put everthin' on it he wanted a body to do fer the day. Mostly none of it made any sense, yet if it weren't done just as he said, somebody'd feel the back of 'is hand—or the toe of his boot. Yet, he let the real bad problems slide right by him. He took your father's operation here—" Jonah made a sweeping gesture with his arm in the direction of the stables, now dark and silent—"and just let it drift to ruin." He snorted, "He sold the stock piece by piece when it suited him, and then—toward the end when things began to go bad for him—he let almost all the remaining animals go for pennies, 'ceptin' fer Warlock, saints be praised." Jonah sighed heavily. "Ah, if only yer da hadn't give up the place to him."

He subsided into a melancholy reverie, but jerked his head up at Jem's next words. "My father didn't give up the place to Carstairs, Jonah. Carstairs stole it."

Jonah's mouth dropped open. "You don't mean t' tell me! But—we was told yer dad got to gamblin' and . . . "

"And lost the place to Carstairs when he defaulted on a loan Carstairs had made to him." Jem was very still, but his voice sliced through the night. He continued in a lower tone. "This must stay between us, old friend. Do you remember Giles Daventry?"

"Oh, aye. Nephew to Squire Fairworthy—used to spend ever' summer here. The Fairworthys are gone now—lost the place some five years ago. Never did cotton much to young Giles, if ye must know."

Jem favored him with a mirthless grin.

"Nor I, Jonah. Nor I. I, er, ran into him in London some time after he left the old homestead, and discovered that he knew a great deal about what really happened between Carstairs and my father."

"Which was?" asked Jonah in fascination.

"It's a long story. Suffice it to say that Emanuel Carstairs stole Ravencroft from my father through a foul piece of trickery, and then murdered him. Then, he made my mother's life such a hell that she was forced to flee one night with my two sisters and me."

Jonah's mouth opened, but for some moments he did not utter a sound.

"My Gawd!" he said at last. Then, after another few moments of thought . . . "Are ye meanin' t' tell me that's what yer here for? T' reclaim Ravencroft?"

"Yes."

"My Gawd," said Jonah again. "But . . . "

"But why didn't I just walk up to the front door and announce to all within that Jeremy Standish, Lord Glenraven has returned to take up residence?"

"Wull—yes."

"Because there are a few minor impediments yet to be cleared. There is, for one thing, the matter of proof."

"But, I thought you said . . . "

"I said Giles Daventry knew a good deal about what happened. In fact, without his help Carstairs could not have pulled off his infamous scheme. And Daventry did sign a statement to that effect, but it's not enough. He made the statement after being arrested for other crimes, and spoke up in return for leniency from the court. A good attorney could make the case that his testimony, therefore is somewhat suspect. However, there is evidence hidden inside Ravencroft, and I must find it before I can prove beyond dispute that the estate is mine."

"And what about Miz Carstairs?"

"Yes," said Jem slowly, "what about Mrs. Carstairs, indeed."

"I dunno what I could do t' help ye, lad—that is, me lord. And if it means pushin' Miz Claudia out inta the snow, I wouldn' want t' do that. Even before Carstairs was killed, she'd taken over the horse-breedin' operation—what precious little there was of it—and she's worked her heart out buildin' it back up. It ain't exactly a gold mine yet, but we're comin' along. She used what little money Carstairs had left her to buy a few good mares fer Warlock t' service. She ain't real knowledgeable about horse flesh, but she has me t' advise her, and when it comes t' the business end of the operation, she's sharp as she can hold together."

"She could do no better than to depend on you." Jem laughed and slapped the old man gently on the shoulder. "Tell me, is the estate still supported in the main by sheep?"

Jonah shuffled uncertainly. "As t' that, I can't tell ye much. Carstairs sold off some o' the land, and the sheep, too. We don't have a reg'lar sheep man anymore. I reckon it's 'cause we don't have all that many o' the animals left. I b'lieve Miz Carstairs runs whatever business there is in that direction herself. She don't say much about it."

Jem sighed dispiritedly. "Things have come to a pretty pass, haven't they?"

After a moment, Jonah asked hesitantly. "If ye don't mind me askin'—me lord, where have ye been since . . . "

Jem laughed briefly. "Why, I took up residence in London. In fact, when I realized that it behooved me to choose a *nom de guerre*, so to speak, I chose the month I arrived there. It was nip and tuck for awhile, but I managed to prize a fair amount of gold from the dross that is life in the metropolis."

"How did ye do that, then?"

"Oh, at first by a little judicious petty thievery. Later I learned to judge to a nicety the cupidity of my fellow man."

The old man stared.

"Gambling, Jonah. It is a passion that rages from the gentlemen's clubs of London to the most abysmal of its gin shops. No." He smiled at Jonah's dubious expression. "I did not personally participate. Suffice it to say, I merely learned how to use those who do participate to my advantage. I am not precisely wealthy, but I have enough blunt to bring Ravencroft back to solvency—and then some."

Jonah shook his head in silent wonderment, and Jem continued briskly. "Getting back to my predicament, I don't know what you can do either, Jonah—at least at this point. What I need most right now is for you to say nothing at all about this to anyone." Jem paused for several moments, considering. "I promise I'll make a fair settlement on Mrs Carstairs."

"I dunno." Jonah shook his head. "I just dunno." He sho another glance at Jem.

Jem drew a long breath. "Jonah, I can understand you wanting to protect Mrs. Carstairs. God knows she's in a wretched position, but it's not as though I'm trying to steal something that belongs to her. Ravencroft is my home, no hers, and I want it back. Is that wrong?"

"N-no, but . . . "

"You're right—I could go to the courts with the documents I have in my possession—the statements from Giles Daventry—and wait for permission to search the house for the one piece of paper that will prove everything he said. But that will take months, during which time both Mrs. Carstairs and myself will exist in limbo."

A deep sigh was Jonah's only answer.

"I tell you again," Jem said patiently. "The widow Carstairs will want for nothing."

"Very well," said Jonah in a troubled voice. "I won't say nothin'. At least for the time bein'. I have to think all this over some." He moved from his position against the fence and stretched stiffly. "And now, we'd best be gettin' to our beds."

Jem sensed rather than saw the ironic grin that spread over Jonah's gnarled features.

"Allow me t' show ye yer accommodations, yer lordship. See that stable buildin' over there? Ye'll be bunkin' in the third stall on the left. It's empty at the moment," he added kindly. "Get a good night's sleep; tomorrow'll be a long day."

But sleep was a long time coming for Jem. He settled himself into the worn blanket Jonah had laid over clean, sweet smelling straw and folded his arms behind his head. Gazing into the darkness overhead, he listened to the faint sounds of mice busy about their nocturnal activities, and the snuffling of the horses as they slumbered nearby.

He smiled into the night. He was home—even though his return was not exactly as he had envisaged it. There were no pennants flying or crowds of eager tenants raising their voices in glad welcome, but then he had known that was nothing more than a dream fashioned by a boy struggling for survival in the hard streets of London.

How many nights had he spent sobbing himself to sleep in one of the countless unspeakable crannies that festered in London's rotten underbelly? How often had he sought shelter in attics and cellars and sometimes in crumbling doorways. For so long, all that had kept him going was his dark, glittering vision of vengeance. He would return to Ravencroft someday to right the terrible wrong that had been done to his family. Countless, profitless hours were spent in imagining Emanuel Carstairs perishing in agony from a sword thrust to the gut, or writhing on the ground as a skillfully wielded whip flayed the very flesh from his bones.

Of course, when he grew a little older, and reality reared its prosaic head, his plans had shifted. Revenge would still be his, but it would take a subtler form. Public disgrace, perhaps, or transportation to a lifetime of misery in Botany Bay. The boy had survived, grown to manhood, and prospered, for even among the grimy, inescapable tentacles of unrelenting poverty there was money to be made if one were quick and bright and not overly scrupulous.

His smile curled ironically. Now, at last he had realized his dream. Sure in his righteous invincibility, he had gathered his accumulation of worldly goods and his precious packet of documents and prepared to storm the battlements of Emanuel Carstairs' evil empire, only to be met at the gate by a sturdy little person with a musical voice and execrable taste in clothing who blasted his grand designs and set him to mucking out the stables. His mouth curved downward, anger still boiling in him that Carstairs was beyond worldly justice. If only it had not taken quite so long to see Daventry punished for what he had done not only to Jem, but to a man Jem had come to call friend.

He rolled over and buried his face in the aromatic roughness of the blanket. The important thing, Jem reminded himself just before sleep finally took him, was that he was home. He was Jeremy Standish, Lord Glenraven, and he had come to reclaim his birthright. No matter that all he had laid claim to so far was a humble little corner of his rightful domain. It would all be his in time. In due time.

* * *

Dawn came early the next morning, announced by the sun slanting in through the window above his head as well as by the hopeful whickering of the other residents of the stable. Yawning, Jem stumbled into the yard and made his hurried ablutions at the pump. He was met there by Jonah, who was proceeding leisurely from the direction of his own quarters, a comfortable lodging above the main stable building. Lucas, too, shambled on to the scene after a few moments. Of Mrs. Carstairs, there was no sign.

"Hurry about yer business this mornin', my lad," said Jonah, after cursory good mornings were said among the three. "The missus wants you up t' the house later on. It appears she has more use of y' as a butler than a stable hand."

Lucas sniffed resentfully. "Or mayhap ye think yerself too good fer stable work, now that you'll be in the big house?"

Jem grinned. "Hardly, but I'll have to take care, won't I? Won't do to be ushering guests into the manor with manure on my boots, will it?"

Lucas guffawed and turned to go about his own chores as Jem faced Jonah.

"Is that what I'm wanted for?" he asked. "To take over Morgan's position?"

"I reckon," returned Jonah laconically. "Miss Melksham—Miss Augusta Melksham, that is, Miz Claudia's aunt, has been natterin' at her to replace old Morgan, and with her sister and brother-in-law arrivin' any time now . . ."

"What happened to Morgan? Did he pass away?"

"Aye, last month. He were gettin' on in years, after all."

"Yes, I suppose he must have been. He was here ever since I can remember. How did he die?"

"Oh," replied Jonah. "He just sort of faded away, ye might say. Them in the house said it was from a broken heart—he wanted to go with yer mother when she left, y' know."

Jem nodded. He remembered with clarity the tears that had stood in the man's eyes as his mother shepherded her children from Ravencroft, never to return.

"On t' other hand, if it was a broken heart, it took long enough to crack open." Jonah's rusty chuckle sounded. "And, after all, he did see Carstairs put into the ground. Happiest day of his life, he said afterward. No, I think old Morgan just plain wore out. Happens t' us all," he concluded philosophically.

"Tell me about the aunt."

"Ah. She come to live here after Carstairs died. Miz Claudia couldn't very well live here on 'er own, after all. She ain't a bad old bird. Kinda lean and gristly, but there's a good heart in her."

"And the sister and brother-in-law?"

Jonah snorted. "Name's Reddinger. Rose and Thomas Reddinger. She's a simperin' wigeon and he's as greedy a maw worm as you're likely t' find under any rock. When Carstairs was alive, we never saw hide nor hair of him from one end of the year t' the other, but now he's here as often as the postman, it seems."

"Oh?"

"The people in the house say his fat fingers are a-twitchin' to get control of Ravencroft."

"But didn't Mrs. Carstairs inherit it free and clear? Theoretically, at least?"

"Yup, but Reddinger seems t' think he can control his sister-in-law like he does his wife. She ain't bendin' so far, but now he's trotted out a feller for her to marry. Name of Fletcher Botsford. He's a skinny, pompous lackwit who's right under Reddinger's thumb, and doesn't even know it. If Miz Claudia marries Botsford, Ravencroft will go to him, which, thinks Reddinger, is nigh as good as it goin' to hisself."

Jem whistled. "High drama in the Cotswolds, forsooth. Perhaps Mrs. C. will be pleased to be out of it all, once Ravencroft is returned to Standish ownership."

Jonah grunted, and turned away.

Thoughts of his upcoming foray into the main house filled Jem's thoughts for the remainder of the morning. He fetched and carried and swept and shoveled and helped Jonah minister to the still unfoaled Jenny, while wondering all the while what changes would be apparent when he finally made his way past the kitchen and scullery into the manor's great hall and the environs beyond.

At last, Jonah signaled him to a halt. "Ye'd best go see what

Miz Carstairs has in mind for ye. Just go into the kitchen, and one of the maids will take ye to her."

Jem touched his finger to his cap and made his way out of the stable yard and through the kitchen garden, and was soon speaking to a young female dressed in a rather shabby semblance of the garb worn by a parlor maid. She eyed him with curiosity.

"If you'll wait here, I'll tell Miz Carstairs you're here."

She ran lightly out of the kitchen, returning a few minutes later to inform him politely that the mistress of the house would meet him in the Great Hall.

Taking a deep breath, Jem followed her out of the kitchen and into the corridor that led to the upper regions of the house. He passed various rooms, whose functions were only dimly remembered by him as sources of homey odors—the fragrance of herbs and fruit from the still room—the scent of beeswax and soap from another small, recessed chamber.

Passing through several doors, they came to an arched hallway from which led several elegantly furnished parlors. Jem glanced cursorily into these, observing them through a haze of memory, until at last they emerged into a huge, vaulted chamber. This was the Great Hall, the entrance to the manor. It was sparsely furnished, and Jem wondered what had become of the suits of armor, the vast oak tables, and the ancient hangings that had been a part of his childhood.

"Mrs. Carstairs will be down momentarily." With a swish of her skirts, the maid hurried away to her duties.

Jem slowly paced the stone flag flooring, finally stopping before a small pier table. An ancient halberd had stood here, which he had once tried to lift, nearly decapitating his sister. He moved to a stone fireplace, large enough to contain a whole tree. It was empty now in the warmth of summer, but in his mind's eye he saw a dancing blaze, with boughs of fragrant greenery hung about to celebrate Christmas.

God, how could things have come to such a pass? His father murdered and his beautiful mother chiveyed out of their home, stealing away in the dead of night to avoid the wicked designs of Emanuel Carstairs.

Suddenly, inutterably weary, he placed both hands on the fireplace lintel and leaned his head on his arms. He stayed thus, motionless for some moments, until a sound behind him caused him to turn.

Abruptly, he jerked upright, his jaw dropping in amazement. There, floating down the great staircase toward him, dressed in a plain muslin round gown, was one of the most beautiful women he had ever seen.

Chapter Three

Claudia paused on her journey down the great stairs, taken by surprise at the aspect of the man who waited for her below. His silver eyes seemed to collect the light streaming in from the long, mullioned windows of the hall, and she was again struck by the air of tension about him. As he continued to gaze, she felt an odd trembling begin deep within her. Their eyes locked, and for an instant she felt an indefinable, almost frightening sense of connection with him.

She blinked and smoothed her skirt self-consciously before continuing down the stairs.

"You stated that you are familiar with the duties of butler," she said rather breathlessly.

He did not reply, but continued to stare at her blankly. Lord, thought Jem, who would have thought that beneath those wretched, smelly men's garments lurked this vision? Her hair was a glorious, wheat color, almost perfectly matched by great, glowing eyes of a light topaz. Her bearing was regal, and as she descended the great staircase, she resembled the carved statue of a goddess, all gold and ivory, sprung to life. He came to himself with a jerk only after several moments had elapsed.

"Yes, Mrs. Carstairs," he murmured at last. "That is true. I am familiar with the duties of a butler, and I am at your disposal."

She flushed, guessing that he had not recognized her at first as the female stable hand he had met yesterday. She drew herself up and addressed him coolly.

"As you perhaps noticed, we have no housekeeper. My Aunt Augusta—that is, Miss Melksham, ordinarily serves in that capacity, however, she is engaged elsewhere at the moment, so it has fallen to me to show you about Ravencroft."

"My pleasure, ma'am," returned Jem smoothly. "This is," he continued, his arm taking a sweeping gesture about the hall, "a most impressive chamber. Might one ask when the residence was built?"

"I'm not sure, Mr. January. I was told it came into being during the time of James the First. It—it was smaller then, of course, but subsequent generations have added to it."

There was nothing in the conversation or in the new butler's demeanor, thought Claudia, that should make her heart pound so, but she felt as overheated and shaky as though she had been running in the hot sun. It was as though they communicated on two levels, one quite prosaic, and the other unspoken and dangerous. She forced her attention to his next words.

"And was the late Mr. Carstairs's family in possession of the manor for all those years?" His voice was bland, but beneath his seemingly cursory interest, Claudia fancied that she heard a certain intensity that put her on her guard.

"No," she replied shortly. "My husband—acquired Ravencroft several years ago. I do not know for how long the previous owner's family had been in residence."

Jem eyed the widow narrowly. God, she was beautiful. Why had he not seen it the day before? Even though she'd been close to obliterated by hat, shirt, and stable dust, such beauty should have been apparent. No wonder Carstairs had lusted after her. He felt a tightening inside as he thought of her in thrall to that swine. He cleared his throat.

"How unfortunate that Mr. Carstairs, er, passed away before establishing his own dynasty."

Mrs. Carstairs made no response to this, but merely turned away with a curt gesture and walked quickly from the room, leaving Jem to follow in some bemusement. In a moment, they stood in a large chamber, illuminated by the light that streamed in from large windows facing the manor's front lawn. They had been an innovation by Jem's mother, replacing narrow, badly crafted panes that had kept the room in a perpetual twilight.

"We call this the emerald saloon," said Claudia, gesturing to indicate emerald-colored hangings. "We receive visitors here, and when I have a moment, this is where I read or take up embroidery or mending."

The rest of the ground-floor rooms were dealt with briefly, and Jem found that after the initial shock of memory suffered in the hall, he was able to view the shreds of his past with equanimity. The great ballroom embraced its history in shadowed majesty, and the music room seemed to echo the strains of simple airs played on the spinet piano by his mother. They trod sedately through the blue saloon, and then the yellow. They peered into the Chinese drawing room and paused to admire the Restoration staircase. Then they reached the library. Here Jem received another jolt, not one of memory, but one much more recent in origin.

His eyes flew to the walls, lined with age-blackened shelves. In his youth they had been packed solidly with books, many of them bound with precious leathers, others dog-eared and spotted with use. In one of these, Giles Daventry had told him, was concealed the evidence of Emanuel Carstairs's wrongdoing. Jem gaped at the shelves in shocked astonishment. At least a third of the books were gone!

Jem swung to Claudia Carstairs. "Where—" he croaked, before shutting his mouth to bite off the question. "Where," he repeated after a moment, "are, um, all the books? That is," he continued in a calmer tone, "there seems to be too many shelves for the number of volumes displayed. If you will forgive my impertinence, ma'am."

Claudia eyed him curiously. She had the oddest idea that it was not the paucity of books in the Glenraven library that had caused that look almost of panic in the pseudo-butler's eyes, but what was it? She was about to squelch his unwarranted interest with a lady-of-the-manor set-down, but decided instead on another tack.

"I sold them," she replied baldly. She noted with interest the expression of amazed anger that leaped into his eyes, quickly shuttered to one of detached interest.

"Not that it is any of your concern, Mr. January," she said crisply, "but my husband left me with very little. I'm sure you have already noticed that we are very down pin around here. I am, however, determined to restore Ravencroft to the prosperity it once enjoyed." She paused for a moment and continued in a low voice. "I cannot tell you how it pained me to dispose of the books, but many of them, such as a first edition of Doctor Johnson's dictionary, were extremely valuable. That particular collection, by the way, enabled me to purchase three mares of good stock."

"I see." Jem's noncommittal reply covered an unpleasant churning in his gut. My God, he was lucky there was a stick of furniture left in the place. The suits of armor and the tapestries in the hall had undoubtedly gone to a dealer in antiques. Were they even now gracing the neo-gothic drawing room of some jumped-up Cit?

He followed her silently from the room, and by the time they had made their assent to the next floor, his emotions had subsided. He could not blame her for taking whatever methods were to hand. He supposed he would have done the same thing. He could always refurnish Ravencroft to his taste later, when the estate was solvent once more. But what about the one damned book he needed? Had she sold that, too? Daventry had been unsure of the title of the volume, recalling only with certainty that it had the word "rural" in the title. It looked to have been little used, he said, and it sounded extremely dull, which is why he had chosen it as a hiding place. At least, Jem reflected a little wildly, the number of tomes to be searched had been effectively diminished.

They had climbed to the second floor by now, reaching what his employer referred to as "the bedroom wing," and Jem was again assaulted by memory. Down that corridor had been his parents' suites, and just two doors along that one there were his sisters' rooms. The young widow opened each door in turn, explaining briefly the use to which the room was now being put. Jem discovered that Mrs. Carstairs had chosen his mother's room for her own, and that the yet unseen Aunt Augusta resided in the older of his sisters' chambers.

In another corridor, Jem held his breath as Mrs. Carstairs paused outside yet another chamber.

"This room has been unoccupied since my husband moved in here twelve years ago. We did not need the space, and since it is in an out-of-the-way location, it was simply left as it was in the days when the—the other family lived here."

She opened the door to reveal a large, airy, sparsely furnished bedchamber.

Jem couldn't stop himself. He moved into the room and twitched at the holland cover that covered the bed. He caught his breath. My God, he might have just risen from it, a gangly youth of twelve years. The colorful quilt lay as though smoothed in place only yesterday. As in a dream, he flung other covers asidc from cupboards, a rocking horse tucked into one shadowy corner, and from shelves on which lay a short lifetime full of treasures. He had nearly broken down and cried in front of everybody when he was told he would have to leave behind his model ship, and the crudely fashioned statue of the Red Indian chief Powhatten.

"I'm so sorry my darling," his mother had said softly, tears springing to her own blue eyes. "We must leave right now, and we can only bring what we can carry. Perhaps someday . . ." But she had choked off the rest of her words and hurriedly finished filling his small valise with things a fellow could very well do without—shirts and underclothing and such.

He held the ship in his hands, lost in thought, until he became suddenly aware that Mrs. Carstairs was staring at him, a very odd expression in those fine, butterscotch eyes. He replaced the ship with an awkward smile.

"Please forgive me ma'am. A room unused for so long—I'm afraid my curiosity got the better of me."

Claudia gazed at him speculatively, but said nothing.

After that, there was little left of the tour, and as they descended via a narrow flight of servants' stairs, Claudia enumerated his duties.

"We have no house steward, I'm afraid, so you will have to double as . . . Oh." She stopped abruptly as a tall, spare figure approached them from the other direction. "Here is Aunt Augusta." She extended her hand to the older woman who, ignoring Jem completely, thrust into Claudia's hands several papers she carried.

"Would you believe," she asked rather breathlessly, "what I found in an old cupboard in the laundry room? A whole parcel of Emanuel's lists!"

When her niece made no response beyond a baffled lift of her brows, the old lady continued. "They all concerned household procedures he wanted put into effect—and it's my belief the staff simply crushed them up and stuffed them in the cupboard where he'd never find them again."

Claudia stared at the papers in her hand for some moments, her expression putting Jem in mind of someone who had just been handed something dead and odorous.

She said only, "Very well, I shall burn them." Turning to Jem she remarked in an odd, controlled tone, "My husband was a rather compulsive note taker. He made lists of absolutely everything. We're still finding them. Aunt," she continued, still in that remote voice, "here is the young man I was telling you about. He is to be our butler, at least"—she glanced at Jem dubiously—"temporarily."

Miss Augusta Melksham inclined her head toward Jem. She appeared to be on the shady side of fifty, and was astonishingly angular. She was tall, with a prepossessing nose, around which her plain features were arranged with precision. Her hair incongruously, was arranged in a profusion of iron-gray ringlets that quivered about forehead and cheeks, punctuating her conversation in a prim dance.

"He seems very young" was her only comment to Claudia. She eyed Jem assessingly. "And very poorly dressed," she concluded.

Jem shifted uncomfortably, feeling like an errant schoolboy brought before the headmaster. "I . . . " he began, but closed his mouth quickly as Miss Melksham lifted her hand.

"I think you are of a size with Morgan," she said, and turned her head. "Claudia, will you show Mr.—January, is it? What an odd name, to be sure. Will you show Mr. January to Morgan's quarters? I would do so myself, except that I am late for my appointment with Mrs. Skinner to go over next week's menus."

"Of course, Aunt." Claudia smiled warmly at the older woman.

"After which," continued Miss Melksham, addressing Jem, "you may come to the kitchen. I will introduce you to Mrs. Skinner—our cook—and the rest of the staff."

Without waiting for a reply, she proceeded on her way with a rustle of bombazine skirts. Jem looked after her in some awe before turning back to his employer. He surprised an amused twinkle in her eyes before she turned to ascend the stairs.

An hour or so later, Jem stood before a patched cheval glass examining his newly butlered self. In his memory, Morgan loomed as an immensely tall, cadaverously thin personage of imposing mien. He was surprised to discover that the man was actually the same height as himself. There was no question, though, that Morgan's shirt and waistcoat were more than a little snug, and there was a definite gap in the fastenings of his breeches. Jem sighed. He had shirts of his own, and with any luck, there would be, somewhere on the premises, a housemaid who plied a talented needle.

Upstairs, Claudia, without benefit of her maid, began to dress for dinner. Standing in the center of her bedchamber, she stripped off the faded blue muslin she had worn all day. She moved to the clothes cupboard and perused her meager wardrobe. Examining each gown in turn, it began to be borne on her that she wished to dress with special care this evening. She wanted to look her best, she realized with a start.

For her butler?

No, not even a butler. A ne'er do well who had appeared out of the sunrise, dressed in a shabby shirt and breeches and who had lost no time in insinuating himself into Ravencroft. What was his purpose? she wondered, and a flutter of panic caught at her throat. Who *was* this man, with hair like night and eyes like a winter morning. And wasn't there something oddly familiar about him? She frowned. Yes, he definitely reminded her of someone, but who? She knew no one who moved with that fluid, yet disturbingly masculine grace, nor was she acquainted with anyone whose gaze was open and guileless yet somehow intimate.

From the depths of the cupboard, she pulled a sarcenet gown of a deep, rich amber. She had not worn it since early in her marriage, in the time when she still tried to please her husband. She dropped the gown over her head, aware of the sensual caress of the silk as it settled over her body. She caught her own glance in the mirror and hastily arranged her hair in a plain knot atop her head. She prepared to leave the room, but on impulse, turned back to the glass, and in a swift motion, pulled a few tendrils of dark gold to curl about her cheeks.

Not long afterward, Claudia entered the dining room, her aunt on her arm. Without volition, her glance flew to her butler, who opened the door and ushered the ladies into the room with great dignity. He seated them silently and ceremoniously at the enormous mahogany table, burdened under the weight of several weighty candelabra and assorted epergnes that marched down the center of the board like an advancing army.

As the meal commenced, Claudia was intensely aware of her new servant standing at a discreet distance behind her chair. She felt that he was aware of her as well. It was as though waves of intensity emanated from him, washing through her in a warm current. She turned to her aunt, but found herself unable to initiate conversation. Aunt Augusta, it appeared, labored under no such restraint.

"I have," she began prosaically, "prepared the green and blue bedchambers for Thomas and Rose. I assume they will be bringing servants to see after the children, but perhaps we should bring in a girl or two from the village, since they always seem to generate a great deal of extra work for the staff here."

Jem, standing erect near the door leading to the kitchen, folded his hands behind his back and prepared to glean some much-needed information during the half hour or so that the ladies would be at table.

He had been surprised to discover, in his earlier meeting with Cook and the rest of the domestic staff, that the two women not only dined at an unfashionably early hour, even for the country, but spent remarkably little time in consuming their meal. The frugal repast usually consisted of one of the humbler portions of lamb or mutton, or pork, or possibly some species of poultry, accompanied by whatever vegetables were in season or could be found potted in the jars lined neatly in rows in the still room.

Claudia frowned. "I suppose you're right, Aunt, although I begrudge the expense. Perhaps Annie Sounder and her sister will come. Do you think we need put on another footman?"

"I think not, even though I suppose Thomas will be affronted. The man's a veritable squeeze-turnip, but when he visits others, he expects to be treated like traveling royalty. Thank the Lord," she continued abstractedly, her iron-gray curls stirring about her cheeks, so that one almost expected the sound of clinking metal to issue forth, "we'll have plenty to feed them. The kitchen garden is in full spate. What about meat, Claudia?"

"Hmm," replied her niece, brows drawn together. "We're not butchering yet, of course, but we have chickens on hand," She lifted a hand, unconsciously counting on her fingers. "We have several pigs ready for the chopping block, and there's always mutton."

Ah, sheep, thought Jem, who had been impatiently shifting from one foot to another during this exchange. He waited hopefully for her to embroider on the mutton theme, but she persevered in her domestic plans for some minutes.

It was not until the two were well into a creamy syllabub that Claudia broached a subject that caused Jem to prick up his ears once more.

"I had a note from Squire Foster today. He wishes for a meeting this week."

Aunt Augusta uttered an unladylike snort. "That confounded man! Who does he think he is to treat you in such a skimble-skamble manner? He did make an agreement, after all."

"Yes, but it was never put in writing. Now if he chooses to turn my flock off his property, I fear I shall have no recourse."

The figure standing in the shadows behind Claudia stiffened imperceptibly.

"He did offer to sell you the land?" Miss Melksham queried diffidently.

Claudia's laughter was brittle. "Oh yes, indeed—for twice the price he paid when he brought it from Emanuel several years ago." She sighed. "I suppose I cannot blame him for wanting to make a profit, after all. But," she continued, her voice hardening, "I intend to purchase that land someday, as well as every other last acre that Emanuel let slip from his fingers. The time will come when you and I shall see Ravencroft restored to its former beauty and prestige."

Jem listened in some astonishment as he watched Claudia's firm chin rise with these words. Why, one would think that Ravencroft was her ancestral home. What could have bred such a love for the place in her? For the first time, he knew a twinge of guilt at the thought of expelling her from the only home she knew. For it did not sound as though she would find a haven elsewhere.

She spoke of retrieving Ravencroft's lost acreage. Jem frowned. Just how much was left of the estate? Apparently Emanuel Carstairs, finding himself in low water, had sold off huge chunks of the place. What if . . . He came to himself with a start, realizing that the ladies had finished their repast and were ready to leave the table.

Much later, Jem lay sleepless in the small, but comfortable bedchamber set aside for the butler's quarters. He was biding his time until nothing stirred in the rest of the house, waiting to search the few remaining volumes left in the library. Good God, what was he going to do if he could not find the evidence described to him by Giles Daventry?

The hands on the small clock on his bedside table pointed to half past one before Jem considered it safe to slide from the covers. He had not undressed, and in shirt and breeches, he made his way silently through the downstairs corridor. Reaching the library, he began a methodical perusal of each volume, noting that they seemed to be arranged in no particular order. A book on household hints rested next to one on sixteenth-century philosophers. Next, came a brief history of the Standish family. Hm, he'd never seen that. He tucked it under his arm to take to his room.

He reached for yet another tome, but was stilled suddenly as the noise of scurrying feet struck his ears. It sounded like more than one person, and they were headed for the library.

Chapter Four

The footsteps approached the library door rapidly, and just as quickly receded in the other direction. Jem expelled a deep breath and opened the door just enough to let him peer into the corridor. Moving in an envelope of candle glow were a man and a woman, already some distance away. The woman was speaking, her voice high and anxious.

Jem slid into the corridor and pursued them at a discreet pace. To his surprise, the couple strode toward the rear of the house and out the door that led to the kitchen garden. From there, they moved to the stable area, and in a few moments, they were lost to sight within one of the stable buildings. Seconds later, the windows were flooded with lantern light.

He strode to the building and opened the door. Two faces turned to him as he entered, but his gaze was captured first by the sight of Jenny, the mare, standing motionless in the center of a large stall, in which had been laid a thin bed of fresh straw. Claudia stood nearby, watching, as Jonah remained close to the mare, stroking and probing and murmuring gently to the perspiring animal.

"I heard you in the house—ma'am," Jem said to Claudia, who was garbed in her shapeless shirt and breeches. Minus the large, floppy hat, she was disturbingly appealing, with her eyes huge and vulnerable and her hair tumbling down her back in a tawny cascade.

"The mare's begun to foal," said Jonah succinctly. "Everthin' appears to be goin' well, but if she runs into any trouble, an extra pair of hands wouldn't come amiss. Lucas is gone to visit 'is sister along Wybeck way."

Jem glanced at Claudia, who said nothing, but added a silent appeal of her own. Jem turned to look at Jenny, and the three watched for a moment as the mare began to pace in the large stall constructed for just this purpose. Every now and again she gazed over her shoulder at her swollen body as if in some puzzlement as to how she had arrived at this ludicrous state of affairs.

"She doesn't seem to be experiencing any pain," said Claudia after a moment.

"No," chuckled Jonah, "it's only human leddies that make such a to-do over a simple thing. Animals just work hard for a few minutes and get the job over with."

"Spoken like a typical man," snorted Claudia, glaring at Jem's muted outburst of laughter. "Oh!" she gasped, as Jenny stiffened suddenly and her sides seemed to cave inward.

"Foal's movin' about," grunted Jonah. "Gettin' ready to squeeze itself into the world."

For almost an hour, the mare paced about in her stall before coming to an abrupt standstill.

"Look!" cried Jem, pointing to where a stream of liquid gushed out from beneath Jenny's tail. "My God, what's happening?"

Jonah's voice was gruff and contemptuous. "Thought you said you knew somethin' about horses. She's broke her water only—the little 'un will come soon now."

Jenny lay down on the straw, breathing heavily. She had begun to work hard, and her sides heaved as she pushed in conjunction with the contractions that could be seen convulsing her whole body.

"Poor thing," said Claudia. "She's just like a woman in labor." She looked up at Jonah. "Do you remember? I helped Hannah Waverly deliver her child last December. She went through the same thing—the water, the contractions . . . "

As Jonah's creaky laughter sounded, Jem knew a moment of astonishment. His acquaintance with gently bred females was minimal, but he was quite sure none of them made it a practice to assist in the delivery of their tenants' children, nor would any of them be likely to discuss the procedure in the presence of a man, even if the man in question were merely a member of her domestic staff.

"Aye." Jonah's voice was an amused rasp. "The Good Lord figgered out the best way to produce bebbies, and that's the way it's done, whether the mama is a mare or a leddy, or a cow or even a gy-raffe. There," he continued. "There's the birth sack a-comin."

A bluish-gray bulge, streaked with blood, appeared from under Jenny's tail. For some moments, the mare panted and heaved, but nothing further happened. A worried frown creased Jonah's face.

"What is it?" cried Claudia. "What's happening?"

"It's what ain't happen'. One of the foal's feet should be pokin' through by now."

He knelt beside Jenny and stroked the beast's nose, calling gently to her as she heaved and strained. The mare was becoming increasingly restive, and her eyes rolled wildly as she threw herself back and forth in the straw. In another ten minutes, when her efforts still produced no results, Jonah thrust both of his arms into the mare's birth canal. After only a few moments of exploration, he looked straightly at Claudia.

"Little feller's got one leg bent back," grunted Jonah. "You," he said to Jem. "Come down here."

Jem, galvanized into activity, knelt beside the grizzled stable man.

"I'm gonna have t' see that Jenny don't go berserker on us. She'll kill that foal if she gets the wind up any more. I got t' gentle her. I'll stay at her head while you go in and see t' that leg."

"What?" Jem went rigid with shock. "Me? But I don't know anything about . . . I mean, I can't . . . "

"Yes, ye can, boy, or that little colt's goin' to' die. Jenny's got t' be calmed down, and I'm the only one she'll listen to. All you have t' do is reach in, push the foal back up the birth canal, and straighten out its leg. I'll guide ye through it. There's not time t' git anybody else here. Now," he finished, piercing Jem with his glance, "are yer hands clean?"

Jem knew a moment of abject panic. "Yes, they're clean," he gulped finally, "but . . . "

Jonah was not listening. He jerked his head toward a nearby table on which lay several jars and a selection of instruments.

"There's some lard there. Find it and slather it on your hands, all the way up t' yer elbows."

"But . . . " repeated Jem in a strangled gasp. Under Jonah's minatory stare, however, he took the canister in numb fingers. Claudia moved into the stall and, kneeling down, began to stroke Jenny's heaving sides.

"Miz Carstairs, she's liable to do you damage, flailin' about like that," said Jonah peremptorily. Claudia merely continued to massage the animal's flanks in a downward motion, dodging Jenny's hooves as they came perilously close to her head.

"Miz Carstairs," repeated the old man firmly "get the lantern and hold it up so's we can see."

Claudia hurried to do Jonah's bidding, and as light flooded the stall, Jenny twisted her body in a spasmodic attempt to rise, prevented only by Jonah's casting his body atop her head and holding her firm.

Jem had never felt so helpless. What in God's name was he doing here? He knew a blind urge to flee the stables, but as he turned to expostulate with the old man, he met Claudia's eyes. In their amber depths, he read a mixture of fear for Jenny's well-being, an anguished plea for help, and scorn for his own ineptitude. Swallowing hard, he gulped and attempted a reassuring smile. Breathing a silent prayer to God, who as far as he knew had never listened to him before, he bent to the task at hand.

With another momentary surge of panic, he pushed the tattered remnants of the birth sack aside and probed into the dark, pulsing passage behind it.

"Feel for feet," admonished Jonah, the tendons on his neck visible as he wrestled with the panicky mare.

"What?"

"Feet," replied Jonah through gritted teeth. "Bebbies come head first, but with foal's it's feet. Ye should come to one foot first, then the head. Push the head back till ye can feel the second foreleg. Then pull it forward—gently."

Jem swallowed hard. "Right." He shifted position to gain better purchase in the slippery warmth of Jenny's interior, and in a few minutes, to his wondering surprise, he began to recognize the shape of the little animal struggling so hard to be born. After a small eternity, a tiny point, sharp and insistent, thrust itself into his hand. A hoof! He felt along the incredibly fragile little limb. Yes, a foreleg. And there, surely, was a small, equine head, and this, then must be his shoulder. Now, where was the other foreleg? There! It was twisted back so far, he could not feel the second hoof.

He signaled to Jonah, and with infinite caution, pushed the head back toward the mare's uterus until at last he was able to gain purchase on the bent foreleg. He began to pull it into position, when he was stopped by a cry from Jonah.

"Wait! She's goin' into another contraction. If ye pull now, the leg could break."

Jem ceased his exertions, and the next moment Jenny's muscles tightened around his arms in an incredibly powerful grip that made him gasp in pained astonishment. The contraction seemed to go on forever, and Jem thought his bones must be cracking, but at last the mare relaxed. He discovered to his dismay, that the spasm had sent the foal's head down again so that it pressed against the leg that was properly positioned.

Concerned that another such contraction would expel the head from the birth canal completely, tearing the badly positioned foreleg as it did so, he moved the head back as hastily as he could. With numbed fingers, hc straightened the bent leg and slowly pulled it into position. At once, he began easing the hoofed feet toward the cervix. God, they were like twigs that could be snapped with a single, wrong move. Gently, he repositioned the foal's head so that it rested between the forelegs.

After another endless period of achingly slow shifting, accompanied by Jenny's wild neighs of distress, Jem was able to draw the forelegs out of the mare's body. Claudia uttered a small sob of relief, and Jem cast her a look of mutual pleasure.

The foal's nose appeared, then, and Jenny quieted dramatically. Jonah left her head for a moment and, with a cloth he'd kept ready to hand, he wiped the colt's nose free of mucus. He held his palm against the quivering nostrils, nodding to Claudia to indicate that the colt was breathing normally. Jenny's body stiffened into one more contraction, and the rest of the angular little form slid into the straw almost at once. Claudia drew a long, shuddering breath of her own.

Oh, you little miracle! were the words that hummed in her brain as Jonah leaned back against the wall of the stall and said with a tired sigh, "Ye've got a new stallion, Miz Carstairs." She watched as Jenny, in a last, convulsive thrust, expelled the afterbirth and then struggled to her feet. The mare was still uneasy, but the wildness had left her eyes. The colt, too, in what appeared to be an impossible feat, rose to stand, wavering on straw-like legs, and freed himself from the still-throbbing cord that had been his lifeline for eleven long months. He was the color of night, and as he made his unsteady way to his mother's side, he reminded Claudia of a wobbling pool of spilled ink.

"Look," she said with a gurgle of laughter, as the colt made it his first order of business to acquire a bit of dinner. Despite Jenny's un-maternal efforts to avoid the eager little mouth that searched her underside, he soon found what he was looking for, and in another moment, the stable was filled with sounds of his greedy suckling.

The three impromptu midwives laughed together in a mutual venting of happy relief.

"I'm glad ye showed up, me lo—lad." It appeared that Jonah's wide grin would crack his seamed face. "We woulda been hard put to manage on our own."

Claudia, her face alight, whirled to stretch out both hands to Jem before recalling herself. "Oh—yes—er, January," she said in what she hoped was a tone of great propriety. "I must thank you for volunteering your help." She found herself unable to suppress the smile that rose to her lips. "Tonight, you have gone far beyond what is expected of the average butler."

Jem knew an urge to cup that bright face in his hands and press his lips against her curving smile. Instead, he bowed.

"I believe the first line of the butler's code is an admonition to offer one's services wherever and in whatever capacity necessary," he said gravely, massaging his aching arms, and Claudia found herself nearly undone by the compelling twinkle in his eye.

"So what're ye goin' t' call the little feller?" asked Jonah.

"Oh. I hadn't thought. Let's see, he's the first colt born of Jenny and Warlock. Perhaps we could call him Number One. No," she decided with a shake of her head. "That's much too prosaic. How about Premier? Or maybe," she added, laughing, "First and Foremost. Oh, dear, now I'm becoming ridiculous."

"I think," said Jem softly, observing the glow that shimmered about her, "you should call him Claudia's Pride."

"The very thing!" exclaimed Jonah.

Claudia gasped in confusion, and felt a tide of heat rush to her cheeks. "Oh, no—I couldn't. Could I?"

"Don't see why not," returned Jonah. Jem said nothing, but the smile in his eyes spoke for him.

Claudia turned to look once more at the colt, still intent on the business at hand. Jenny stared at him bemusedly before extending a long, pink tongue to clean the birth residue from his dusky coat.

"All right," said Claudia slowly, her eyes shining with pleasure. "I think Claudia's Pride sounds wonderful. Although," she continued, still gazing at the colt, "I think from the looks of him—he's black as an imp of Satan, after all—his stable name will no doubt be Goblin."

Jonah stirred himself and moved to the nearby table and took up a bottle of cleaning solution, which he applied to the stump on Goblin's belly where the umbilical cord had been severed. He turned to the other two, watching avidly.

"There ain't much left t' do here. Whyn't you two run along? I can finish up."

Claudia suddenly realized how very tired she was. It must be after three in the morning, and she had not yet been asleep when she was summoned by Jonah. It had been a long, eventful day. She smiled gratefully at her stable man and turned to leave the building, Jem in her wake.

Once in the house, she turned, but the brisk good night she had been about to utter died on her lips as Jem placed a hand under her elbow and guided her farther along the dark corridor. She was instantly conscious of the strength of his fingers and fought a panicky urge to pull away from him.

"You know," he said meditatively, "after all this excitement, you'll never be able to get to sleep. I think what you need right now is a very large glass of some very good brandy. Luckily, I know precisely where such a commodity may be obtained."

Without giving her an opportunity to resist, he led her into the butler's pantry.

"Oh, my!" said Claudia. "No, I don't think . . ."

"Nonsense," replied Jem in a severe tone of voice. "You don't want to offend the help, do you?" Going to a cupboard in the corner, he fetched a decanter. "I wouldn't like to hazard a guess as to how Morgan came by this excellent cognac, or the armagnac next to it, but I applaud his taste."

It was impossible, of course, thought Claudia in a spurt of desperation. What kind of a woman would be found sitting in a secluded chamber in the middle of the night drinking with her butler, for heaven's sake? To her astonishment, however, she found herself sinking into the chair pulled out for her in one, smooth motion. Well . . . the words crept cravenly into her mind . . . perhaps this was the opportunity she had been looking for to find out more about this mysterious young man.

She surveyed him nervously as he took tumblers from the cupboard and poured a more than generous dollop of brandy in each. Placing the glass before her with a flourish, he sat down opposite her at the small table occupying the center of the room. Her glance skimmed over the black hair tumbled in disarray, and fell unawares into the silvery eyes that returned her gaze with amusement. Startled, she looked elsewhere and was brought up short by the sight of the strong column of his throat exposed by his open shirt. That garment, which by the way, was fashioned of a rather more luxurious grade of linen than would be found on the average servant, did little to conceal the splendid set of muscles that moved sinuously beneath it. His slim elegance was most deceiving, she considered warily. She took a deep breath.

"How—?" she began in a great rush, but was forestalled by Jem's own words.

"Tell me, ma'am . . . " His eyes showed nothing beyond a courteous interest. "How long have you been active in the horse breeding business?"

"For a few years only," she answered, taking a sip of the brandy he had poured for her. "I became interested in the operation before my husband passed away."

"I understand that the former owners of the estate raised sheep. As do most of the gentry hereabouts."

"Yes, that's true—and we still do. That is, as well as we can with the land we possess. Sheep, as you may know, require a great deal of pasturage."

Jem topped off her glass, and hesitated a moment before continuing. "I could not help overhearing your remarks about Squire Foster. You rent land from him?"

"Yes," Claudia replied with more than a hint of bitterness. "And it's all land that should belong to us. It did belong to us, until . . . " She took a deep breath. "My husband sold quite a bit of the estate in the months before he died."

"But surely . . . " Jem probed delicately. "The loss of a few acres should not mean the curtailment of . . . "

"It was not a few acres." A voice inside Claudia bade her to mind her tongue, but the feeling of companionship that had developed during Goblin's birthing process lingered, and besides, it felt good to discuss her problems with one who seemed to show a genuine interest. "Ravencroft is now less than a third the size it was before Emanuel began slicing off pieces of it."

Jem sat in appalled silence for several moments. My God, he had come home to financial disaster! It was sheep that had kept Ravencroft solvent for centuries. His father had created a thriving business from his horse-breeding efforts, and it had come to rival the profits reaped from sheep, but . . . My God, he repeated.

Claudia wondered at the bleak expression on the young man's face, and she continued hurriedly. "We are by no means poverty-stricken here. I lease the other land for sheep production, and the horse-breeding operation is going very well, considering we have been at it for such a short time. I am plowing all our profits back into the estate."

Jem unobtrusively refilled Claudia's glass. "It seems quite an undertaking for a young woman alone."

"Oh, but I'm not alone." She sipped at her brandy, grateful for the curling warmth it created in her body. "I have Jonah. And, of course, Aunt Augusta."

"Ah, yes, the redoubtable Miss Melksham. But why horse breeding? Why a business of any kind, for that matter? Surely, if you are getting by . . . "

"I do not wish," answered Claudia sharply, "to merely get by, nor am I content to live in greatly reduced circumstances for the rest of our lives." She took a convulsive gulp of the liquid fire in her glass.

"Does it mean so much to you to live extravagantly?" Jem's voice held only mild curiosity as he casually added another dollop of brandy to her tumbler, but in it Claudia read a note of criticism.

"Not at all." Good Lord, what was the matter with her, discussing her personal life with a person who was virtually unknown to her. She continued austerely, "It is Ravencroft with which I am concerned. When I arrived here, it was already in considerable disarray, but it—it was obviously once a magnificent residence. Beauty and grace can be seen at every turning—in the staircases and in the design of the rooms. I wish to see it returned to what it was."

"But why?" Jem watched her intently. "Even as it is, you could probably sell the old pile for a tidy profit, and you and Aunt Augusta could live a life of ease in London, or Brighton, or even Bath."

"Because I love this place." Claudia drew in a sharp breath. "Because I want to live here. I—I am thinking of adopting children." She paused startled. She had never thought any such thing, but then again, it did seem like a good idea. Why, she wondered, not for the first time since Emanuel's death, had their distasteful couplings never borne fruit? She continued in a rush. "I would like to have children—squads of them—and I would like something beautiful to leave to them," she finished. Dear Lord, she thought, what had she just said? She rose so abruptly that Jem was forced to move quickly in order to prevent her glass from toppling to the floor.

"I must go," she gasped.

"Are you all right, ma'am?" he asked solicitously, encircling her waist with one arm. "May I assist you?"

"You become impernament, Jennary." She tried again. "You are impert—inant, J—my good man. I am perfectly capable of leaving—this room—now."

Claudia pulled away from him, and swayed only slightly as she hurried from the room, leaving Jem to stare after her.

After a long moment, he made his way once more to the library.

Chapter Five

Morning came very early for Jeremy, Lord Glenraven. In fact at cockcrow, his eyes had not yet closed in sleep. Last night's rapid search of the library's remaining volumes had proved fruitless. There were two books containing the word "rural" in their titles. One was Cobbett's *Rural Rides*, which Jem had read some years ago. The other was a series of short poems extolling the pastoral life, and neither contained a small wad of crumpled paper stuffed between the spine and its leather cover.

When at last he returned to his chamber, more sleepless hours were spent in consideration of the time he had spent earlier with the beautiful Widow Carstairs. Beautiful, yet seemingly unconscious of her loveliness. An unusual quality in a woman, he mused. Against his closed eyelids her image remained startling clear, stroking the laboring mare, Jenny, and crooning reassurances to her, unmindful of the lateness of the hour or the blood and animal sweat that stained her garments. And then, later, as she had sat across the small table from him in his chambers, a brandy glass cradled in her slim fingers, he had been drawn despite himself to the shining spirit that lay beneath the beauty.

It was only with her comfort in mind that he had poured her that enormous glass of brandy, but when in her fatigue she had begun to succumb so rapidly, becoming so very forthcoming in the process, it had been beyond his admittedly limited supply of scruples to refrain from taking advantage of the situation. At least, he thought virtuously, he had not attempted to take advantage of the widow.

His eyes took on a faraway look. What was he going to do about this utterly fascinating creature?

When, on his arrival in the village of Little Marshdean, he had learned that Ravencroft was in the possession of Carstairs's widow, he had prepared to transfer all the loathing he felt for her husband to her. After all, was it not reasonable to assume that the person married to the monster must be a hard-eyed harridan with grasping tendons for hands and a heart of obsidian?

He had been entirely unprepared to find a small, determined person of serious mien, dressed in stable hands' garb occupying the position of lady of the manor, and he had been equally startled at the vision into which she was later transformed. Jem reviewed the moment he had seen her descending the great staircase, dressed in a plain, rather shabby muslin gown, and bearing herself with the grace of a princess royal. Her hair had been caught into an obviously hurried knot atop her head, allowing lacy tendrils to fall about her cheek, and he had known an almost irresistible urge to stride to her and pull the shining fall from its constraint so that he could bury his face in it.

Jem shook his head dazedly. Good Lord, what was he thinking of? This woman was a lady, and not for dalliance. Moreover, she was the woman he was planning to evict from her home. He had spoken the truth to Jonah when he had assured the old man that Mrs. Carstairs would not have to live in penury, but the revelation of her deep love for Ravencroft had come as an unwelcome shock. She spoke of children. A new dynasty at Ravencroft?

The thought skittered through his mind, there was a method other than adoption that could provide Mrs. Carstairs with her squads of offspring, and such an effort could prove most pleasurable.

He flung his bedcovers aside and planted his feet firmly on the polished wooden floor. He was sorry for the Widow Carstairs, and in other circumstances would have set himself to the enjoyable task of consoling her in her sad straits. Things being as they were, however, he would simply see her on her way with a suitable stipend. He would be fair, but that's as far as he was prepared to go. He was not a heartless man, but he had survived twelve years in the meanest of London streets by looking out for himself, assiduously and with great persistence, and he saw no reason to change his modus operandi at this time in his life.

Dispelling the memory of a cloud of disheveled golden hair, and warm caramel-colored eyes gazing at him from across the top of a brandy glass, he strode to a nearby commode where a pitcher of water and a basin awaited him.

Upstairs, Claudia greeted the day with somewhat less equanimity. Consciousness arrived slowly, and as she squinted at the sun slanting through her windows, she rolled over with a moan. After a few moments, having come to the decision that she really could not spend the rest of the day with her head stuffed beneath her pillow, she sat up and was immediately sorry she had done so. Pressing her fingers against her temples, she waited for the room to cease reverberating.

Abruptly, a horrified expression fell upon her features as memories of last evening flooded to her. Good Lord, had she really allowed herself to lounge about with her butler in his pantry in the dead of night? What in heaven's name had possessed her to speak so to—to that man. He was her butler, for Lord's sake. Not that that made any difference, of course. She was not in the habit of exchanging confidences with perfect strangers, after all. Come to think of it, it was her opinion that this particular stranger was far from perfect. If she were not very much mistaken, Mr. Jem January had been plying her with liquor.

But why? Had he designs on her virtue? She snorted. Enveloped in her stable boy rig, and covered with blood and horse sweat, she hardly presented the picture of a damsel ripe for seduction. There had been straw in her hair, and she was sure there was a definite whiff of manure clinging to her person.

Then, what *was* he after? Why had he come to Ravencroft? He had said he was competent to act as a footman, or a valet—or a butler. She had to admit that so far, aside from the very personal way in which he looked at her, he had slipped very easily into butlerhood. He had claimed to be a horseman, too, but he had shown his claims in that area were a lie within five minutes after he had begun ministering to Jenny. She smiled. His panic had been obvious, and she had expected him to flee ignominiously. But he hadn't. He had stayed to help, and in doing so, he had saved Goblin's life.

But she did not trust the man.

She finished dressing in an uneasy state of mind. Surely she had seen him somewhere before. Had he been among her husband's acquaintances? No, she would not have forgotten had they met before. She chose not to consider the implications of this thought. It was not until she stood before her mirror, sweeping her hair into its usual bulky chignon that recognition flared in her mind. Flinging the comb down on her dressing table, she whirled and ran from the room.

She flew along the corridor and up a flight of stairs until she came to a door that opened to a room containing odds and ends of furniture that had been discarded by Emanuel because they did not fit his standards of what a country gentleman should display in his home. In one corner stood several paintings, stacked against each other like a winter's supply of firewood, and Claudia struggled to free one of them. Dragging it to the window, she stood staring at it in mute horror.

Wide-eyed and with heart beating in great, lurching thuds, Claudia studied the picture in her hands. It portrayed a slender, arrogant young man, dressed in the silks and laces of the previous century. It was not precisely a mirror image of Jem, but the resemblance was strong. Eyes of a peculiarly luminous gray were shadowed by hair black as evil. The portrait, she knew, was of the fifth Lord Glenraven, and she could only conclude that, judging from his style of clothing, he must be the grandfather of the man who currently resided in her butler's quarters.

So, Jem January was in reality a Standish. Was he merely a relative of the family who had lived here? Or was he—? She recalled the familiarity with which he had prowled the child's bedroom down the corridor from her own, and an icy finger curled within her.

She knew the previous owner of Ravencroft, Lord Glenraven, had sired only one son, and that the child had left with his mother and two sisters shortly after Emanuel had acquired the place.

"*. . . And after I offered her and her brats the opportunity to live here as long as they wished. She crept out of here like a* *thief in the night—well, she was a thief, wasn't she? Takin' items that rightfully belonged t' me . . . "*

Claudia shivered as she recalled Emanuel's words, spoken in pious indignation. From what little information she had been able to glean, Claudia strongly suspected that the still-beautiful Lady Glenraven had been hounded from her home by a man who insisted that in sharing his home, she would be sharing his bed as well. As for the "items," which appeared promptly on a list that Emanuel kept by him until the day of his death, they apparently consisted of clothing and a few keepsakes.

Claudia returned to the portrait, and she stared transfixed at the gray eyes whose gaze seemed to lock with hers. Cold as a northern sea they were, and seeming to hold an unspoken threat.

Was the stranger truly Lord Glenraven? She paced the room thoughtfully. Her first instinct was to charge into the butler's pantry, banners flying, to accuse the spurious servant to his face and to evict him peremptorily from the premises. Reflection served to alter her purpose. She had no real proof that the dark-haired stranger who had tried to fill her full of brandy last night was in truth the current Lord Glenraven. Even if he were, would she not be better off keeping him under observation? She must learn why he had come to Ravencroft in disguise.

She chewed her lip thoughtfully. Yes, that was odd indeed. Why come in disguise? If he wished to visit the old homestead, why not just knock at the front door and request entrance? No, the man had an ulterior motive, and the only one that she could think of was that he planned to take Ravencroft from her.

She clenched her fists. By God, he would not! Ravencroft was hers by right. She had the papers, and she had the law on her side. She would face him down no matter what his claim.

She shifted uneasily. Hers by right? She remembered other words Emanuel had spoken—phrases absently mouthed in drunken maunderings and bitten off as soon as they were uttered. She rose abruptly. No, she would not think about that. She must focus on the issue at hand, which was to keep Ravencroft as her home. My God, where else would she go? She could not return to her parents' home where she would in all probability be forced into another distasteful marriage by her ne'er-do-well-father, while her mother stood in the background wringing her hands ineffectually.

Nor could she make her home with Rose and her husband. Thomas seemed to have his own agenda for her, equally unappealing.

No, Emanuel had willed Ravencroft to her. It was the one thing he had done in all their married life to stand her in good stead. She stiffened, and a smile hard as iron curved her mouth. If my Lord Glenraven had designs on Ravencroft, he would be in for the war of his life. One, moreover, he had no hope of winning. With a rustle of her skirts, which sounded in her ears like a clarion call to battle, she turned to leave the room, glancing once more at the portrait of Lord Glenraven. Smiling serenely into the cold, gray eyes, she gestured a small salute before closing the door firmly behind her.

Descending to the lower regions of the house, she hurried first out to the stables. Jenny and her colt were still in the birthing barn, and Claudia watched mother and son in bemused delight.

"A beautiful sight, aren't they?" She whirled to face Jem and Jonah, just entering the building. Jem was dressed in work clothes and boots, and carried a pitchfork in his hand.

"I didn't think you needed a full-time butler," said Jem in response to her lifted brows. "So I thought I'd spend the morning hours out here. If that's all right with you, ma'am," he added respectfully, fingers touching the brim of his shabby cap. There was no hint in his eyes of remembered intimacy.

Claudia nodded coolly. "Yes, I think that's a good idea. We rarely receive guests until the afternoon. Well," she amended, "we rarely have guests at all. In fact, January"—with an effort, she forced her voice to a calm courtesy she did not feel— "I would prefer you to confine the major portion of your duties to the stables. I feel you will be of much more use here."

Was that a flash of disappointment she caught in his eyes?

"Of course, ma'am. Do you still wish me to serve at dinner?"

"Of course." She most definitely did not, but the man had to come into the house sometime, she supposed. If nothing else, Aunt Gussie would insist on it. "And," she continued, "when my sister and her husband arrive in a few days, we will need you in the house all the time."

"Yes, ma'am," replied Jem, with a bow, he turned to the task at hand.

Whew! he thought, exchanging a glance with Jonah. The widow was certainly coming all over the lady of the manor this morning. Last night's tentative rapport had apparently evaporated at some time during the dark reaches of the night. He sighed. Back to the stables, eh? Actually, if it weren't for his desire to broaden his search for the "rural" book, he wouldn't mind maintaining his status as a stable hand. He rather enjoyed the mindless but energy-consuming tasks he'd been set to as providing a sort of lull before the storm. It would be soon enough that his heart and mind would be set to an altogether different sort of task. It was fortunate, he concluded, that his quarters were in the main house. He would have to use the midnight hours to continue his search.

He watched the widow in conversation with Jonah, struck again by the luminous beauty that clung to her like a casually worn cloak. She was a widow—had been a wife—yet, there was something rather touchingly virginal about her, as though her spirit had remained untouched by whatever carnal demands her husband had inflicted on her.

She finished her talk with Jonah and, with a nod to each of the men, walked away toward the house. He watched the delicate sway of her hips as she moved, and his throat tightened. Well, perhaps not all that virginal.

Back in the house, Claudia went about her duties somewhat absentmindedly. Mid-morning found her seated in the linen room with Aunt Augusta, carrying out an inventory, but such was her preoccupation that she came to herself with a start when Miss Melksham let out a small squeak.

"One hundred and thirty-seven pillow slips? In need of repair?" asked the distracted lady?

"What?" responded Claudia blankly. "Oh—no, that should be thirty-seven pillow slips, and six in need of repair." Flushing, she placed the offending items in the to-be-mended pile, and plucked the list from her aunt's nerveless fingers. "I'm sorry," she said, hurriedly scratching in a correction.

"Child, what's got into you today?" Miss Melksham peered

severely at her over the tops of her spectacles. "First you nearly threw out three dozen of our finest candles, and now you have got the linen inventory all higgeldy-piggeldy."

Claudia raised a hand to her head, which was beginning to ache again. "I'm sorry," she repeated. "I just can't seem to concentrate."

"It's Thomas and Rose, isn't it?"

"Oh, no—that is, yes," Claudia replied, prevaricating. "I do want everything to be just so for them."

"Why, for heaven's sake? You're expecting your sister and her husband, not the Prince Regent." Claudia essayed a small, not entirely successful smile. "Yes, but I don't think the Regent is quite as demanding as Thomas."

Miss Melksham sniffed. "I certainly hope you aren't going to accede to his constant need for attention. Rose is bad enough with her megrims and her collywobbles." She cast a penetrating glance at her niece. "At least," she continued meaningfully, "while they are here you won't be outside mucking out the stables."

Claudia flushed, but felt herself to be on firmer ground here. "I don't do that anymore. January has taken over that task."

"Our butler?" queried the older woman in bewilderment.

"Yes, well—" Claudia went on in rather a rush. "He was originally hired as a stable hand—did I not tell you?" Without giving her aunt a chance to answer, she continued hastily. "It was only when he assured me that he was eminently qualified—which, I'm sure he is, don't you—at any rate, since his duties are so light here in the house, he will be spending his mornings in the stable with Jonah and Lucas."

Thrusting the remainder of the pillow slips on a shelf, she rose and made as though to leave the room. Her aunt, however, stayed her with a minatory glance and a hand on her arm.

"What do you mean, my dear, about his duties being so light? We've been without a butler for too long, and there are many things he should be attending to. Since we have so few other men about the place, he must take over chores that we have let slide for too long. The chandelier lusters are in desperate need of cleaning, and—what *is* his name again—January—must see to lowering them for the maids. Since we have no housekeeper, I always depended on Morgan to help oversee the maids in their duties—have you looked at the upstairs parlors lately? An absolute disgrace! Dust you can write your name in, and—and the silver is in a deplorable condition. Morgan took it upon himself to polish it, you know. Oh, there are a hundred things that need doing."

"There, there, Aunt," replied Claudia soothingly. "When Thomas and Rose come—and that is in just a few days, now—January will spend all his time in the house."

Miss Melksham threw up her hands. "Most unsatisfactory, but if it keeps you out of the stables, I suppose we can manage. Gracious, the sight of you in those dreadful clothes, with a pitchfork in your hand is enough to send me into a purple megrim."

Laughing, Claudia escorted her aunt from the room. Once in the corridor, the two ladies parted, Miss Melksham to see to activities in the kitchen, and Claudia, beeswax and polishing rag in hand, toward the great hall.

En route, she passed the library, and on impulse, stepped inside. During her tour yesterday with January, she had noticed how the dust was beginning to accumulate in this room. Appreciatively, she breathed in the scent of vellum and leather and old wood. Odd, she felt more in tune with the spirit of the old house in this room. It had cost her a great deal to sell off so many of the books, but there were still many left. Enough, certainly, to provide her with pleasurable reading during the brief periods when she had time for such an activity. She walked no more than a few steps into the room, when she halted. There, on one of the tables, were several volumes, and next to them, a candlestick containing a burned-down stub. She frowned. Surely, when she had been here yesterday, all the books had been shelved.

She brushed her fingers through the recently disturbed dust on the table. Two books had been set aside, and she glanced absently at their titles. Cobbett's *Rural Rides*—she was familiar with that one, having read Mr. Cobbett's curmudgeonly comments on the state of the nation some years ago—and another volume with which she was unfamiliar—*Observations on a Rural Scene*.

Uneasily, she reshelved the books, dusting them as she did so. Perhaps Aunt Gussie had come down to the library for something to read before retiring for the night. She herself had removed several books to her room for this purpose. However, Claudia thought it highly unlikely that her aunt would do so, since Aunt Gussie was not a reader, and relied on a tisane if she needed something to make her drowsy. After a moment's thought, she moved lightly from the room, pausing only when she reached the butler's quarters.

Feeling inexplicably guilty, she pushed the door open and slipped inside. There, on a small table lay a leather-bound volume. So, it had indeed been he who had been helping himself to her books.

Not that she minded, of course. She had told all the servants they were welcome to select volumes of their choice at any time. Not that any of them had ever taken her up on her offer. Still, it made her uneasy to think of the man prowling about the house in the dead of night. Idly, she picked up the book and glanced at the title. *A History of the Standish Family*! She let the book drop from her trembling fingers and rushed headlong from the room.

Back in the hall, she mechanically applied beeswax to the balustrade of the great staircase. How was she to go about discovering what January was up to? Emanuel had employed an attorney of sorts, but she was loathe to confide in him. She had not trusted Cornelius Welker when Emanuel was alive, and she trusted him even less now. She recalled the ill-concealed eagerness he had displayed at her husband's obsequies.

"If you'll just put everything in my hands, my dear young lady," he had pronounced in tones so oily that she could almost see the words sliding down his chin, "I shall be happy to assume the duties of running the estate, a burden that no person of your youth and inexperience should have to shoulder."

My dear young lady, indeed! She had sent the man off with a flea in his ear, and had gone to his office a few days later to retrieve all Emanuel's important documents from his unwilling hands. She had not heard from him since, and she could scarcely go to him now and ask for his help in ridding her of a possible threat to her ownership of Ravencroft.

She supposed she could go to Thomas. She almost smiled as she pictured Thomas's reaction to the merest hint that her possession was in jeopardy. Unfortunately, his method of dealing with the problem would most likely only make things worse, Thomas being in favor of the confrontational approach to matters.

No, she was all alone in this. She gave an involuntary shiver at the thought of going against the unknown Standish by herself. He was not precisely sinister, yet she had received the definite impression that crossing swords with him would be dangerous and would irrevocably alter the course of her life.

She turned to her polishing, when a faint noise from outside made her lift her head. In a moment, the sound became identifiable as hoofbeats and the harness jingle of a carriage. Curious, she moved to the great front door, pausing to peer through one of the mullioned windows that overlooked the drive. Gasping, she dropped rag and polish and ran toward the kitchens, calling "Aunt! Aunt Gussie!"

Chapter Six

Responding to the frantic note in her niece's voice, Augusta Melksham burst into the great hall before Claudia had taken very many steps. She, too, paused as she heard the gathering commotion outside. The crunch of gravel could be heard, as well as upraised voices calling for attention. Miss Melksham paled.

"Never tell me—!" she began.

"Yes, it's Thomas," cried Claudia. "They're here!"

"But . . ."

"I know. None the less—they're early, but they're here." Claudia grasped her aunt by the shoulders and turned her about in the direction from which she had just come. "Go find January." The words tumbled from her. "Then send someone to the village to get the Sounder sisters. And Thelma Goodall if she'll come. In the meantime, hustle every available housemaid upstairs to see that the guest rooms are at least habitable. Tell Cook she'll need four chickens for dinner—Clem, the boots and knives boy, can wring their necks." She drew a deep breath. "I'll greet our guests."

Aunt Augusta took off at a run, almost tripping on her bombazine skirts in her haste. Claudia affixed a determinedly bright smile to her lips and strode to the massive door. Pausing a moment to bring an instinctive hand to her hair, she flung it open.

"Thomas!" she cried to the large gentleman making his way ponderously down from the carriage. "Rose!" she added a moment later, as the gentleman assisted a lady to disembark. She was small and fluttery, and held a large, lacy handkerchief pressed to her nose. Behind her tumbled two children, Master George, nine, and Horatia, a few years younger. They were engaged in a pitched battle, apparently over who was going to carry the small dog presently clutched in a death grip under George's arm.

The smile fell abruptly from Claudia's lips as a second man, tall and reedy, disentangled himself with some difficulty from the coach's leather stirrups as he lurched from the carriage to the ground. "Oh, no!" she quavered. How *could* Thomas have done this to her? "Mr. Botsford," she finished weakly. "How very nice to see you."

Fletcher Botsford nodded distractedly, but by now Claudia had turned her attention back to her sister and brother-in-law.

"What a surprise," she cried weakly. "We were not expecting you for another two days."

"Two days?" replied Thomas Reddinger, his florid face round with umbrage. "Nonsense. Told you we'd be here Tuesday—day after the Tentrum races."

"Oh, but dearest," interjected his wife, handkerchief held aloft in trembling supplication. "I *told* you we were to come on Thursday."

"Nonsense," Thomas repeated with finality. "You there!" he bawled. "Crumshaw! Get those valises out—step lively!"

"But, where is your butler, my dear?" asked Rose in faint, but scandalized tones. "Surely you do not answer your own door now?"

"Oh," replied Claudia distractedly. "The—ah—January will be here momentarily. He is occupied elsewhere at present, and since I was—oh, dear!" This as the puppy relieved himself on Master George's coat.

Rose uttered a muted scream. "Grample! Nanny Gr—where are—oh. Do take the children upstairs—and take that wretched animal with you."

A plump woman, wearing a long-suffering expression, labored to extricate herself from the large coach just lumbering to a stop behind the vehicle that had disgorged her mistress. Silently, she gathered up her charges and, to Claudia's great relief, herded them into the house.

In a moment, the area before the entrance door became virtually impassable, as the hapless valet, Crumshaw, and Rose's maid, Binter, collided with the servants sent out by Miss Melksham. That lady herself appeared the next moment, and with apparent delight, embraced Mr. Reddinger and his distracted wife. Turning to Fletcher Botsford, she smiled distantly and offered two fingers of her mittened hand.

It was some minutes before the guests were assisted out of wraps, hats, canes, bonnets, and gloves, and the entire party shepherded into the emerald saloon.

"Tea will be here momentarily," said Claudia rather breathlessly, shooting her aunt an agonized glance of inquiry. She breathed a small sigh of relief at Aunt Gussie's nod, and settled the newcomers in chairs and settees.

"Did you have a good journey?" she asked brightly.

"Oh, tol lol," replied Thomas.

"Simply dreadful," said his wife at the same time.

"For God's sake, Rosie, don't be such a ninnyhammer," bellowed Thomas jovially. "Rose suffers from headaches, you know," he confided loudly to Miss Melksham. "Always quacks herself into a megrim with her everlasting nostrums and potions."

Claudia surprised a flash of resentment in Rose's eyes, but it was quickly veiled behind her pale lids. She bowed her head and after a moment, sat back in her chair and looked around the room.

"My, you never did get rid of that stain on the Egyptian sofa, did you?" she remarked in a high, sweet voice. "How fortunate that I brought something for it. My housekeeper makes it up, you know. Wonderful stuff. Perhaps it might help bring back some of the color in the hangings, too."

Claudia clenched her teeth. Rose had perhaps forgotten that the stain was a result of Master George's accident some months previous with a cherry tart that he had been expressly forbidden to bring into the room. It was a perfectly hideous sofa, anyway, one of Emanuel's acquisitions, purchased when he had moved into Ravencroft.

"But, my dear," continued Rose. "You are not wearing your blacks."

"No," replied Claudia shortly. "Had I known you were arriving today, I should have put on something more suitable, but I decided to put off my blacks long ago. I never did wear them except for company, or when out visiting. At any rate, Emanuel has been dead for almost a year."

Rose pursed her lips, but said nothing. She was a nondescript-looking woman, faded and dispirited—as Claudia saw it, living with Thomas for ten years had taken its toll—who seemed to disappear into whatever background she was set against.

"I say, Mrs. Carstairs," a nasal voice piped up. Fletcher Botsford had seated himself next to Claudia on a straw-colored satin settee, and now captured her hand. "You're looking, er, very nice." He pressed a moist kiss on her fingers, and beamed nearsightedly at her.

"I'll wager you were surprised to see Fletcher, what?" barked Thomas. "Had to winkle him away from the pleasures of city life, doncher know. The pretty ladies there don't want to let him go."

Botsford cast down his eyes modestly without relinquishing Claudia's hand. Easing her fingers from his clammy grip, she smiled. "How nice to know you are wanted, Mr. Botsford," she purred. "We will certainly understand should you wish to hurry back to Gloucester."

Guiltily, she observed his painful blush. Fletcher was not a bad sort, after all, but Thomas surely must know by now that she had no intention of marrying the poor twit. Why did he keep forcing her into the young man's company? *You know very well why.* The thought curled into her mind with cold irony. Even as she watched Thomas, his eyes flickered about the room in an unpleasantly proprietary manner.

A soft sound behind her caused her to twist in her seat, and her eyes widened. Proceeding majestically into the room, pushing a tea table laden with gleaming silver and china was January, garbed meticulously in all his butlered splendor.

"Madam wished tea?" he queried austerely. Claudia could only nod mutely as Miss Melksham unfolded her angular form and rose to wave him forward.

"Yes, indeed, January. Over here." She turned to speak to Claudia with an air of elegant condescension. "Would you like me to pour, my dear?"

Claudia looked again at January, who raised his eyes to hers for one swift glance of humorous mockery. She nodded again. Thomas raised his quizzing glass to inspect Jem, who moved with smooth grace to distribute tea and cakes without so much as rattling the delicate Spode china of which Claudia was inordinately proud. "This the feller who replaced whatsizname?" asked Thomas.

"Morgan. He replaced Morgan," replied Claudia, her fingers clenching.

"He seems very young." This from Rose, surveying the young man as, with a respectfully lowered gaze, he bestowed a cup of Bohea on her.

"Yes," replied Claudia somewhat unsteadily, "but he came to us with excellent references." Only she observed the slight twitch that turned up the mouth of the seemingly oblivious butler.

January remained until the ladies and their guests had been served. Then, with a deferential bow, he glided silently from the room. Claudia breathed a grateful sigh.

"Seems to know his job, at any rate," said Thomas expansively. "Glad you finally replaced whatsiz—er, Morgan. Now then," he rubbed his hands together, "tell us how you've been going on? Have you settled anything with Foster about your sheep yet?"

Claudia, loathe to discuss her business affairs with her brother-in-law, turned an inconsequential answer, then searched for a topic with which to turn the conversation.

She bent her attention to Rose. "George is becoming quite the little man, isn't he? Perhaps later, when he is, er, cleaned up, I shall take him to the stable to see our new colt."

"The stables!" cried Rose, with a little gasp. "I don't think—"

"Colt?" rasped Thomas, as though she had not spoken. "Has Jenny foaled then?"

"Last night," Claudia responded, allowing the pleasure of this thought to leaven her ill temper. "A little stallion. We're very pleased."

Thomas looked very pleased, himself, as though someone had just informed him he'd won the lottery. "If he's well formed, we could get a pretty price for him from Selwyn Morthwaite," he said eagerly. "You've met him—he lives not five miles from me."

We? Claudia caught her breath in anger at his inadvertent slip.

"He's not for sale, Thomas. We plan to use him for stud when Warlock is no longer capable. Jonah says he will—"

"Tchah!" interrupted Thomas. "Are you still listening to that old fool?"

In her armchair of emerald-striped silk, Rose twittered ineffectually, while Aunt Augusta stiffened. Claudia shot her a smiling glance as she rose to face her brother-in-law.

"I always listen to Jonah," she said, her features a smooth mask except for tawny eyes that glittered dangerously. "He is, after all, well worth listening to." With an effort she dropped the subject and gestured to Rose. "Now, I know you will wish to repair to your rooms. We have prepared the chambers you always use. Rose, George and Horatia will be in the nursery."

Thomas opened his mouth as though he would say more, but after a glance at Claudia's rigid form, apparently thought better of it. He rose and, offering his arm to his wife, made a dignified exit.

Claudia sank back down in her chair. "Aunt, I am liable to do mischief to that man someday."

"And I would enjoy helping you, my dear"—Miss Melksham enveloped her niece in an impulsive embrace—"but he is kin. Or at least, he's married to your kin."

Claudia gulped in wordless dismay. Rose was her only sister, though at nine years her senior, she had always seemed more like an aunt. An aunt, moreover, whose personality was the opposite of hers in every respect. Where Claudia was wild and stubborn to a fault, Rose was meek and biddable. Claudia, the rebel, vowed she would not be told whom to marry, while Rose at eighteen had blushed and declared herself more than willing to wed the prosperous landowner her father had chosen for her. There were other, less critical differences. Claudia loved books; Rose, except for the occasional volume on household advice was totally disinterested in them. Claudia loved long tramps in rain-washed, fragrant meadows; Rose squealed at the prospect of getting her feet wet. The catalog could be continued at some length, but Claudia preferred not to reflect any further.

She loved her sister, of course, but it took a great deal of effort sometimes to remember this fact.

Rising again, she smiled at her aunt. "But not nearly such

beloved kin as you are, Miss Augusta Melksham. I am still thanking Providence that you agreed to come here and live."

Miss Melksham, suffering a rare moment of discomposure, adjured her niece not to be a goose, and led the way from the room.

The rest of the day passed with little further event. As promised, Claudia took George, and Horatia, who insisted on accompanying them, to the stables to view Goblin. This resulted in Jonah's taking unprecedented action when Master George insisted he be allowed to ride the little animal. The boy's outraged screams when Jonah picked him up bodily and carried him from the building brought his mother on the run. She skidded to an abrupt halt when she reached the edge of the kitchen garden, and from the relative tidiness of its border, she railed first at Jonah and then at Claudia for allowing this attack on her son. Horatia provided an antistrophe of screeches and earsplitting demands for attention. Thomas, whether through determined deafness or disinterest did not appear, and without his bluster at her back, Rose soon subsided into a series of resentful sniffs. George and the iron-lunged Horatia eventually quieted as well. Claudia basely fled to her bedchamber.

Entering the dining room that evening, her eyes flew to Jem and as quickly turned to Thomas as that gentleman progressed directly to the chair at the head of the table. It was a source of intense irritation to Claudia, that it was Thomas's habit to sit there when he visited. To keep peace in the family, she had never disputed his appalling presumption, but this night Jem was ahead of him. Placing his hands on the back of the chair, and thus making it inaccessible to Thomas, he waited until she approached before pulling it out with a flourish for her to be seated. Thomas reddened, and he swelled visibly, but said nothing, accepting with an air of bruised dignity the chair to Claudia's right, drawn out for him with a profound bow by Jem.

From there, Claudia was pleased to note, dinner went much more smoothly. She was pleasantly surprised at the stature lent to her table by Jem's presence. He had evidently coerced Lucas into service as a footman, although the only task entrusted to the young man was the carrying of food into the dining room and the removal of plates. January himself served each dish in turn, circling the vast table with inspired dignity, proferring the food as though he were ladling out precious gems.

As before, Claudia was vitally aware of Jem's silent attendance—of his every move. She told herself that the heightened sense of vitality she felt whenever she was in his presence was due solely to her concern over his nefarious schemes.

"This is excellent soup," remarked Rose in a tone of rather affronted surprise.

"Yes, Cook is famous for her vichyssoise." Which might very possibly be true, reflected Claudia, except that she had certainly never prepared it before for the Carstairs family. She shot a sidelong glance at Jem, standing with unconscious grace at his position near the door. She rather thought it was he, rather than Aunt Augusta—who was not given to display—who had cozened the staff into providing this elegant feast. She breathed in the scent of the fresh-cut flowers that adorned the center of the board.

Her hand stilled in its course from her soup plate to her lips. The word she so often uttered when contemplating the mysterious Jem January—or Standish—leaped into her mind. *Why*? What possible difference could it make to him if Rose and Thomas Reddinger were served vichyssoise or mutton broth? Was it because he could not bear to see any standard beyond that of excellence prevail at his old home? She risked another peek toward the shadowy corner by the door, but could find no enlightenment in her butler's stony features.

Jem intercepted the glance, wondering what was behind it. The widow had been casting him some extremely odd glances all day, or at least during the portion of it that he had been given the opportunity to observe her. He watched her unobstrusively, noting the graceful tilt to her head as she maintained a courteous conversation with Thomas Reddinger. Lord, what a nodcock the man was. And yes, definitely a greedy muckworm as any he'd ever seen—and God knew he'd seen quite a few. As for the other guests, Rose Reddinger was such a nonentity that it was hard to consider her as anything beyond a taker up of space, and Fletcher Botsford was enough to make a person cast up his accounts.

Botsford was seated on Miss Melksham's left, but she might

have been invisible for all the attention he paid her. His slightly protuberant eyes focused solely on his hostess, and he responded to her every word with a bray of laughter that set Jem's teeth on edge. Lord, did the booberkin really believe he stood a chance with an incomparable like Mrs. Carstairs? Jem's gaze caressed her again, following the pure line of her cheek to the delicate tracery of her lips, and down the slender column of her throat. The gown she wore tonight was the amber-colored affair she had worn the night before, and his breath caught as she moved slightly, causing the roundness of her breasts to shift enticingly under the silk. Abruptly, Jem came to himself as Lucas came to stand beside him, swearing softly under his breath in discomfort at the livery he'd been forced into.

After dinner, Thomas declined the port decanter and accompanied the ladies to the music room, where Rose favored the company with a selection of rigid little études that had Claudia yawning behind her teeth.

It seemed a small eternity to Claudia before Jem once more put in appearance with the tea table. It was a little early for this, the final refreshment of the day, and she shot him a glance of abject gratitude, which he returned with the merest lift of his brows.

Later, as she wearily crawled into bed, she wondered how she would manage to get through the next week or so. She supposed she should be grateful that, since they lived less than a day's drive, the Reddingers did not stay long when they came. On the other hand, she thought wistfully, if they lived farther away, she might not have to see them so often. She shrugged her shoulders in a rueful gesture, realizing that the chances of her sister and brother-in-law moving to the Antipodes with their awful offspring were woefully slim. Yawning, she nestled her head in her pillow and prepared to give herself up to sleep.

But no.

She sat up. She had forgotten to tell one of the maids to leave a candle burning in the hallway outside Rose's bedchamber. Being a light sleeper, it was her habit to rise frequently in the middle of the night to check on George and Horatia. The fact that Nanny Grample reposed in a room next door to the children, and could be depended on to awaken at a sound bore no influence with Rose.

"A child waking terrified in the dead of night requires the presence of his mother," she was fond of saying in a tone of long-suffering sweetness. Privately, Claudia considered that it was the recounting of her nightly forays at the breakfast table, garnering murmurs of awed commiseration from her listeners, that provided the momentum for this evidence of maternal devotion.

No, she definitely had not given instructions for the candle, and in the morning Rose would comment plaintively on the oversight.

Sighing, Claudia flung aside the covers, and, not bothering with robe or slippers, she lit her own bedside candle from the glowing embers in her fireplace and tiptoed from her room.

Moving quietly along the gallery that spread from the great staircase to create a balcony on the second level of the house, her gaze was caught by a flicker of light from below. Curious, she peered down into the cavernous blackness of the hall and discerned in a moment that someone was approaching from the service area.

With a quick breath, she extinguished her candle and waited. In a moment, a figure could be discerned walking swiftly into the huge chamber. His face was clearly visible in the pallid light surrounding him, and Claudia realized with a start that the late-night wanderer was Jem January.

Holding her breath, she watched him traverse the hall in his circle of light, moving with a silent intensity that brought her sharply to mind of a slender, elegant panther sliding through a midnight jungle.

With only a moment's hesitation, Claudia descended the stairs. She made no sound as she kept her eyes fixed on the faint radiance that bobbed ahead of her in the corridor leading to the library. When she herself reached the library, January was no longer in sight, but from inside the room came sounds of movement. Drawing a deep breath, she placed her hand on the door handle and, taking care not to make a sound, cautiously opened it.

Chapter Seven

Claudia stopped just inside the door, her eyes drawn immediately to where Jem stood near one section of the bookshelf. She watched as he selected a volume and brought it near the taper, and she let out the breath she had been holding for what seemed like several minutes. How ridiculous she had been. Of course, he was only here to find some reading material.

The first book he chose was evidently not to his liking, for he—what on earth was he doing? Holding the book in both hands, he raised it above the candle and opening it, he peered not at the pages, but along the volume's spine. He shook the book a little, and thrust a finger inside the space between the spine cover and the page binding. He shook his head, muttered something to himself, and chose another volume, whereupon he repeated the same procedure.

A chill crept over Claudia that had nothing to do with the draft that floated over her bare toes. January was not here to borrow a book. He was searching for something! She stood motionless for another few minutes as the butler removed several more books from their places and subjected them to the same scrutiny. He paused once to sneeze as a cloud of dust from an upper shelf enveloped him.

Claudia turned to steal out of the room, but suddenly changed her mind. It was time, she decided, to find out more about this interloper. She must discover his purpose. She slid back out into the corridor and soundlessly closed the door behind her. Then, she swung about, and with a determined clatter of the door latch, entered the library once more.

January turned as she entered. He did not appear discomposed at being found outside his quarters at this late hour, but raised the candle in an effort to discover who had interrupted him.

"Ah, Mrs. Carstairs. I hope I did not disturb you."

"Not at all, January. I remembered something I omitted to do for my sister and rose to tend to the matter. I heard a sound and came to investigate. Are you unable to sleep?"

Jem surveyed the young woman as she glided into the room. With her hair streaming over her shoulders, and her ruffled cotton night rail brushing her bare toes, she looked almost childlike. As she grew closer, however, the soft curves that proved her to be all woman could be seen beneath the cotton. Jem swallowed.

"Yes, ma'am. With all the excitement today, I found it difficult to compose myself to rest. I thought perhaps a book—"

"Of course, I often read to make me sleepy. After all"—she glanced at him from beneath lowered lashes—"books contain treasure that appeals to all of us, do they not?"

The butler made no response, and Claudia drew closer to him. "Tell me, January, are you happy here so far?"

Jem caught the faint scent that enveloped her. Lavender, he thought, with something else sweet and fresh blended in. Her hair caught the candlelight in golden reflections as it fell over her shoulders in a silken rope, and her eyes as she gazed at him were large and mysterious. She moved with an unknowing, sensuous grace, like a young woodland deity from the depths of the forest.

Noting the extinguished candle in her hand, he took it from her, and her fingers trembled slightly as they came into contact with his. He lit the little taper from his own, then set them both on a nearby table. He gestured to a chair, and when she had seated herself, he took another close by her.

"To answer your question, ma'am, yes, so far I like it here very much." He smiled, and to Claudia it seemed that the light in his eyes came not from the candle flame, but from an inner compelling luminescence. "I thought butlering might be boring," he continued with a laugh, "but such is far from the case."

Claudia returned his smile. "We endeavor to keep our employees entertained here at Ravencroft. Tell me, Mr. January, what do you do when you are not buttling? Or delivering colts?"

Jem paused for a moment, the laughter dying on his lips. "Oh, a little of this and some of that," he replied.

"And where do you accomplish a little of this and some of that?" Claudia made an effort to keep her tone casual. "I first thought that you must be from Gloucestershire, but now I am not so sure that is true."

"Indeed," replied Jem easily. "I am originally from this part of the country, but I left many years ago and have only recently returned." He had learned a long time ago that the best way to perpetrate a deception is to tell the truth whenever possible.

"Ah." Claudia's nose wrinkled disarmingly. "Did you go to London to seek your fortune?"

"In a manner of speaking."

"But the Cotswolds called you back."

"Indeed."

Claudia felt perspiration break out on her brow. This was like trying to nail a blancmange to the wall. Faint but persistent, she continued. "But, why did you not return to your own village—wherever that may be?"

January did not rise to the bait, merely lifting his brows as he remarked, "Jobs are scarce, and a man must eat."

Abandoning this line, Claudia waved her hand toward the books lining the walls. "And apparently a man must read as well. Were you looking for anything in particular, January? We have a wide range of selections."

"But not nearly as extensive as it was before," replied Jem, indicating the many gaps that appeared on the shelves. "How unfortunate that so many are gone."

"Yes, but I've found that we still have less valuable copies of most of the volumes that were sold, and I feel that the substance of a book is its most important feature."

"Very true," agreed Jem gravely. "The value of a book lies in what the author has to say rather than the fact that it is bound in Moroccan leather, or that it was the first copy to be printed. I was looking for, ah, *Tristram Shandy*, but I do not see it. Would there perhaps be a copy somewhere else in the house?"

Puzzled, Claudia stared at him a moment before answering. "Well, there are quite a few books in the study. Those are mostly volumes on farming and country life in general."

"Ah, I find rural subjects most interesting," said Jem, his attention fully caught.

"Really? Let me see . . . " Claudia rose and went to the bookshelves, lightly brushing his arm as she passed. "Yes, up there"—she pointed to a thick tome resting on a shelf high above her head—"is a book on agricultural practices, published in the last century."

She made a futile effort to reach the book, and Jem moved to stand close behind her. He plucked it from its position, bringing it down so that they could both read its title.

"*On Maintaining a Country Estate in the Cotswolds, with Instructive Treatises on Agriculture, Animal Husbandry, and Hints on Household Management*," read Jem. "Whew! That seems to cover the subject pretty thoroughly."

He was very close to her, and a tremor passed the length of Claudia's body at the warmth of his breath on her cheek. Lord, he smelled good—of soap and his own peculiarly musky scent, and very faintly of horse. Had he just come in from the stables? She laughed shakily. "Yes, indeed. I leafed through it a year or so ago, hoping to find some useful information."

"And?" His voice had taken on an odd, husky tone and Claudia had the sensation that the rest of the world had vanished into the darkness surrounding them, leaving the two of them standing alone in a warm, glowing pocket of intimacy. She tried to move away from him, but found herself alarmingly enclosed by the bookshelf, the butler, and the volume he was holding. She glanced up and encountered a gaze containing, she thought, amusement and a certain tenderness.

Hurriedly, she dropped her eyes again to the book. "And," she replied in a voice she hardly recognized as her own, "I did find some helpful facts on raising horses—and sheep—and . . . " Unable to help herself, she lifted her head once more and found herself caught, helpless as a rabbit pinned beneath a predator, staring into eyes that held all the brightness and all the mesmerizing promise of morning starlight.

Slowly, and with infinite tenderness, Jem lifted his hand to where her hair met her cheek. She was appalled at the shudder of response that shot through her at his touch, but she seemed incapable of withdrawing from him. His head bent to hers until his lips rested on her mouth with a softness that was at first tentative, but which flamed immediately into urgency.

Frightened at the need she felt to press against him—to offer him the welcome of her body, she drew back with a startled gasp, and at her withdrawal, January stepped abruptly away from her.

"I'm sorry." His voice was a rasping growl, and he appeared almost startled as his hand dropped to his side. "I—I don't . . ."

But she did not stay to hear. Whirling, she ran from the room. Stumbling blindly through the silent house, she reached her bedchamber at last and flung herself on her bed.

What had just happened? The library, she reflected wildly, was neutral territory—at least—surely more so than the servants' quarters, but she was very certain that kissing one's butler in the former was a far greater solecism than swilling brandy with him in the latter.

Of course, he wasn't really a butler, was he? Not that that made things any better. Good God, she had vowed war against this man, and her defenses had crumbled at the first skirmish. To make things worse, she berated herself, she had no doubt brought the whole episode on herself. She had been conscious the whole time she was in the room with him that her appearance, barefoot and in her night rail, without so much as a robe, was highly improper. She had consoled herself with the thought that the night rail was very concealing and made of the sturdiest cotton. Apparently, she was mistaken in this concept. Lord, she must have looked the veriest wanton. It was not surprising that the interloper had tried to force his attentions on her. The man had no morals, after all, or he would not be here with the purpose, in all probability, of preparing to throw a practically destitute widow out of her own home.

A moment, my girl. Forced his attentions on you? The small, cool voice spoke in the back of Claudia's mind, and she stilled in the act of punching one of her pillows. Well, not forced precisely, but if she had made the slightest resistance, he no doubt would have . . .

Ah.

She rose from the bed slowly and padded across the room to her mirror. She lit the candle resting on her dressing table and stared for several moments at her reflection.

No, she had not resisted. In point of fact, when his mouth had brushed hers with such tender authority, it had taken every scrap of willpower she possessed to refrain from burying her hands in that silky, dark mane and pulling him into her very being. She had never thought of herself as being "that sort" of woman, but with his kiss, she knew she wanted to feel the length of his body against hers. Her tongue curled with the desire to know the flavor of that lightly bronzed skin.

It must be sheer lust—mustn't it? She certainly felt no tender sentiments toward him. She hardly knew him, for heaven's sake. Was this aching—this fire in her veins merely the result of her own innate passion, too long repressed?

She thought of her distasteful couplings with Emanuel Carstairs. On their wedding day, as she had stood beside him at the altar, she had felt cold at the appalling realization that the hour was fast approaching when she would have to undress before this man—when she would be forced to endure his embrace, which she had already learned was a sweaty, smothering invasion of her senses. The reality had proved even more repellent.

She shuddered and drew the high neck of her night rail tighter about her neck. The memory of Emanuel Carstairs's touch inspired nothing in her beyond a sick horror and a sense of relief that she would never again have to submit to a man's advances. Why then should she feel a vastly different response to the touch of Jem January's strong, slender fingers on her flesh?

Determinedly, she blew out the candle and scuttled across the room, fairly leaping into bed. She would waste no more time thinking of silvery eyes and hair like night. With an effort, she turned her thoughts to his replies—or lack of same—to her questions. He had admitted that he was a native of these parts. Was he telling the truth? But, why would he lie? She turned his words over in her mind, and realized to her chagrin that his supposed origin was the only bit of information she had been able to prize from him. And she already knew that he must be from around here. He very well might be one of the former residents of Ravencroft, if not Lord Glenraven himself. Lord Glenraven. She shivered, wishing that name did not have the power to cause a frisson of panic to skitter up her spine.

And what had he been searching for in the book spines? What could be hidden in such a small space? Well, any number of things, she supposed. A small utensil, a piece of paper, jewelry, coins . . . She sighed, realizing that she was wasting her time, time that could much better be spent in sleep, for morning would come early.

She rolled over resolutely, but it was many minutes before her eyes closed in sleep.

Downstairs, Jem stood for some moments, motionless, after Claudia's flight. After a long while, he made his way back to his own quarters and again, stood in the center of the room, staring dazedly about him as though he had strayed into a foreign universe.

He had never considered himself to be a ladies' man. There had been brief moments of brightness in the bleak chill that was life in London's underbelly, occasions of warmth and pleasure, but they had been few and fleeting. In the main they had consisted of solace given and taken. He had never loved, and, he rather thought, had never been loved. He did not consider this an unfortunate state of affairs. It was his observation that those who fancied themselves in love appeared to be among the most wretched of creatures, always miserable at the slights, real or imagined, inflicted on them by the objects of their affection, and eternally eaten by petty jealousies.

That was not to say he did not like women. A coquettish smile, a lilting voice, the gratification—and temporary oblivion—to be found in a warm, scented embrace, were all pleasures taken by him with gratitude and, yes, even friendship. However, he had never given anything of himself in these encounters. He had little to give, after all, and it didn't do to let oneself become too close to another. Down that path lay only disillusionment and grief. No, he had always known just where he was in his affairs. In all of them, everything had been above board and spelled out ahead of time, just the way he liked it.

Then what had he been about tonight? Granted, the lady was supremely enticing, and to find oneself alone in a candlelit room with such a creature—one in a fairly advanced state of undress to boot—was surely an incitement to dalliance. But he had already established in his own mind that this particular lady was not for seduction. After an initial leap of anticipation, his pulse had slowed, and he had felt himself fully in control.

Then she had drawn near, and his detachment had exploded like a bolt of flame rising from the sun's surface. Her beauty, the scent of her, robbed him of coherent thought, leaving him a shaken, unthinking mass of desire. He could no more have stopped himself from at long last giving into the temptation to see if that glorious hair really felt like coiled satin than he could have voluntarily elected to stop breathing.

From there, of course, it was not to be expected that a man could resist the temptation to taste the warmly curving lips raised to his. It had been an experience like nothing else he had ever known. In an instant, he had become lost in the wonder of her mouth and the sweetness that lay within. If she had not pulled away . . .

Hmm.

Had he detected a response in the lovely widow? Her eyes, just before she turned to flee the room, had not been angry, but rather almost frightened. Perhaps she had been concerned about the possibility of being discovered in the arms of her butler. She had seemed as startled as he at his sudden transformation from respectful servant to importunate lover.

He slumped into a handy chair and listened to the silence around him. This must not happen again. He would be on his guard in the future against taffy-colored hair that seemed alive with a vitality of its own and huge eyes filled with a blend of childlike vulnerability and womanly wisdom. There would be no more candlelit encounters. No more confidences shared over brandy.

In a matter of weeks, if all went well, Claudia Carstairs would be out of his house and out of his life. As would her appalling relatives, he added, reflecting on the contretemps he had witnessed earlier between Jonah and young Master George.

He began his preparations for bed and felt, for the first time in many years, an odd sense of loneliness.

Chapter Eight

The next several days passed in relative calm. Despite Claudia's best efforts, she and January met each other frequently in the chambers and corridors of Ravencroft, as well as the stables, but his demeanor toward her reflected nothing beyond the most neutral of servant-employer relationships. Claudia was relieved, of course, that the man did not again attempt to importune her, yet she was forced to admit that she felt somewhat bereft as well. The memory of his lips pressed against hers remained with her in startling clarity.

Claudia entered the breakfast room one morning, after the Reddingers had been at Ravencroft for a week. It was a small, sunny chamber on the south side of the house, giving onto a charming garden, and as she entered, she was relieved to note that January was nowhere in sight. A respectable repast, including eggs, ham, kidneys, and toast ready to be spread with fresh, country butter, was laid out on the sideboard, and a footman, one of the young men drafted from the village community for the duration of the Reddingers' stay, stood by to give assistance.

As she moved farther into the room, Claudia's relief turned to dismay as she noted that the only other person at table was Fletcher Botsford. Her heart sank within her. She knew that ordinarily he was a late riser, and must have left his bed early with the express purpose of waylaying her. She had been successful at evading his clumsy attempts to get her alone, but now she was virtually trapped.

Observing his expression of pleased delight at her entrance, she forced her lips into a smile.

"Why, good morning, Mr. Botsford."

Mr. Botsford's somewhat vacuous features fell into what

could only be termed a smirk. "I have asked you repeatedly to call me Fletcher, my dear lady. Surely our acquaintance is of long enough standing to permit ourselves this small informality."

"Oh, I think not, Mr. Botsford," she replied breezily. "I'm afraid I was raised to set great store by the proprieties."

The smirk faded, to be replaced a moment later by a hopeful grin. "It is a lovely day," he began, pausing to wait for a gesture of encouragement that never came. "Um, that is, I was hoping that you would come for a drive with me. Perhaps we could even pack a pic—"

"Oh, I'm terribly sorry, Mr. Botsford," Claudia interrupted, looking not in the least regretful, "but Lord Winlake is driving over this morning to look at one of our yearlings. He is visiting friends nearby, and will only be in the area for a day or two."

"Clau—Mrs. Carstairs!" His lips pursed in astonishment. "Surely you do not handle the business matters of your estate. You must have retainers for that sort of thing."

"Of course, she does." A jovial voice sounded from the doorway, and, as was becoming a habit, Claudia's fingers clenched instinctively. "What can you be thinking, m'dear? Of course you will accompany Botsford. Jonah can take care of his lordship."

As though the matter were settled, Thomas turned to the sideboard and proceeded to mound large portions of food onto his plate. He waved at the footman to indicate his desire for coffee, then settled himself at the table across from Claudia. "Do you good to get out," he finished, speaking through a mouthful of eggs and ham.

Before Claudia could reply, Rose fluttered into the room. Directing the footman to procure fresh toast, *very* lightly buttered, and a cup of tea brewed from a simmering, but not boiling kettle, she perched on a chair next to her husband.

"Gracious," she declared in a faint voice. "I vow I did not sleep a wink last night. Claudia, dear, you really must instruct your housekeeper to replace the mattress on my bed. It has such a large lump in it that my back is one large welt this morning."

"We do not have a housekeeper," responded Claudia quietly, her fingers now in a permanent cramp, "but I shall relay your message to Aunt Gussie."

Rose's hands waved in a petulant gesture. "Oh yes, I had forgotten. Well, never mind then. I do not wish to add to Aunt Augusta's burdens. I shall make do." Her eyes lifted ceilingward in pious resignation.

"Nonsense," Thomas said. "I'm sure your aunt will not regard the matter as any trouble. After all, this is your home, too." He shot a sidelong glance at Claudia, and at her expression of affront, he added, "That is, we are all family, are we not?"

Claudia did not reply, but abruptly rose from the table. "If you will all excuse me," she said, fighting to control the anger that bubbled within her, "I must go out to the stables and see that all is in readiness for Lord Winlake's visit."

"But what about your drive with Botsford?" Thomas's voice was high with vexation, and the piece of toast he held in one beefy hand paused in its journey to his mouth.

"I'm afraid that will be impossible," said Claudia tightly. "For I do, indeed, find it necessary to see to the business of running the stables myself."

Hurrying from the room, she practically flew down the corridor and did not stop until she had reached a small service room into which she darted for haven. Slamming the door behind her, she leaned against it with closed eyes, breathing deeply.

"Is anything amiss, ma'am?"

Startled, she whirled about to discover January standing at a table at the far end of the room, garbed in a voluminous cloth apron. Claudia stared unbelievingly. He was polishing silver!

Carefully placing a gleaming sugar bowl next to the creamer he had just finished, he repeated his question in a manner that perfectly blended concern with deference.

She did not answer at once, merely staring for a long moment at her hands, which she slowly stretched out before her. At last, she bestowed a fiery glance upon the butler.

"Yes, January," she said in a controlled voice. "There is something very definitely amiss. I am surrounded by persons who appear to have made it their main goal in life to steal Ravencroft from me."

To Jem, the young widow seemed to be in danger of simply exploding in a burst of lightening bolts. She advanced, her eyes taking on the color of polished shell casings. "I'll tell you something else, Mr. January. *Nobody* is going to take this place away from me. Do you hear? *Nobody.*" Without waiting for a reply, she turned on her heel and strode from the room.

Jem could have sworn he heard a sound of trumpets as the door clicked soundlessly behind her.

Well, he mused as he picked up a tarnished butter boat and thoughtfully applied polish and cloth. Well and well, indeed. The situation was growing interesting. Was he to infer that Mrs. Carstairs suspected his true identity? He smiled to himself at his Gothic interpretation. The smile faded. He had by now searched through nearly all the volumes in the library. He was still hopeful that he would find the information he needed to prove his claim to Ravencroft. He admired the widow's tenacity and her fearless determination to fight all comers, but if matters turned out as he hoped, it would be to no avail. In the end, she would have to admit defeat, and her departure would take place soon afterward. He would miss her, but . . . He paused in his ruminations, surprised. He would miss her. What a ludicrous thought—it implied that her presence was of importance to him. Which it wasn't. He had learned long ago the importance of being sufficient unto oneself, and the idea that a woman he had known but a few days could creep into his life was—well, ludicrous.

Still, the house would seem empty without her clear laughter and the warmth of her ready smile. His brief conversations with her left him smiling and wanting more. Her wit and intelligence—her generosity to those around her—had admittedly got under his skin. And he rather regretted that he would not have another opportunity to feel the brightness of her hair beneath his fingers, or the softness of her body pressed against his.

He shook his head and applied himself with renewed vigor to the butter boat.

After she left Jem, it took some moments for Claudia to recover her equanimity, but her mood improved measurably some hours later when Lord Winlake purchased the yearling with a minimum of haggling. When his lordship left, he declared his cheerful intentions of recommending the Ravencroft stables to his friends.

The remainder of the day was consumed in discussing with Jonah how the purchase price was to be spent, and in delighting Aunt Gussie's soul with the promise of a new closed stove for the kitchen. Just before it was time to dress for dinner, Claudia left the service area of the house and, entering a quiet corridor on the ground floor, she slipped into a small, pleasant little room that lay at the far end of the east wing. Emanuel had used it for a study, and once she had removed all traces of its previous occupant, she had appropriated it for her own use. In one corner stood a small, elegant Sheraton desk, and here she sat to do the estate accounts. On a table nearby rested an untidy stack of books culled from the library. They were her favorites, and many a reflective hour was spent perusing their contents or simply daydreaming in a comfortably shabby chair drawn up to catch the window light.

It was into this chair that she now sank gratefully, and settled back to review the day's events. She murmured aloud the figure she had received for Cloud, the yearling, and lovingly rolled it around in her mind. This was the second large sale she had made in a month. There were four yearlings yet to be sold, in addition to one or two mares, and the prospect of . . .

Her thoughts were interrupted by a knock at the door, followed immediately by Fletcher Botsford's balding head, peering into the room.

"Dear lady," he said breathily, whisking the rest of his thin frame inside. "I hope I do not intrude?"

Since she was slouched in a chair staring at nothing, she could hardly claim the press of her affairs as an excuse for fobbing the man off. Claudia managed a weak smile and a "No, of course not, Mr. Botsford."

She rose to greet him, hoping that if they both remained standing, his visit would be of short duration. He grasped her hand and pressed it to his lips. Restraining an urge to wipe her fingers on her skirt, Claudia stepped back hastily.

He wandered about the room, riffling the papers on her desk and turning over the books to examine the titles. Stifling her irritation at his familiar behavior, she asked, "Was there something you wanted, Mr. Botsford?"

He turned back to face her. "No, no—I merely wondered where you had got to. Haven't seen you all day, after all." His gaze traveled over the little chamber. "So this is where you keep so busy all the time."

"Yes, here and in the stables, and often in the fields."

"The fields?" He glanced about again, as though expecting to see a plow standing in the corner.

"Yes," she replied smoothly. "I like to go out now and then to see how the work progresses. Harvest is not far off, and there is much to be done to insure a good crop. We are expecting an exceptionally good growth of corn this year. Our alfalfa is shoulder high already and the clover is doing well, too. Would you like to come with me tomorrow?" she asked innocently. "I plan to help with the sheep delousing."

She watched with malicious pleasure as he paled. "De . . . ? Uh, no. I think not. I have a delicate constitution, you know. I shouldn't wonder if I'm not allergic to, er, sheep."

Claudia assumed an expression of regret.

"But I didn't come in here to talk to you of corn and sheep," he continued with an air of injury. He advanced on her once more, and again availed himself of her hand. "My dear," he continued throatily. "You must know of my feelings for you. My, ah, long-standing feelings, that is. I want . . . "

Claudia gave a little shriek. "Oh, my goodness, look at the time! I must dress for dinner. What will Thomas think if I am late?" She endeavored to remove her hand from his rather damp grasp, but Mr. Botsford was not to be deterred. He brought his other arm about her waist, and despite her concerted effort to the contrary, he pulled her to him.

"Mrs. Carstairs," he said, by now panting a little with exertion. "Claudia," he amended firmly, "about my long standing feeling for you—your brother-in-law has advised me that you stand in need of a husband, and I wish to offer myself to you in—in that position."

Claudia tried once more to wrest herself from Fletcher Botsford's grip, but he proved to be surprisingly strong. "Mr. Botsford, please!"

But the gentleman was well and truly in the throes of passion, and instead of releasing her, went so far as to press a moist kiss on her cheek. He uttered a disgruntled sound, for he had been aiming at another target. He made another try.

"Mr. Botsford, you must let me go this instant!" Claudia wriggled in his embrace, but this served merely to inflame her would-be suitor. He wrapped both arms around her and proceeded to rain kisses upon her face.

Claudia was beginning to feel somewhat alarmed. She was not afraid of the wretch, but the situation was becoming severly embarrassing. She flexed her leg in preparation for a well-placed thrust of her knee.

"You rang, madam?"

Such was Claudia's relief at the sound of the familiar voice, that she nearly crumpled as Mr. Botsford, jerking spasmodically, released her.

"What the devil . . . ?" he began, turning on Jem in outrage.

"January!" gasped Claudia, attempting to smooth a strand of hair into place.

"Nobody rang for you, you looby," blustered the thwarted lover. "Go about your business."

"No!" The word burst from Claudia. "That is," she continued in a quieter, albeit breathless tone, "We were just about to leave to dress for dinner. Thank you."

Fletcher opened his mouth as though to expostulate, but catching January's bland, unwavering stare, he turned to Claudia, only to find her expression no more promising. With a muttered oath, he wheeled about and strode from the room.

There was a moment's silence.

"Will there be anything else, ma'am?"

Claudia searched January's face, but his imperturbable features showed no recollection of the intimacy of several nights ago. Had that kiss meant nothing to him? Not that she cared, of course. He meant nothing to her except as an enemy to be vanquished. What had happened in the throbbing silence of the library was best forgotten.

She inclined her head, and said cooly, "Thank you, no, January." Gathering her skirts, she swept past him, her eyes lowered, knowing that if she were to raise them to his, she would find that amused twinkle that made her go weak.

How had he known where to find her, she mused as she hurried along the corridor. How had he known that she needed him just then? How foolish she must have looked struggling in the arms of that ridiculous twit. A thought struck her suddenly, almost causing her to stumble. Surely January did not think she had been encouraging Fletcher Botsford in his misplaced ardor? Immediately she chided herself for once again allowing herself to be concerned over what January thought of her.

Upon reaching her room, she moved straight to her wardrobe, where she selected another of the gowns she had not worn since early in her marriage. She attempted to ignore the uncomfortable truth that waggled for attention in the back of her mind—that she was not garbing herself in her most becoming gowns for the edification of Thomas and Rose, and certainly not for Fletcher Botsford.

Entering the emerald saloon some minutes later, she found that she had indeed put in an appearance behind Thomas and Rose. Taking advantage of the fact that Fletcher had not yet arrived, she advanced on Thomas, who stood before the fireplace, sipping gustily at a glass of port.

"A word with you, brother-in-law," she said, her eyes glittering. Rose scuttled to a chair some distance away, where she plunged into some embroidery and became apparently oblivious to all else.

"I wish you to stop giving Mr. Botsford to believe that I am amenable to his suit. For I am not, Thomas, and never shall be."

Thomas shifted uncomfortably. "I don't know what you're talking about, Claudia." He coughed as though something had stuck in his throat. "Oh, well," he continued after a moment, "perhaps I have encouraged him—a little. And what's wrong with that?" His voice held more than a hint of bluster. "You are my responsibility, after all."

Claudia went rigid. "No, Thomas." She spoke quietly, but her balled fists were pressed tight against her sides. "You are not responsible for me. I am accountable to no one, least of all you. You have nothing to say to my affairs. I do not wish to marry again, and, and rest assured, even if I did, Fletcher Botsford is probably the last person in the world I would choose."

"Now, see here, my girl . . . " Thomas began, while in her corner, Rose twittered agitatedly. "Dearest sister—" she breathed, but was cut off as Thomas plowed ahead. "You are becoming entirely too hot at hand. You are a woman living alone, and I am your nearest male relative. You must see that gives me some say-so in the ordering of your affairs."

"I see nothing of the kind," snapped Claudia. "I am of age, and I am the sole owner of a prosperous estate—or at least it will be so in a few years. As *you* must see, I am managing quite nicely on my own, thank you."

Thomas stood for a long moment, his feet planted wide apart, staring speculatively at her. When he spoke again, it was in a quieter tone, but it seemed to Claudia that it held a note of menace she had not heard before.

"You delude yourself, my dear child, if you think you do not need the guidance of someone older and wiser. You believe yourself to be an astute businesswoman, but how many clients will flock to your stables if it becomes known that the proprietor is naught but a flighty young girl who flies in the face of custom? Or worse. There are those who might think you mentally and emotionally incompetent to handle such an operation."

Claudia stared at her brother-in-law unbelievingly. "Are you threatening me?" she gasped.

For an instant there flashed in Thomas's eyes a look of such naked hostility that Claudia found herself momentarily breathless. It vanished so quickly, however, that she thought she must have imagined it, and in the next instant, he waved an impatient hand.

"Of course I'm not threatening you," he said pettishly. "I am merely looking out for your interests."

"For no doubt you believe them to be yours as well, but let me tell you, Thomas . . ."

She broke off as Fletcher Botsford entered the room, followed closely by Aunt Augusta. Claudia bade a distant good evening to Mr. Botsford, who was still looking somewhat disgruntled. After greeting Thomas and Rose, he began edging toward his prey once more, but Claudia was spared further incursions on her patience by the entrance of January. Through happenstance, he paused only a few paces from Botsford, and Claudia was struck by the contrast between the two. January, in his plain servant's garb stood slender and elegant and every inch the gentleman, while poor Fletcher had a stretch merely to appear adequate. As though she were the only person in the room, January directed his dark gaze toward her and announced in mellifluous tones that dinner was served. Unsuccessfully attempting to quell the sudden and unwelcome increase in her pulse rate, Claudia followed him sedately.

As might be expected, the meal was not a happy occasion. Its only redeeming feature, at least to Claudia's mind, was the fact that Thomas had relinquished whatever rights he considered were his to the head of the table, obviously feeling it was beneath his dignity to race the butler to the table. He settled himself in the chair to her right and proceeded to complain over every dish that was set before him. In this, he was ably seconded by his wife. She whined consistently about everything from the soup, which she said was too salty, to the custard, which was declared watery. In between, the lamb chops were pronounced to be underdone, the asparagus stringy, and the pigeon pie too spicy. Even Aunt Augusta, who had earlier chided Claudia on her inability to keep her tongue between her teeth, took umbrage.

"We consider ourselves extremely fortunate in our cook," she informed Rose austerely, her curls almost rattling in her displeasure. "It is unfortunate that you do not share our appreciation, but how nice it is that you are able to overcome your sensibilities," she finished, casting a pointed glance at Thomas's plate, which had been wiped clean of his third helping of the maligned pigeon pie.

Fletcher Botsford tittered into his napkin, subsiding quickly as Thomas shot him a minatory glare.

Claudia scarcely followed this exchange, so conscious was she of January's presence behind her chair. Why, she fumed silently, when she was in his presence, did she always feel as though she were attached to him with invisible, silken cords? As he helped her to one dish after another, small shocks sizzled through her body at his every casual touch. It did no good to tell herself she was behaving like the veriest schoolgirl. Firm reminders that this man was her enemy were useless.

No sooner had the final drop of wine been sipped and the last crumb of pastry been nibbled than Claudia pushed her chair back and rose abruptly. She accompanied Rose and Aunt

Augusta to the music room, but, pleading a headache, she soon fled to the sanctuary of her bedchamber.

"Mercy, Miz Carstairs," cried Phoebe Dodge, one of the girls from the village, who was temporarily filling in as lady's maid "You had a bad day? You look strung up like my Uncle Fred's fiddle. Here." She bustled about the room, disrobing her mistress and enveloping her in another cotton night rail. "Let me brush your hair. That'll take your kinks out."

Claudia accepted these ministrations with silent gratitude, but it was not until the little maid had finished with the brushing and had scurried from the room that she finally took a deep breath and began to relax.

She felt utterly exhausted, but it was too early to go to bed. Outside, the late summer sun had not quite set, and Claudia stared from the window at lawns and gardens turned to flame in its rays.

Turning, at last, she moved to a small shelf near her bed and began to peruse the books that lay there. She had brought them up from the library some weeks ago, but, since her evenings were usually long and work-filled, she ordinarily fell asleep almost immediately after retiring; thus she had not opened even one of the little horde.

Yawning, she selected a small volume of Milton's pastoral odes. Feeling that this was just the soothing sort of reading matter she needed, she placed it on her bedside table along with a candle. Settling herself among the pillows, she reached for the book and as she opened it, an odd, crackling noise came to her ears. What in the world . . . ? She opened and closed the book a few times. Yes, there was something . . . Drawing closer to the candlelight, she probed into the space between the spine of the book and the page bindings, and in a moment drew out two crumpled sheets of paper.

She smoothed them out on the coverlet, and her breath caught as she noted that the sheets were covered with a familiar handwriting. Why, it looked like one of Emanuel's lists . . . Yes, there was his name scrawled at the bottom of one of the pieces of paper. But, who would have stuck such a thing inside a book? She scanned the first page rapidly, and suddenly went rigid. Dear God, what *was* this? "Look at G. signat. for copying . . . must at night . . . Glenraven—cards Tuesday . . . D.

must finish his work that night . . . forged title in my hands by morning . . . must put Glen. in his cups . . . "

Her hands were shaking so badly by now that she was barely able to maintain her grip on the papers. After she had read every word of the scrawl that covered both sides of each page, she fell back against the pillows. She felt as though the floor had opened beneath her, sending her plunging into a terrifying abyss. The meaning of the scraps of paper was damningly clear. Emanuel Carstairs had stolen Ravencroft by the wickedest piece of deception imaginable and had killed its owner. The estate belonged by right to the murdered Lord Glenraven's heir—and Emanuel Carstairs's widow had no claim to it.

Chapter Nine

For a long moment, Claudia sat still and cold as the implications of her discovery rolled over her in great, icy waves. Ravencroft did not belong to her! It was not her home—it was that of the man who had taken up residence in her servants' quarters. No—not *her* servants' quarters, for it was she who was the interloper, not the gray-eyed stranger who was in all probability Lord Glenraven.

She pressed her fingertips to her temples, trying to think, but she could not seem to get past the appalling words, "Ravencroft is not mine. I do not belong here." The thought grew and swelled in a great, throbbing ache until it seemed to fill her entire being, pressing down on her until she thought she might simply fall to the floor under its weight, unable to rise.

"Oh, God!" Her anguished cry echoed through the room as she put her head in her hands and sobbed.

She looked again at the pieces of paper still crumpled in her hand. Her eyes followed the progression of events, detailed in Emanuel's heavy, untidy hand, that had led to the unseating of the previous Lord Glenraven and his eventual death. Emanuel and his everlasting lists, she thought grimly. The habit that she had always considered merely an irritating eccentricity had proven her undoing.

Everything she had worked so hard for was gone. The pride she had taken in the revitalizing of Ravencroft—the horses, the sheep, the reacquisition of land and tenantry—all blown away on the bitter wind of loss.

Emanuel, she reflected numbly, had been an evil man—but never stupid. Why had he not destroyed this proof of his villainy? What reason could he have had for concealing it—

where anyone might later find it? She shook her head dazedly and turned the pages of the list over in her hand, noting that the edges were partially charred. Had he begun to burn them and then changed his mind? But why? None of it made any sense.

And none of it made any difference, she realized with chilling clarity. It was obvious that this was what the Standish heir had been searching for. This was why he had crept into Ravencroft in disguise—why he had not simply ridden up to the front door with barristers and bailiffs and magistrates at his back. For how long, she wondered, had he suspected that his home had been stolen from him through greed and chicanery—and, yes, murder. How had he discovered that there was hidden somewhere in the house . . . No, his search had been specific. He knew the information was concealed in a book—but he did not know which one. She smiled in grim amusement. No wonder he had been dismayed to find so many of the library's volumes gone. It must be that without the evidence he sought, the rightful heir had no legal claim to Ravencroft.

No legal claim to Ravencroft.

The words slid into her mind slyly, like a thief reaching into a pocket. She was the only person in the world who knew of the existence of the papers. My lord butler could search till his eyes bubbled, but without her help, he would never find the information he so desperately sought.

Who, she reflected fiercely, had the greater right to Ravencroft? The stranger, who had not lived here for years, and in all probability remembered little about the place, or herself, who had labored to bring the estate back to beauty and prosperity? Surely, this man could never love Ravencroft with the passion and single-minded dedication that now seemed part of her soul. Surely, except for a legal technicality, Ravencroft was hers by any moral or ethical standard that could be applied to the situation.

She rose and strode to the window. For a long time she gazed blankly at the lawns and lakes of Ravencroft, and the fields that lay beyond, all folded in the rolling landscape of the Cotswolds piedmont.

* * *

Belowstairs, Jem entered his chambers and wearily stripped off his stable clothes. As had become his habit, he had spent the hours between dinner and bedtime working with Jonah and Lucas. He was daily growing more impressed with Claudia Carstairs's business acumen. Despite her lack of horse knowledge, she had made remarkable progress in restoring the stables to the reputation they had held when his father had been the owner. Under Jonah's tutelage, she had made intelligent decisions in the breeding end of the operation, and her management of cost and income was astonishing. She had an excellent grasp of sales principles. As she increased her stock, she had contacted a select group of his father's old customers with highly satisfactory results. These men—or their sons—all renowned for their knowledge of prime horseflesh, had purchased colts, geldings, and mares, and had returned to buy more. Their friends were now beginning to appear at the Ravencroft stables, as well.

Mrs. Carstairs had accomplished all this in only two years, reflected Jem. She had worked at accounts night after night in the loneliness of the hours when everyone else slept. No task was too menial to turn her hand to, and she inspired the same devotion to the estate in those who worked for her.

He sighed deeply. It was becoming more and more difficult to face the prospect of turning Claudia out of Ravencroft. The fact that he would make an adequate settlement on her no longer seemed appropriate. She had poured her strength and her sustenance into this place, and he had the feeling she would be miserable living out the rest of her days in genteel boredom in Bath or Brighton. Or Gloucester.

With her beauty, she would not be condemned to live alone with her aunt for very long. Perhaps she would marry that insufferable twit, Botsford. Lord, he thought with revulsion, surely she would not consider that. When he had interrupted their embrace that afternoon, she looked as though she were about to become ill. But, if not Botsford, there would be someone to covet her golden loveliness.

Of course, Jem reflected with a grim smile, her brother-in-law would not be so assiduous in providing her with a compliant bridegroom when she no longer owned Ravencroft. On the other hand, Jem had no doubt that Thomas, bereft of the chance to virtually own Ravencroft would salvage what he could of the situation by attempting to sell his beautiful sister-in-law to the highest bidder. Claudia was pluck to the back-bone, but for how long could she resist her brother-in-law's constant pressure?

He sighed again, thinking again of the indomitable spirit clothed in that slight, lissome frame. It was unfair that she must be forced to make her own way in the world. He brought himself up short. That was the way of things, wasn't it? He had learned long ago that life is not fair, and Claudia, having been married to Emanuel Carstairs for four years, must realize it as well.

Jem moved to the washbasin near his bed and began sluicing away the day's grime, wondering uneasily as he did so how long it might take him to find the papers he sought. He had so far managed to thrust the dismaying possibility from his mind that he might not find them at all, but he had been through nearly every volume in the library with no result. There were other books in the house, to be sure, but what if the volume he needed had been sold?

He shrugged resignedly. Surely, with the evidence he had already accrued, he would eventually see himself settled in as master of Ravencroft. Wouldn't he? He had the sworn statement of the man who had aided Carstairs in his filthy scheme. That statement had been wrung from Daventry, however, under the threat of a lifetime spent in jail, as opposed to transportation to the penal colonies in Austrailia. Would it hold up in court? The fact that Daventry was now halfway around the world would not help.

There were still people—such as Jonah—who could testify as to Carstairs's villainous character, but would that be enough?

Jem sat down on the edge of his bed and ran his fingers through his hair. Dear God, he could not have come this far merely to have Ravencroft snatched from him again. His head sank into his hands, and he sat thus for a long time before slowly beginning to remove his boots. So immersed was he in his unpleasant thoughts that at first he did not hear the soft knock that sounded at his sitting room door. When it was repeated, he lifted his head, and rising, shrugged into his shirt. His first thought was that Jonah had sent for him, and in stocking feet, he padded to the door.

His eyes widened as he beheld the small figure standing there, the candle she carried creating russet highlights in her tumbled hair.

Claudia took a deep breath. "I must talk to you," she said baldly.

Silently, Jem opened the door to admit her and gestured her to a small armchair. When she was seated, he sank into one nearby.

Claudia stared into eyes that returned her gaze with a certain quizzical amusement. She flushed as she realized he must think she was seeking an assignation with him. She stiffened, and perched on the edge of the chair. At her first words, the amusement faded abruptly.

"I think it is time we had an honest discussion, my lord."

If she had expected to discompose him, she was disappointed. His eyes were calm and unreadable, and he said simply, "I beg your pardon?"

"No need for that," she said flatly. "And no need for further dissembling. I know who you are and why you've come."

In the long pause that ensued, Jem did not take his eyes from Claudia's face. "I see," he said at last. "And may I ask what has led you to this, er, surprising conclusion?"

"You bear a striking resemblance to the portrait I discovered of one of your ancestors."

Claudia was startled at his sudden laughter. "Of course. That would be Great-uncle Philip. My mother often noted our similarities. I always thought him a rather shambling fellow, myself."

"And," continued Claudia, "it is obvious that since you have gone to such lengths to gain access to the house, you must be the heir."

"I see," repeated Jem. "May I ask why you have chosen this particular time to announce your discovery?" His tone was light, but Claudia had no difficulty in discerning the tension that lay beneath it.

"I believe I shall not tell you that just at present, my lord," she said composedly. "It is equally apparent that you have come with the intention of establishing your ownership of Ravencroft."

This time, Jem made no response, but his eyes had taken on the glitter of rainwashed pebbles. Claudia simply stared at him until at last he nodded in an unwilling gesture of assent.

"May I ask," she proceeded, feeling as though she were making her way along a tightwire, "on what you base your claim to the estate? As you must know, my late husband—acquired it from your father in payment of a gambling debt."

Jem rose and paced the floor, his thoughts tumbling over one another like stones flung into a pool. Good God, he had known from the start of his charade that he could not keep his identity a secret for very long, but he had not expected the widow to penetrate his disguise so soon. What was he to do now? His mind raced, assessing the implications of her discovery, and in another few moments, he reached a decision. He returned to where Claudia sat, rigid and tense.

"You have arrived at the correct conclusion, Mrs. Carstairs, and I do indeed owe you an explanation of my admittedly bizarre activities." He sat down again and pulled his chair near, gazing at her with that intensity she found so unnerving.

"To begin with, my name is Jeremy Standish, and yes, I am Lord Glenraven. Ravencroft was my home for the first twelve years of my life." He paused for a moment of reflection. "That life was a relatively happy one, until the day that Emanuel Carstairs swung into the orbit of our family, which consisted of my father and my mother and my two sisters.

"Carstairs was the guest of one Giles Daventry, the nephew of a neighboring squire. Daventry used the squire's estate as a second home, to which he repaired frequently from his, er, busy life in London. Daventry and Carstairs had found each other sometime before, and had become partners in various unsavory enterprises. When Carstairs found himself the target of a group of gamblers he had duped, he found it prudent to rusticate for a bit, hence his presence at the squire's house."

Again Jem paused, and for the first time, Claudia sensed a slight uncertainty in his demeanor.

"Father," he said at last, "was—a good man, but more than somewhat weak. He rarely visited London, being uncomfortable with the ways of the Polite World, and supremely content with his horses and his estate and the family he loved dearly. But he did share one flaw that besets so many of the *ton*; he was addicted to gambling. This being the case, it was perhaps inevitable that he would come to the notice of a man like Carstairs, who had, by the way, grown immensely popular in the neighborhood. He had a gift—as you no doubt know—of drawing people to him, with his hale-fellow-well-met joviality and his ability to counterfeit the air of a prime go. A regular top-of-the-trees, everyone thought him."

Claudia said nothing, but nodded in grim agreement.

"He became a frequent visitor in our home, and when my father was not about, he made my mother the object of his gallantry. During this time, I grew to dislike him, though I knew not why. I learned much later that he was pressing his attentions on my young, still beautiful mother."

"Dear Lord," murmured Claudia.

"Father enjoyed many late-night card sessions with Carstairs and Daventry, and somehow did not find it strange that he was so frequently in debt to these gentlemen at the end of the evening. At about this time, things began going badly in the stables. Mysterious illnesses and accidents cost us our finest stud and several mares. In a short time, Father found himself in serious financial difficulties."

Claudia writhed in her chair, and listened in growing apprehension.

"He could not stop gambling, however, and the card games with Carstairs continued. He began to drink heavily, as well." Jem rose and crossed to the window, where he stared into the night. "To cut a long story short, it came to pass that the point was soon reached where Father could not pay what he owed to Carstairs. Carstairs, being the good fellow he was, brushed all that aside, and allowed Father to pile debt upon debt, until one night, he made a kindly proposition.

"As incredible as it sounds, he persuaded Father to put up Ravencroft as security for the amount owed. Ravencroft, unlike the estates of most peers, had never been entailed. It had originally been a minor holding for the Lords of Glenraven, their primary seat being in the Scottish border country. Weary of the constant skirmishes that threatened life and harmony there, they abandoned it some two centuries ago and settled here. For some reason, they never saw to the entailment of Ravencroft. Thus, it was possible for my father to sell it at will. Carstairs assured him that things would surely come about, and that it was simply not possible that Carstairs would ever feel the need to actually call in the debt."

Jem swung about to face Claudia, his face a mask of despair in the candlelight. "And my poor, weak father believed him. He was in his cups, of course, and he signed a note that very night, promising to sell Ravencroft to Carstairs for the sum of one pound, if his entire debt were not paid by a certain date."

"Dear God," gasped Claudia. "What did your mother say?"

"He never told Mother—or anybody else—anything about it. Matters went from bad to worse after that. Father, of course, did not come about, but the drinking became worse, and the debt mounted. The day of reckoning came and went."

By now, Jem's voice had sunk to a rasping growl, but Claudia had no difficulty in catching every word.

"It was not long after this that Father went for a late-night walk, and tumbled into an abandoned well that lies not far from the house. He was found the next morning, with his neck broken."

Claudia reached her hand involuntarily to him, but Jem continued, oblivious.

"He was drunk, of course, and the coroner had no hesitation in ruling his death an accident. A week later, Carstairs came to my mother and showed her the title to Ravencroft. It had been signed over to Carstairs."

White-faced, Claudia uttered a little moan. "But . . . " she began, only to be silenced by Jem's curt gesture.

"My mother refused to believe the legitimacy of Carstairs's claim, but it was all in order—notarized and all the proper steps taken. Carstairs moved into Ravencroft almost immediately, but he magnanimously declared that he would not force Mother and us children out of our home. Of course not! Was he a monster, after all? He would be happy to marry Mother, and adopt her children as his own.

"Mother, who had read his true character long ago, refused his offer, and stole away in the dead of night, with my sisters and me, to live with her sister and her husband in Stepney. My uncle was a fairly prosperous merchant, and for two years we lived in reasonable comfort. I—I grew rather fond of them. Then, unfortunately, hard times befell him, and he and my aunt declared themselves unable to keep us in their home. Mother moved to spartan quarters in an unsavory section of London and took up a career as a seamstress. I was fourteen then, and my sisters were twelve and nine.

"It was here that I began my education, for it was quickly borne upon me that life in Seven Dials"—here a sound that might have been a whimper escaped his listener, but again, Jem continued as though oblivious—"was far different from anything I had experienced in Gloucestershire, or even Stepney." He smiled grimly. "I took my surname, by the way, from the month we arrived there. Nice touch, that, don't you think?" Claudia shivered, but he went on, unheeding. "I was, fortunately, a quick learner, and it was not long before I was able to contribute my mite to the family income. To my mother's questions about the source of my funds, I resolutely returned the most innocent and false of answers, for it would not have done for her to discover that the heir to the barony of Glenraven had become an accomplished pickpocket."

Claudia was crying openly now, but Jem still ignored her as he continued doggedly.

"Two years after our removal to London, my mother contracted a fever and died. My younger sister followed within a few days. I did my best to take care of Beth—my only remaining family." Jem's voice broke, and for a moment, Claudia feared he would break down, but after a moment he continued dryly. "I was able to protect her for a time from the ugliness around us. I managed to find us a place to live in an unused nook above a tavern. Beth helped out in the scullery while I—followed my own pursuits. At night, we would escape to our corner, hardly big enough to shelter the two of us, and I would tell her stories of Ravencroft—of the trees that I climbed and the meadows I roamed, and I promised I would take her back someday."

Jem rose abruptly and returned to the window. "One day I returned from my day's activities to find Beth gone. I—I searched for her for days, pelting the tavern keeper and his wife with frantic questions and wandering the neighborhood streets calling her name and asking passersby if they had seen a young girl with straight dark hair and blue eyes. Only thirteen, she was. At last I discovered from another girl who she talked to from time to time that she'd been kidnapped. The two had been looking in a pastry shopwindow, when a man came up behind them and simply scooped Beth up and threw her into his waiting carriage."

"But, I don't understand. Why would anyone . . . "

"Beth was a very beautiful child, Mrs. Carstairs," returned Jem harshly. "And very young—just the sort in such demand in some of the more select brothels lining, for example, St. James's Street."

This time, Claudia was bereft of speech, merely staring at Jem in horror.

"I never saw her again," he continued quietly. "I did, however"—here his voice took on a note Claudia had not heard before—"discover that there was a man known to be working in the area whose specialty was abducting likely prospects for the delectation of some of the more jaded customers of these brothels. He worked for a man named Giles Daventry."

"Oh!" cried Claudia, her hand to her mouth.

"Despite my continuing efforts, I never saw Beth again," finished Jem, his words dropping into the stillness. He returned to his chair, and as though disturbed at having revealed so much of himself, assumed a lighter tone.

"As you can imagine, I became intensely interested in Giles Daventry's activities—and not simply because I was trying to discover Beth's whereabouts." He leaned toward Claudia, resting his arms on his knees and steepling his fingers. "An ugly suspicion had festered in my mind ever since my father's death. You see, the well into which he had fallen had been carefully covered with wooden planking some years before. It was meticulously maintained and had always been considered safe. In fact, I had stood upon it only the day before he died. As I crossed it, I jumped up and down, as I always did, because I liked the satisfying thump of hollow wood it made. The covering showed no signs of giving way, and was, as far as I could see, whole and sturdy. Yet the day after father's death, the planking over the well could clearly be seen to be rotted, with a gaping, jagged hole in the center."

Claudia moaned softly as the words flashed before her eyes, "Tues, nt.—repl. boards" written on the crumpled pages she had left upstairs. She had an urge to leap from her chair and run from the room.

As though he had read her thoughts, the man before her said in a voice devoid of expression, "Do I disturb you, Mrs. Carstairs? But there is much more. So very much more."

Chapter Ten

"Over the years," continued Jem, "the suspicion grew in my mind that Father had been murdered. I thought of returning to Ravencroft and accusing Carstairs to his face, but even at fourteen, I knew the futility of such an action. I had no proof, and Carstairs would have simply laughed in my face—or killed me as well. Therefore, I made the study of Giles Daventry my life's work, so to speak. I found where he lived and followed him everywhere. When I began to see some small success in my own slightly nefarious activities, I formed a network of associates who helped me in my research and watched him when I could not. I made records of his associates—of all his comings and goings—who he spoke to, and what dealings he had with whom. I began to compile a dossier of his criminal activities with which I hoped to blackmail him into revealing all he knew of Carstairs's plot against my father."

Jem glanced at Claudia for the first time since he had begun his monologue and smiled faintly at the expression of horror that lingered in her eyes.

"Don't take it to heart, my dear. It all happened so very long ago, after all."

"Oh, but Je—my lord," the words erupted in a sob. "You have—"

He placed his hand over hers, cutting off her speech. "Jem will do very nicely, don't you think, under the circumstances?"

She found his words cryptic, but so aware was she of the pressure of his fingers on hers that she merely lifted her brows. He continued without haste.

"Then, a few months ago, an opportunity dropped into my lap. I had begun receiving some odd information of Daventry's association with a young man, one Chad Lockridge, who was apparently in love with a woman Daventry had staked out for himself. An earl's daughter, and very wealthy. Daventry, by the by, had cut a swathe for himself in the Polite World and was received by the highest sticklers in the *ton*. He had, however, due to his proclivity for cards, women, and other expensive pastimes, found himself in very low water recently and was in desperate need of an advantageous marriage. Lockridge had left the country suddenly some years ago, and I believed Daventry had something to do with his departure. Then, Lockridge returned, much wealthier than when he had left, and it became apparent to me that Daventry had once more taken an interest in the fellow. One evening, as I stood outside a house in Mayfair waiting for Daventry to emerge from a party, I observed Lockridge leave the place first—by himself. He strolled away from the house, and on a hunch I followed him. Thus, I was on hand when he was set upon by a band of thugs, and was able to give him a hand.

"Lockridge and I formed a sort of partnership, the happy result of which was the ultimate arrest of Giles Daventry for a number of things, including theft and attempted kidnapping. It turned out that Daventry had indeed done his best to ruin Lockridge, employing some highly illegal methods in doing so."

Claudia drew a shuddering breath. "And Giles Daventry told you . . . ?"

"Everything I wanted to know. Under pressure from Lockridge, who had become an extremely influential man by then, the magistrate agreed to transportation for Daventry instead of a death sentence. For three days, information spewed from him like poison from a lanced boil."

"But what part had he played in Emanuel's scheme?" asked Claudia, afraid to hear the answer. Her hands were still clasped tightly in Jem's, and she found herself without the will to disengage them.

"Ah. Giles Daventry, among his other accomplishments was a skilled forger. He had done a bit of work for Carstairs from time to time, and the two had formed an extremely profitable association. When Carstairs arrived in the neighborhood and met my father—and my mother—the idea for taking Ravencroft apparently leapt into his brain full-blown. Father was an innocent, you see, with no idea of the evil that could lurk in the hearts of other men. He saw Carstairs as Carstairs wished to be perceived, a bluff, kindly soul who was fond of the occasional game of cards. Father was also weak—and overfond of the occasional game of cards. In short, the perfect mark.

"It did not take long for Carstairs to plunge my father into debt, and like all gambling addicts, the more he lost the more he believed that the next hand would see him come about. He apparently had no idea of how deep he had fallen into your husband's clutches, for when Carstairs pointed out the sum to him one evening, he was appalled. It was a few days after this that Carstairs suggested Father put up Ravencroft as security. Father, of course, believed him when he said that Ravencroft would never actually pass from Standish hands. There was no question, said Carstairs, but that Father would soon recoup his losses. And Father believed him. He had papers drawn up promising Carstairs full ownership of Ravencroft if his debt were not paid by a date some two months in the future. Father, you see, felt that if worse came to worse, he could sell off the horses to pay what he owed." Jem's voice hardened once more. "This may well have done the trick, but Father never had a chance to resort to this option."

He gazed down into Claudia's stricken face. "I told you this would not be a pleasant story. As I said," he continued without giving her a chance to reply, "Father had begun to drink heavily, and on one of their visits to Ravencroft—how my mother dreaded those visits, by the way, for as a guest, Carstairs left a great deal to be desired. He lost no opportunity to waylay her as she moved about the house, touching her in a familiar manner and making every effort to establish a liaison with her."

Jem felt Claudia's fingers tremble beneath his, and without volition, he brought them to his lips for a moment. Hastily, he continued.

"On one of their visits to Ravencroft, Carstairs and Daventry prevailed upon Father to show them the small wall safe in his study, where the deed to the estate was kept. The date agreed upon came and went, with still more drunken card games taking place here.

"One night, after a particularly boisterous session, Daventry returned to the house, much later. Did I tell you he was also an expert cracksman? A safe robber," he explained, at Claudia's expression of puzzlement. "He removed the title from the safe and within a matter of minutes, had forged Father's name to a transfer deed."

"But how . . . ?" Claudia felt as though she could not bear to hear more, but the words seemed forced from her. "Do you mean Emanuel . . . ?"

"Yes. The next day he came to Ravencroft and with the utmost regret began to speak of 'what happened last night.' In the face of Father's blank ignorance, he said, 'Oh, my dear fellow. Do you not remember?' Well, of course Father remembered little of the previous evening's occurrences, having spent most of it in a semi-drunken stupor. Carstairs then informed him that the two of them had reached an agreement in which Father signed Ravencroft over to Carstairs. As you can imagine, Father was stricken. Carstairs, however, hastened to assure him that he, being a good friend, had no intention of taking possession of the estate. No, no. He would merely hold the title, and allow Father more time to repay the debt.

"It still did not occur to Father that Carstairs had duped him. Numb with grief, but like an obedient child, he accompanied Carstairs to the magistrate's office, where he filled out the appropriate papers and had the deed notarized. By the end of the day, Ravencroft belonged, lock, stock, stables, and lands, to Carstairs."

"Dear God," said Claudia again. "I know what Emanuel did was vile, but how could your Father have let himself be so duped?"

Jem laughed shortly. "Do you not think I have not asked myself that question a thousand times? I could almost loathe him for his—emasculation, yet, he could not help being as he was. I still remember him as the laughing man who threw me in the air only to catch me in his arms for an enveloping embrace. He loved my mother—he loved my sisters and me, only—"

"He loved gambling and drinking more," finished Claudia

harshly. "I know—my father was such a one. He bartered his daughters to feed his appetites."

Jem looked at her, startled. "Yes," he said gently. "I heard that was the case. I am sorry."

Claudia glared at him. She snatched her hands away and let them form into fists. "Well, don't be," she replied fiercely. "I survived Emanuel Carstairs, and I will survive this. I am beholden to no man now, and I thank God every night for it."

To this, Jem made no reply, but continued softly. "I'm sure you have guessed the rest of my story. A month or so after signing Ravencroft away, your husband replaced the solid planks over the dry well with rotted boards and the next day, Father had his 'accident.' The well lies near our orchard, and it was one of Father's favorite walks. Carstairs immediately began his persecution against my mother."

Jem paused, a bitter smile curving his lips. "I confronted him one day and in the blithe ignorance of my twelve years, ordered him to 'stop bothering Mama, for she would rather die than marry you.' He roared with laughter and with one swoop of the back of his hand, knocked me to the floor. I did not tell my mother what had happened, but she saw the bruise on my cheek and drew her own conclusions. Within a week, she and my sisters and I were on our way to Stepney, taking only what we could carry with us."

There was a long silence in the little room, as Claudia gazed steadily at her fingers and Jem gazed even more fixedly at Claudia. She looked, he thought, in the purity of her features, like an early Christian martyr waiting for the ax to fall—not in terrified submission, but with a dignity so profound that it almost hurt to watch her.

At last she lifted her head and looked at him straightly. "You are telling me, then, that you are the true owner of Ravencroft."

"Yes." He said the word simply, but behind it she could hear the exultation of the weary traveler who has at last reached sanctuary.

"You have Giles Daventry's statement verifying all you have said."

"Yes." A certain wariness crept into Jem's voice.

"Do you think this sufficient to convince the authorities of your claim?"

Jem felt perspiration break out on his brow. No fool she, the widow Carstairs. She had unerringly put her finger on the flaw in his program.

"Yes," he repeated, with what he hoped was an air of surety.

Claudia rose, and this time it was she who paced the worn carpet. She turned finally, and faced him. "I think you have not told me quite everything, my lord. You have yet to explain why you did not, as you say, march up to the front door with the full weight of the law at your back."

For the first time in many years, Jem felt himself completely at a loss. He said nothing, however, merely cocking his head in courteous attention.

"I believe," continued Claudia, speaking carefully, "that you came here to find something. Something hidden in a book—though I don't think you knew precisely which book." She shot a quick glance at Jem and was gratified to observe that he had grown rigid. She permitted herself a small smile. "I could not help but note your pointed interest in the fate of our library volumes, and your uncommon interest in late-night reading."

Jem drew a deep breath. It appeared he would have to tell this golden witch everything. Perhaps, he concluded hopefully after a moment's consideration, he could turn the revelation to his advantage.

"You are most perceptive, Mrs. Carstairs." Claudia did not at all care for the grin that curled on his lips. "Giles Daventry related another occurrence to me. It seems that your late husband was in the habit of making lists. Almost compulsive about it, he was. Daventry said that even in his illegal activities he made it a practice to outline in writing the project at hand. He was always careful to destroy any paperwork that might be incriminating, of course."

"Yes," said Claudia, her features hardening. "I remember."

"When Carstairs sat down with Daventry in the squire's house to plan Glenraven's downfall, he made one of his usual meticulous lists. Afterward, when all was finalized, he crumpled the two sheets of paper he had covered with his writing and tossed them in the dying hearth fire. Later, when the two men were ready to leave the room, Daventry noticed that the sheets had missed their mark and lay unburned just in front of the nearly extinguished fire. Not knowing why he did so, he scooped them up, unseen, and thrust them into his pocket before following Carstairs from the room.

"Much later, when Carstairs was established at Ravencroft, Daventry decided to return to London to attend to his own business matters there. In his opinion, Carstairs had been overly thrifty in his renumeration for services rendered, and, recalling the crumpled papers in his possession, he determined to try a little blackmail.

"He approached Carstairs one afternoon in the library. Carstairs was apparently dumbfounded at Daventry's effrontery, and merely admonished him for his stupidity, considering that the notes implicated Daventry as well as himself. On reflection, however, he rang for a footman—also a longtime henchman, and in Daventry's presence ordered a thorough search of the young man's rooms. As it happened, Daventry had the papers in his pocket—admittedly not very wise, but in this case it saved his bacon, for it never occurred to Carstairs that Daventry would commit such a blunder. However, Daventry knew with chilling certainty that Carstairs's next step, having discovered nothing upstairs, would be a thorough search of Daventry's person.

"Fate intervened just then in the person of the vicar, who had chosen this moment to call. Carstairs was forced to leave the room, just long enough, it appears, to virtually drive the man from his door, and in that time Daventry secreted the papers in the spine of the dustiest volume he could find on a shelf in the darkest corner of the room. In his haste, he barely discerned the name of the book, recalling later merely that it had the word 'rural' in the title."

At a slight sound that could have been smothered laughter, Jem bent a keen glance on Claudia, who had settled again in the little armchair. She shook her head. "I was merely reflecting on the 'great ripples from little stones' theme," she said unsteadily.

He gazed at her for another moment before continuing. "Daventry thought he would be able to retrieve the papers at his leisure, but such was not to be. Not only did Carstairs refuse to dispense any largesse, but he evicted Daventry from the premises with all possible speed, promising dire retribution should he reveal any of Carstairs's sordid secrets. Daventry never set foot in the library again. This, needless to say, weakened his position considerably, and nothing further came of the scheme."

Claudia's eyes fixed on Jem's in unwavering intensity. "So, you are saying that proof positive for your claim is concealed in one of the books in the library."

Jem sighed. "Yes. That was my reason for this ridiculous charade." His arm flew up to encompass the butler's quarters. "I thought it would expedite things if I could add those papers to the stack of documents already in my possession. I—I did not wish for a long, drawn-out court battle. I must confess that I had myself talked into the idea that you would not wish for such an eventuality, either."

"And now, my lord," asked Claudia quietly, "do you expect me to simply fold my tent and slip away from Ravencroft in defeat?"

Jem shifted in his chair. "Well, yes, I do rather. For, with the information I have collected I believe I shall have no difficulty in convincing the magistrate to allow me to search the house thoroughly. I assume you have kept records of your sales of the various volumes no longer in your possession. If I have no luck with what's left, I'll seek those out as well." He hunched forward. "In the long run, you understand, I must prevail."

Jem's gray eyes contained nothing but a courteous, waiting attention, but she knew she was in the presence of a force so dangerous to her position that she should be shivering in her seat. Yet somehow she felt exhilarated, as though a fresh wind had blown into her settled existence scouring out all that was weak within her and honing her strength and defiance to a diamond-hard weapon. So absorbed was she in the depths of his gaze that it was several moments before she comprehended what he was saying.

"Recompense?" she asked stupidly.

"Of course. I do not plan to turn you and your aunt out penniless into the cold, cruel world, after all. I am prepared to make a generous settlement upon you."

"How very kind of you, my lord. And how, may I ask, did

you come by the wherewithal to make such an offer? From all you have told me, you have been living in dire poverty since you left Ravencroft."

"If that is the impression I gave you, Mrs. Carstairs, I misspoke. My first years in London were dire, indeed. However, as I said, I was not overly nice in my choice of occupation to keep body and soul together. I took to the dub lay, you see. I became a pickpocket. And a very good one," he added, in response to Claudia's expression of disbelief. "Unlike most of the other denizens of my neighborhood, I did not waste my ill-gotten gains on gin. I was perhaps fortunate that the, er, gentleman to whom I was apprenticed was a fairly decent chap—unusual in those environs—and he kept me fed and housed. At least until the day when the authorities caught up with him and he scarpered, leaving me holding the bag. No, no," he said, a crooked smile curving his lips. "I escaped transportation—by an unpleasantly narrow margin, and in the end, I took over my preceptor's position. I became myself a fence for stolen goods.

"It was not until I entered my late teens, however, that I discovered in myself a talent for figuring odds. As in gambling," he explained kindly, lifting Claudia's drooping jaw with one slender finger. "Everyone in London gambles, you know, from the most exalted peer to the grimiest of street rats. One who can calculate the odds of any given occurrence happening over another is in the position of scooping in an enormous amount of money."

"What kind of occurrences?" asked Claudia in unwilling fascination.

"Well, horse races, for one. I studied the history of every nag that ever ran on four legs and became an expert. I also became rather adept at taking wagers on situations where I already knew the outcome."

"I don't understand . . . "

"If I laid out a row of bottles in front of you, and produced a mouse from my pocket, and then offered to wager which bottle the mouse would run into when set before them, would you not say that was an unexceptionable wager?"

"I most certainly would not!"

"Well, you would if you were an inveterate gambler," he

replied somewhat impatiently. "My point is, that I had plenty of takers in every gin mill where I set up operation. And," he concluded modestly, "I won every time."

Claudia could not resist. "But how?"

"Because I happened to know that a mouse is loathe to tread where no mouse has been before him, but will take the path he knows has been trod before him by his fellows."

"That tells me nothing," Claudia said with a sniff.

"It tells you everything. It was my practice to provide freshly washed bottles for my wagers—all except for one, which I would rub very lightly with mouse droppings. When placed on the table, the little creature would nip unerringly into the bottle exuding the scent of his mousy friends."

"Ugh!"

"Disgusting but effective."

"Are you saying you amassed a fortune in this manner?" asked Claudia disbelievingly.

"Well, no, but that's how I got my start. And I did not say I amassed a fortune. I have a fairly comfortable sum put by. What fortune I gain will come from Ravencroft. I have enough to buy back the land from Squire Foster and to buy stock for raising sheep. And," he added prosaically, "I plan to marry well."

"What?" asked Claudia dazedly.

"I am hopeful," replied Jem patiently, "that my title and my estate will gladden the heart of some wealthy landowner, or merchant, with a marriageable daughter."

Claudia shook her head disbelievingly, attempting to ignore the unexpected pain his words had caused. "That's the most cold, cruel, calculating thing I ever heard!"

"Are you a romantic then, Mrs. Carstairs? Well, I am not. I have survived by being eminently practical, and I do not see why a reasonably happy union could not be contrived under such circumstances. At any rate," he continued hastily, observing the dawning indignation and contempt rising in her eyes, "the main point of my discourse was to impress upon you the fact that you will not leave Ravencroft destitute."

Claudia whirled on him, the corners of her mouth lifting in a brilliant smile. "I do not plan to leave Ravencroft at all, my lord."

"But, I have just told you . . . "

"I know what you have just told me, now you will please have the courtesy to listen to what I have to say to you. For, my lord, I have a proposition for you."

Chapter Eleven

For a stunned instant, Jem gaped at her. "A w-what?" The word fell awkwardly from his lips.

"A proposal, my lord." Her heart thundering in her breast, she smoothed her skirt. She wondered how easy it was going to be to live with her decision not to tell Lord Glenraven of her discovery of Emanuel's list. She stiffened her resolve, for the compromise she had reached with her conscience was equitable, she told herself. After an hour's bitter soul-searching, she had come to the realization that she had no right to keep Lord Glenraven from taking possession of his own home. She had no right to Ravencroft at all.

"But it is my home, too!" she had cried aloud into the silence of her room. She may not have been born here, but she loved every stone of the place, and she was *not*, by God going to be turned out.

She marveled at her control as she returned to her seat with no outward show of the turmoil that raged within her.

"You were talking about a long court battle," she continued. "You seem very sure of your chances of winning such a war, but I am not at all certain I agree." She shot a glance at him from under her lashes and was not reassured to note that his eyes now resembled storm clouds blown before the wind. She went on hastily. "However, I am no more eager than you to engage in a protracted struggle."

"Then, the only sensible thing to—"

She held up her hand, and rather to her astonishment, he subsided, contenting himself with what sounded like a thwarted growl.

"As I was saying, I do not wish this thing to drag on forever, so I am offering to give up any claim I have on Ravencroft, in re—"

"What!" Lord Ravencroft wore a ludicrous expression in which relief and astonishment were blended in equal measure. "You are surrendering?"

"Not precisely, my lord," replied Claudia, a sharp edge to her voice. "I will give up my claim on one condition—well, two, really."

The edge transferred itself to the voice of her opponent. "Which are?"

"That you allow Aunt Augusta to remain here—as your housekeeper, and that you retain me to manage the stables."

His lordship's features registered astonishment and angry disbelief. "You're not serious!" he exclaimed.

Claudia did not deign to reply, but returned his outraged glare with the sweetest smile at her disposal.

"But—but, this is ludicrous!" Jem said after a moment. "Why would I agree to such an outrageous proposal? I can run my own stable, I believe, and, while your aunt has done very well as housekeeper, I believe a local woman—"

"Of course, you can run your own stable," Claudia interrupted impatiently. "However, judging from your present knowledge of its operation, it will take months for you to understand its management. In that time, the business will backslide. Are you sure you can afford that? Besides," she continued, "your time would be much better spent in rebuilding the sheep herd."

Jem considered her words silently. She was right, but . . . "You don't know much more about horses than I do," he said, irritated at the pettish note he heard in his voice.

Claudia heard it, too, and smiled. "That may have been true a few years ago, but I have learned a great deal. Aside from that, I am very good at handling the accounts and spending the profits to the highest advantage. I am a good salesman, as well," she added, casting her eyes down in an assumption of modesty.

Jem suppressed an involuntary grin. He was forced to admit that her proposal appealed to him vastly. The next moment, the grin faded. He must be all about in his head. The continued presence at Ravencroft of this lissome charmer was a sure ticket to disaster. He could just imagine the gossip that would circulate, and while he did not care for himself—he would surely not be the first-landed gentleman to install a beautiful young woman in his house—it could prove a tragedy for the young widow. Any chance she might have for a second, and hopefully happier marriage, would be doomed at the outset.

"If you are concerned about the proprieties, my lord . . ." Jem started. Good Lord, was she a mind reader in addition to her other witchery? " . . . I shall, of course, cease to live in the house. Aunt Augusta and I will remove to Hill Cottage. It is situated far enough away to prevent any untoward speculation by the neighbors, but it is close enough so that Aunt Gussie and I can perform our duties without undue difficulty. I know that it is customary for the housekeeper to reside in the domicile, but perhaps you could overlook this very small discrepancy."

Jem waved his hand irritably. He had the feeling that, like the crafty pitchman she had become, she was focusing on a small facet of the problem, knowing it to be one that he could easily overlook, in order to ease him into acceptance of the larger issue. Lord, if she thought that moving into a house in his demesne, not a quarter of a mile from his own home, would still the wagging tongues of a rural community, she was woefully mistaken.

On the other hand, he mused, Miss Augusta Melksham was undoubtedly a figure of unimpeachable virtue and propriety. Her austere presence in the main house during the daytime and at Hill Cottage at night would go far to make the situation acceptable. In addition, from what he could gather, Claudia Carstairs herself had established a blameless reputation during her tenure at Ravencroft that would stand her in good stead.

He shook himself. What was he thinking? The idea was impossible—quite ridiculous. And yet . . . A picture formed in his mind of himself huddled over the account desk across from the delectable widow—of hours spent in her company discussing plans for the expansion of the stables—of days of listening to her musical voice and gazing into her topaz eyes and perhaps allowing his fingers to drift over her silken, taffy-colored hair. He was forced to give himself another mental shake.

"I'm afraid your plan would not at all satisfy the proprieties,

Mrs. Carstairs. Just think, you will wish to remarry someday, but I'm afraid any gentleman worthy of your hand would look askance at a female stable manager, living in such close proximity to a bachelor."

"I have no plans to remarry, my lord." Her tone was bleak and sharp, and such was her expression that Jem forbore to probe further. "In any event"—she crossed her arms and began to tap her foot on the carpet—"you are talking nonsense—and you are evading the issue."

"Which is?" asked Jem, fascinated.

"That it would be in your best interest to hire Aunt Augusta and me. We have all the clothes we need for years to come, and our other requirements are minimal, so all that we would ask in renumeration, besides permission to live in Hill Cottage—which is already adequately furnished, by the way—is our board and a trifling sum for pin money." She folded her hands in her lap and smiled serenely as though awaiting his capitulation to the overwhelming force of her logic.

He rose to pace the floor swiftly, running his fingers through hair that already looked as though it had been set upon by mice, and made the shocking discovery that he was actually thinking of accepting her proposal! He turned to face her, and was struck for the first time by her attire. She really should not make it a habit to accost susceptible butlers in the middle of the night wearing her nightclothes. To be sure, this time she was bundled in a serviceable dressing gown of what looked like woolen homespun, but with the candlelight reflected in that glorious hair hanging down her back in a satin fall, and her eyes full of ancient, womanly mystery, it was almost more than a man could do not to stride to her and pull her up from that chair and— He took a deep breath.

"Mrs. Carstairs, it is late. I appreciate your coming down and—and giving me an opportunity to explain my actions. As to your proposal, I simply cannot give you an answer tonight. If you will give me a few days . . . "

"So that you may think up more unreasonable excuses for not accepting my offer?"

"So that I may come to a reasonable conclusion regarding your highly unorthodox proposal."

She cocked her head. "It's odd, my lord, but somehow you

do not seem the sort of person who would be overly concerned with the orthodoxy of a situation."

Jem was beginning to feel harassed. "I'm not, but . . . "

Claudia tried to quell the churning that had begun again in the pit of her stomach. Dear Lord, this had to work! She breathed deeply. "You know very well, my offer is to your advantage, my lord. And do but consider. If you refuse, I shall retain legal counsel and will fight your claim to the end. Despite your display of confidence, I think you are wondering if the proof in your possession is sufficient to convince the authorities of the validity of your claim."

Jem observed her in growing wrath. The chit thought she had him squarely beneath her thumb, didn't she? He ran his hands through his hair once more. Well, there was no getting around it, she did have him in a corner, and as he examined that corner, he found little room to maneuver. Bloody hell!

He took several more turns around the room before he turned to her at last. "Very well, Mrs. Carstairs," he said stiffly. "I will agree to your proposal."

For a long moment they stared at each other in a silence so charged that Claudia felt it almost as a physical presence. At length, she extended her hand, and after an instant's hesitation, Lord Glenraven clasped it with his own. Her fingers were very cold, he reflected irrelevantly, and having given his hand a slight shake, she withdrew her own hastily and stepped back.

"I shall notify Aunt Augusta of our new situation," she said briskly, "and after that I shall tell Thomas and Rose." Her mischievous smile startled him. "I fear that Thomas will take all this very much to heart. Why, he shall probably whisk Rose away from Ravencroft—and he may vow never to speak to me again."

"May I take it, that your reflections fall into the every-cloud-has-a-silver-lining theme?"

Her mouth curved engagingly, but her voice was demure as she said, "I would never admit to such an undutiful turn of phrase, my lord. However, upon considering that Fletcher Botsford will no doubt withdraw his suit, I think we might add to our collection of pithy sayings the one about those same clouds raining pennies from heaven."

He joined her in a burst of laughter that died almost as soon as it had begun. An awkward silence descended upon them, and their expressions grew somber once more.

"Tomorrow," said Claudia, her throat tightening, "we will go to Gloucester, if you wish—if we start early, we can be back by nightfall—and find an attorney who can help us with the business of t-transferring the deed." She could feel tears gathering behind her eyes, and she blinked fiercely. She was determined she would not cry before this man. "You will not be sorry for your decision, my lord," she continued unsteadily. "I will do a good job for you. As will Aunt Augusta."

"I'm sure you will, Mrs. Carstairs," he replied gravely, then hesitated. "I am truly sorry to be the means of removing Ravencroft from your ownership. Your love for it has saved it from certain ruin, and I—I hope that your continuing presence here will be a source of—fulfillment for you. I know that everyone here will benefit." *Particularly myself*, he almost added, but refrained.

She could not answer, but merely nodded, and turning on her heel, she hurried from the room.

Jem remained for a long time gazing at the closed door. He was filled with apprehension at the commitment he had just made, but beneath it a strange exhilaration bubbled. Silently, in his stocking feet, he did a slow waltz about the room. He told himself that the happiness he felt was due to the knowledge that at last, he would be able to take possession of Ravencroft, full and clear. He finished removing his clothes and fell into bed, exhausted. Still, it was a very long time before he closed his eyes in sleep.

As she hurried through the darkened corridors of Ravencroft to her bedchamber, Claudia allowed some of her gathering tears to fall, then wiped them away determinedly. No, she was not going to cry, for tears would not help. In truth, the urge to weep passed almost as quickly as it had come, leaving her strangely lighthearted. Losing Ravencroft was a blow almost unbearable in its cruelty, but her relief that she would still have a roof over her head—and that the roof would be on the Ravencroft estate—acted as a powerful stimulant, raising her spirits immeasurably.

Reaching her room, she extinguished her candle and sat in the darkness to reflect upon her coming change in station. In all likelihood, she mused, she would want to leave Ravencroft eventually. She could not hang about forever, dependent on Glenraven's good graces. Besides, when he married, his bride might wish to choose a new housekeeper, and might resent the presence in such close proximity of another young woman.

Would he? she wondered. Marry?

The thought caused a flicker of dismay to curl through her, and after a moment she chided herself. How silly she was being. Of course, he would marry—it was his duty to do so. He had declared his intention of contracting an advantageous match, and he must produce an heir. At this thought, the flicker became a major quake, which she suppressed with difficulty. What in the world was the matter with her? Lord Glenraven was her employer, for Lord's sake, and nothing more. Nothing more at all.

This being the case, she thought purposefully, she had better be prepared to serve him to the best of her ability. And, she considered further, she'd be wise to put what was left of the night to good use. Flinging off the woolen robe, she climbed into bed—where she spent a good hour staring at the ceiling.

Despite the lateness of the hour at which she had finally fallen asleep, Claudia awakened before cockcrow. For an instant, she stared into the grayness about her with a strange sense of disorientation. Then she remembered. She looked around the room, as though memorizing its familiar contours against the time when she would no longer have the right to so much as enter this chamber.

She sighed, and slipping from her bed, dressed hurriedly and hastened to her aunt's chambers. Before she and Lord Glenraven began their journey to Gloucester, she must take the time to inform Aunt Gussie of all that had transpired.

Reaching Miss Melksham's chambers, she was forced to knock twice before she heard her aunt's summons from within.

"Whatever is the matter, child?" asked Miss Melksham in bewilderment. The old lady sat up in bed, her voluminous cap askew over one eye.

Claudia hurried to sit on the bed, taking both Miss Melksham's hands in her own. "Oh, Aunt, I'm sorry to awaken you at such an ungodly hour, but I have something terribly important to discuss with you."

Pausing only to reach for her spectacles from the bedside, and having adjusted them on her nose, she adjured Claudia to continue. She did not interrupt Claudia's tale, except to interject an "Oh, my heavens!" at close intervals and in increasingly higher frequencies. After much soul-searching, Claudia had decided to tell her aunt of the discovery of Emanuel's lists, and at this the older woman threw up her hands in horrified amazement.

"Oh, my heavens, Claudia!" she gasped. "I knew the man was a monster, but I never realized the depths of which he was capable."

Her reaction to her niece's further revelations was no less profound. "What do you mean you didn't tell him! My dear, you have committed a terrible sin! Surely you must—"

Claudia managed to soothe the old lady's sensibilities, but it was some time before she was able to launch into the final portion of her tale. When she was finished, Miss Melksham flung herself back on her pillows with a moan.

"Oh, Claudia what have you done? To perpetrate such a deception—"

"But, don't you see, Aunt Gussie? I had no choice. If I had given Lord Glenraven the papers, I would have had no bargaining power, for with them, he has all the proof he needs to take over Ravencroft—leaving him free to turn us out without a second thought—for I put no credence in his talk of a fair settlement. Promises are easy to make, and it's my experience that a man will proceed to do as he pleases. And I did not lie, after all. If I sinned, it was one merely of omission. You must admit, it's not as though I have brought his lordship any harm. We have served Ravencroft well, and there is no reason why we should not keep on doing so."

She was obliged to continue in this vein for many more minutes before her aunt finally flung up a hand in concession.

"Yes, very well," she sighed. "I'm not sure you acted wisely, my dear, but it seems the die is cast. I will say nothing of Emanuel's wretched list to—to Lord Glenraven. Gracious, it will seem strange to call him by that title. Who would have thought that one's butler could become so elevated?"

"Certainly not I," responded Claudia, chuckling despite herself. She then explained her plans to travel into Gloucester with Lord Glenraven to arrange for the transfer of the title. "For," she concluded, "I wish to present a fait accompli to Thomas."

Her aunt sat bolt upright in her bed. "Oh, my heavens, I had not thought of Thomas. He will be absolutely livid!" Her mouth wrinkled into a sour smile. "Yes, I can see your point. Left to his own devices, he would never see you turn over Ravencroft to another without a cataclysmic battle. Well," she concluded, at last flinging the bedcovers aside. "We have much to do today, so we'd best get started. Would you ring for my maid, dear?"

As Claudia complied, her aunt drifted about the room, uttering aloud the plans that seemed to be fairly assaulting her. "The first thing we must do is make the master's bedchamber ready. I'm sure his lordship will not wish to spend another night in the butler's quarters. Then . . ."

Claudia raised a hand to still her aunt's busy ramblings. "We'd best wait until the day after tomorrow, Aunt, when we have concluded our business in Gloucester. I do not wish Thomas to get wind of my decision to relinquish Ravencroft until the deed is done."

"Oh. Yes, of course. Well, I shall merely peek into the master's suite, just to get an idea of what must be done. It's been empty for so long, you know. What a fortunate thing we just inventoried the linen room. I shall select what will be needed. Oh. What about clothes? Surely, he will require new coats and—and everything. I shall be thinking of who he might hire as a manservant, too."

Claudia tiptoed from the room, gently closing the door behind her.

It was not very much later that Claudia found herself seated next to the master of Ravencroft, tooling along the road to Gloucester in the gig that served as the means of transportation for those living at Ravencroft. Emanuel's curricle and phaeton, and even the fashionable barouche that had once graced the Ravencroft carriage house had been sold many months previously. They might have ridden in the ancient landau that still squatted in the shadows, but Claudia had been loathe to take Lucas away from his stable duties to act as coachman. She prayed that it would not rain, although the skies hanging grayly above them did not look promising.

She was acutely conscious of the close proximity of the man seated next to her, wielding the reins of the gig rather inexpertly. He had not, he explained rather sheepishly at the onset of their journey, driven a horse beyond two or three times in his adult life. Despite this, he drove with a definite panache, and if occasionally the horses misinterpreted his direction, he was able without undue difficulty to make his wishes known and eventually obeyed. Claudia had the feeling that it would not be long before Lord Glenraven became as adept a whip as he had been a confidence trickster in his bad old days.

A thought struck her suddenly, and she twisted about to look at him. "Would you like to stop at a haberdashery today, my lord, to purchase some new clothes?"

Jem glanced down at the serviceable but obviously inexpensive outfit he had worn at his first encounter with her. "New clothes?" he asked in surprise. Then, he laughed. "Are you saying, my dear Mrs. Carstairs, that I don't present the picture of a peer? You are right, of course," he concluded. "This, ensemble, however, is not the only suit of clothes that I own. I left most of my things in London, and after I have got myself officially announced as Lord Glenraven, I shall send for them." He laughed again. "I promise you, by week's end, if all goes well, I shall be revealed to you in all my lordly glory."

"I shall await your emergence with baited breath, my lord," replied Claudia demurely.

"That reminds me of another thing," Jem said abruptly. "Do you think you might get by without that infernal, eternal 'my lord'?"

She looked at him for a moment in blank surprise. "But I can no longer call you January."

"No, but you might call me Jem."

Claudia drew in a sharp breath. "No, I mightn't."

"I don't see why not. I've been called that by everyone I know for the past twelve years—except when they're swearing at me, of course. I hope you don't plan to do much of that."

"No, of course, not." She was feeling unaccountably flustered by this exchange. "It—it simply would not do. It wouldn't be at all proper. I—" She finished in a rush. "I am your employee."

"Mm, yes. I see what you mean. But, I fear I cannot put up with all this 'my *lord*-ing.' " He mused silently for a moment. "How about Standish? I know it should probably be Glenraven, but even that sounds a bit much, don't you think? I've always thought that title a trifle grandiloquent, as though we were laying claim to half of Scotland."

"You are being absurd, my lord," she responded severely. "I'm afraid from now on you will just have to get accustomed to—my lord."

Jem sighed heavily. "Very well. However, I shall not take that as your final answer. I shall keep chipping away at you. I can be most persuasive, you know."

Claudia permitted herself a smile. "So you've told me. However, I am not a gambler to be fooled by a trick."

He placed a hand on his heart and bent a sorrowful look upon her. "You wound me, Mrs. Carstairs."

Unable to face the warmth she read in his eyes, she hastily directed his attention to the fact that they had reached the outskirts of Gloucester.

Carefully maneuvering the little gig through the narrow streets of the city, Jem gradually arrived at its center. Pulling up in the town square, he looked about him.

"I am afraid I am unacquainted with the attorneys who practice here," said Claudia. "Perhaps we could inquire at an inn or even at the Cathedral Deanery."

Jem hesitated a moment. "I have recalled the name of the man Father used as his man of affairs—and I think I remember where his chambers were located. He was a good man, as I recall. He was unable to stop Father's headlong plunge into ruin, but I do not hold him responsible for that. Would you mind if I try to locate him? Or his successor?"

Claudia gave her agreement willingly, and after a few false starts, they found their way to a small building on Catherine Street, adorned with a modest sign reading, "SCUDDER, WIDDICOMBE AND PHILLIPS, ATTORNEYS AT LAW."

"There," said Jem in satisfaction. "William Scudder is whom I am looking for."

He glanced down at the leather case he had brought with him. It was filled with his very life, he thought, then shrugged at his unwonted fancy. Yet, as he lifted the latch to usher Claudia inside, he was conscious of a lump in his throat and a churning in his stomach, for here was to be found the last hurdle in his journey home.

Chapter Twelve

Claudia and Jem were greeted in a small anteroom by an austere personage of dyspeptic mien.

"Yes?" he inquired haughtily, "May I help you?"

The glance he hastily ran over Jem's shabby suit and Claudia's plain muslin gown obviously had led him to the conclusion these were not the sort of persons to be welcomed with open arms at Scudder, Widdicombe and Phillips.

"We would like to see William Scudder," replied Jem courteously, "if he is in."

The personage sniffed.

"He is in, but I fear he is busy at the moment. Perhaps if you would leave your name . . . " He let the sentence trail off, apparently in the hope that this unsightly pair would take the hint and simply vanish from his ordered world.

"Please," said Jem quietly, but with great firmness. "Tell him that Lord Glenraven wishes to see him."

The personage stiffened. Once more, his rather myopic gaze traveled over them, and he fairly quivered in indignation. "My good man—whoever you might be—please do not try to . . . "

As Claudia watched in fascination, Jem made another of his transformations. He seemed to grow taller, and he drew about him an air of authority that came as naturally to him as pulling on a coat.

"You will tell him that now."

The man opened his mouth as though he would dispute the order, but after one look into Jem's face, he turned on his heel and left the room, shuttering the door behind him with an affronted click.

Claudia had barely absorbed all this, when the door opened once more, and a gentleman in his late fifties hastened into the anteroom. He strode to Jem and gazed at him intently for a long moment before grasping the younger man's hand.

"Lord Glenraven! When Wickerly told me— But—by God, it really is you! Come in, come in, my boy." Sparing barely a glance for Claudia, he took Jem by the arm and drew him into an inner office. It was not a large room, but the stained leather furniture and candles burning to augment the meager illumination provided by a single, grimy window, served to create a comfortable atmosphere. An odor of old leather and vellum hung over the place like a benediction.

His eyes never leaving Jem's face, Mr. Scudder gestured the young man to a seat near a large, paper-strewn desk. Only then did he glance questioningly at Claudia.

"Mr. Scudder," said Jem, bowing, "allow me to present Mrs. Emanuel Carstairs, the present owner of Ravencroft."

After a moment's startled hesitation, Mr. Scudder bowed also, and taking Claudia's hand, he led her to a chair near Jem's. He seated himself behind his desk and drew a deep breath.

"Lord Glenraven," he repeated, smiling broadly. "You have changed considerably from the youngster who visited me once, so many years ago, with your father, but I had no difficulty in recognizing you. Have you come back for a visit, or is there some way in which I can assist you?" He glanced again curiously at Claudia.

Jem sat back in his chair and laid the leather case on the desk.

"Yes, Mr. Scudder, I am in need of your services, and I hope very much that you can help me."

In reply to the older man's questioning stare, Jem opened the packet and began to speak. Mr. Scudder literally perched on the edge of his chair during Jem's recital, and as the monologue continued, his expression grew from surprise, to revulsion, to horror.

When Jem had finished, the attorney collapsed back into his seat, and drawing a large handkerchief from his coat pocket, he wiped his brow.

"This is—I have never heard the like!" he gasped. "To think that one man could cause such misery. Your father—your poor mother! And your sisters—my God! And you. My boy, I simply do not know what to say."

A long silence reigned in the room, broken only by the ticking of an ancient clock resting on a dusty mantelpiece. Mr. Scudder appeared lost in his own thoughts, and came to with a jerk when Jem cleared his throat gently.

"Oh. Ah. Yes, I was just . . . " He straightened abruptly. "You say you have proof of all you have told me?"

Jem removed the papers from the leather case and spread them across the desk for Mr. Scudder's careful perusal. After another lengthy interval, the attorney raised his head.

"This all seems in order. Of course, if there were to be a dispute over—" He bent a sharp stare on Claudia. "You are truly agreeing to return Ravencroft to his lordship without dispute?"

Claudia nodded, and Jem spoke. "Among the items we need to settle today are a contract between Mrs. Carstairs and myself concerning her employment as manager of the Ravencroft stables."

"What?" Amazement was writ large on Mr. Scudder's plump features. "You would hire a female to—but this is unheard of!" He swiveled about to focus his attention on Claudia.

Jem smiled. "Nevertheless, that is what I propose to do. Mrs. Carstairs has made great strides in returning the stables to their former repute, and I feel confident that I could leave them in no more competent hands." He turned to Claudia, who felt an unwelcome heat rise to her cheeks.

"Yes." Mr. Scudder's voice was saturated with disapproval. "I had heard of her activities." He peered again at Claudia from over his spectacles. "Most unsuitable, if I may say so, dear lady."

"Yes, I suppose it is," said Claudia, and at her tone of meek submission, Jem shot her a keen glance. "But, I really had no choice, sir. Perhaps you have also heard that my late husband brought Ravencroft to the brink of ruin."

Mr. Scudder harrumphed, but the gaze he bent on her softened perceptibly.

He picked up the documents that lay scattered on his desk. "There are certain formalities which must be observed in your acquisition to the title, my lord. If you will permit, I shall put these into motion. In a few days, again with your permission, I will call at Ravencroft with documents for your signature. In the meantime, if you wish, I can provide a deed of transfer immediately for Mrs. Carstairs to sign"—he looked at her intently from under thick brows—"if this is what you truly wish to do."

Claudia nodded. "I have no other option, Mr. Scudder. I had vaguely suspected that Emanuel's dealings with the late Lord Glenraven were not precisely aboveboard. Having my suspicions confirmed, I could do no other than to return Ravencroft to its rightful owner. Much as it pains me to do so," she added honestly.

"Well said, Mrs. Carstairs," replied Mr. Scudder, his forbidding expression having phased into one of marked approval. In another few minutes, having conferred with a chastened Wickerly, more documents were brought into the room, and Claudia was handed ink and quill.

Shortly after that, Mr. Scudder notarized her signature with a flourish and pronounced the deed done.

"There will be a few other steps. I shall file these papers with the clerks' office, but as of this moment, Lord Glenraven, you are now the owner of Ravencroft."

These simple words had the power to deprive Jem of speech for several moments. Watching him, Claudia knew an urge to reach out her hand to touch his. Somehow, as she observed the depth of emotion written on his lean face, her own pain at losing the home she had come to love was eased.

The next order of business was Claudia's contract for employment at Ravencroft. She was astonished at the munificent salary offered by his lordship, but her protests were overruled with gruff civility. With shaking hand, she signed the paper.

After that, there was little to be said, and Mr. Scudder ushered the pair from his office with many expressions of goodwill and the promise to appear at Ravencroft within the week to clear up the remaining formalities.

"I wonder," said Jem as they made their way down the winding street that opened out into a wide square, "if the Pelican still exists. When I accompanied Father into town, we always stopped there for luncheon. It lies down—let me see, that street over there."

"Oh," replied Claudia with a little gasp, "but that is the

dearest place in town to dine. I usually go to the White Lamb. Besides, we have little time to spend in the city if we wish to return to Ravencroft before nightfall."

"Nonsense." Jem spoke briskly as he put Claudia's hand in the crook of his arm. "You must strive to be mindful that you are in the company of a nob. No need to worry about paltry things like the cost of lunch."

Claudia eyed him dubiously, but not nearly as dubiously as did the Pelican's host. This burly individual gave them a look that indicated his lack of confidence in them as he ushered them to a table in the coffee room, and Claudia was surprised that he did not ask to see the color of their money before showing them the color of his mutton.

During a hearty luncheon of lamb cutlets, peas, and roasted potatoes, accompanied by a very respectable claret, Jem regaled her with stories of his adventures in London. She felt he glossed over a great deal of the unhappiness he must have suffered, for his stories were lightly entertaining tales of assorted interesting characters he had known, or of outwitting various persons in authority and assorted villains.

When they prepared to leave, Jem was happily able to pay not only for their meal, but to add a little something for the serving maid, who accepted his largesse with astonished thanks.

They parted outside the inn, each to accomplish a few small errands, and the sun was beginning to sink toward the horizon when they again met where Jem had left the gig in the market square.

They rode in silence for some minutes. Jem cast several surreptitious glances at Claudia, who appeared to be sunk in thought. "A penny for them," he said at last in a light tone.

"What? Oh." She assayed a not altogether successful laugh. "I was—looking into the future."

"You do not seem pleased with what you saw there," he said gently.

She made no reply, staring instead with great intensity at her fingertips, clasped tightly in her lap.

"It is not bleak, you know—your future. I believe you will be—good Lord!" His voice rose in consternation. "Don't do that!"

For Claudia, to his horror—and no less to hers—had begun to weep. Once started, she was unable to stop, and tears poured from her in rivulets.

"I'm sorry," she gasped. "I d-don't know what's the matter with me. I know I've done the right thing—and you've been more than generous. It's just that—"

Jem brought the gig to a halt at the side of the road and turned to her. After a moment of ineffectual patting and shushing, he placed an arm around her and drew her to him, oblivious to the curious stares of the few passersby on the road. He said nothing, merely clasping her tightly and stroking her hair.

After some minutes, her sobbing ceased, and after another short interval, she drew abruptly away from him. Gazing at him with drowned eyes, she tried to speak, but Jem lightly placed his fingers over her lips. From his pocket, he produced a clean handkerchief and applied it to her tearstained cheeks.

"Your reaction is only natural, you know," he said gently. "You've been brave and good and, yes, even noble in relinquishing the home you love to a complete stranger. But"—having finished his mopping up, he handed the handkerchief to Claudia, who blew her nose prosaically—"it has been my experience that bravery and goodness and nobility eventually take their toll, and one begins to crack under the strain."

She gave a watery chuckle. "I fear you are r-right, my lord." She hiccuped away a few remaining sobs. "I don't know what possessed me—I am not generally such a watering pot. I fear the fact finally sank home that I no longer own Ravencroft—that I shall live on sufferance on a tiny piece of it. It—it's a very lowering thought," she concluded, her last words muffled as she pressed the handkerchief to her eyes to prevent another freshet.

Jem pulled her hands away from her face and clasped them tightly in his own. His eyes as they gazed into hers, were like a morning sky, she thought irrelevantly, just before the sun appears to color the clouds.

"Listen to me, Claudia. Just because you will not actually live in the house, as you used to, I want you to consider Ravencroft your home. I want you to move freely about the house—play the piano in the music room, if you wish. Read in the library, or any other room you choose. I hope you and your aunt will dine with me on a regular basis—for that is what will make it seem like home to me."

Her eyes dropped before the intensity in his, and her heart, as it always seemed to do when she was close to him, began to beat violently. But she did not attempt to withdraw her hands.

"Thank you," she whispered. "I know I'm being silly." She lifted her gaze again. "I thank you for—"

He cut her off most effectively by leaning forward to brush his lips against hers. She stiffened in shock, but almost before she had time to realize what he had done, he released her hands. Grasping the reins once more, he slapped them smartly against the horse's rump and the gig rattled into motion.

Jem chastised himself as the vehicle gathered speed. He had been as surprised by his action as had Claudia. Good God, what was the matter with him? He had never been the sort of man to be ruled by his emotions—indeed he had spent considerable time and effort in learning to keep his emotions under careful control. Yet, bringing his mouth to hers had been an almost involuntary action, like blinking in a sudden light. Well, he adjured himself severely, there would be no more such lapses. Claudia Carstairs was now his employee. A valued employee, but an employee nonetheless, who must be treated with the detached courtesy that such a situation called for. He turned to her, noting that her eyes were still wide and shocked.

"You have not told me," he said, as though nothing untoward had just taken place, "how you happened to marry Emanuel Carstairs. I understand you were forced into it. You said something about a gambling debt?"

For a moment she simply stared at him. If it were not for the pounding of her pulse and the soft fire that his lips had left behind on hers, she might almost have thought the kiss had not taken place. She should have evinced more displeasure, she thought. She should have let his lordship know in no uncertain terms that she was not a lightskirt to be bussed like a wanton chambermaid. She opened her mouth to put her thoughts to action.

"Yes." She listened in some surprise to the words that emerged from her lips. "My father, like yours, was an inveterate gambler. We lived in Newham, on the other side of Gloucester, but Father had a cousin living in Tetbury, which is not far from Little Marshdean. We were frequent visitors at his home, and that is where he met Emanuel." She shivered. "I can still remember the way Emanuel used to look at me. I had never come up against pure evil before, but I found it in his gaze. His second wife had died a few months before, and I knew he was on the prowl for a replacement. He wanted children, you see, as well as . . . " She shook herself.

"Emanuel soon had Father at his mercy, and, since I was at Father's mercy, I soon found myself betrothed to a man whose very touch caused me to shudder in revulsion. I cried and cajoled and pled, all to no avail. My mother sympathized with my plight, but she was not a strong person. My sister thought my repugnance was the height of stupidity. Emanuel was even richer, or at least so we all thought, than Thomas. This is the standard she sets for a successful marriage, you see. She has never minded being bullied by Thomas as long as she has a nice house to live in, servants to do her bidding, and a little money doled out to her by her master to spend as she pleases."

Jem's expression was startled as he continued to observe Claudia closely.

"At any rate, despite all of my best efforts, I found myself standing at his side in front of the church altar, reciting my vows." She drew a deep breath. "I guess the best thing to be said of the ensuing two years was that they were extremely unpleasant. Without the stables to manage, I think I would have lost my mind."

"And yet," said Jem carefully, "according to Jonah, you fared better with your late husband than did his previous wives."

To Jem's surprise, Claudia uttered a rusty little chuckle.

"Yes, well things started out badly. He beat me one night. I—I actually thought I was going to die. After he left me, I lay on the floor for hours, and by the time I pulled myself up, I had resolved that this was never going to happen again. I formed a strategy, and the next morning I bearded him in his study. Oh, Jem, it was the hardest thing I've ever done in my life."

Jem's heart lifted in absurd pleasure at the sound of his name on her lips, even though spoken unconsciously.

"I pushed open the door," she continued, "and strode in as

though I were the master and not he. I planted myself in front of his desk and said, 'Emanuel Carstairs, I have come for your apology and to tell you that what happened last night will never occur again if you value your life.'

"He simply goggled at me for several moments, and then came up at me like a hurricane. I stood my ground and simply held up my hand with an expression of great—and totally false—confidence on my face. He stopped, as though confused, and I began to speak. I told him that I had inherited certain powers from my grandmother on my mother's side. People, I said, who crossed Granny soon wished they hadn't. I listed a few examples—the bailiff who stole from her and was later found dead from unexplained causes, the neighbor who did her a trifling wrong and was struck down with a pain too horrible to describe.

"Like so many bullies, Emanuel was a coward, and a superstitious one, to boot. He blustered at me for a time, but I could tell he was uneasy. Then I pulled my coup de grâce. In my best otherworldly tone of voice, I told him I would give him a portent. I pointed dramatically to a large plant that stood in the window of the study. Muttering a brief incantation, I waggled two fingers at it, then informed him that in three days time, the plant would be dead. He sneered and said that anybody can kill a plant. I retorted that he could keep the plant under guard during the specified time to assure himself that I would not touch it. Which he did! He locked it up in his dressing room! It began to wilt almost immediately, however, and three days later it was totally and undeniably defunct.

"After that, Emanuel gave me a wide berth. He would still lose his temper with me occasionally, but all I had to do was waggle my fingers to render him a spent force, so to speak."

"But . . . " interjected Jem.

"How did I kill the plant? Earlier that morning, after I was able to move, I limped into his study and dosed the plant with massive amounts of salt water—enough to kill a tree, I think. By the time I confronted him the next morning, the poor thing was already on its way to plant heaven."

At Jem's shout of laughter, Claudia folded her hands in her lap and shot him a demure glance.

"And I thought *I* was a confidence trickster extraordinaire," he gasped. "You are priceless, my dear, and I shall take great care never to get on your wrong side."

So absorbed was he that he forgot for a moment to mind his driving. His inadvertent slap of the reins against the horse's flanks caused some confusion in the animal, with the result that he hastened his stride at precisely the wrong moment. As they flew around a curve, two wheels of the gig went off the road into a shallow ditch, causing the vehicle to come to an abrupt halt, tilting precariously.

Jem slid with some force across the seat, and the next moment found his arms full of delectable widow. He gazed into her butterscotch eyes and was lost. Oblivious to anyone who might be passing by, he brought his mouth down on hers.

Chapter Thirteen

When Jem's arms encircled her, Claudia knew she should pull back. The contact was unavoidable, of course. Indeed if it had not been for Jem's embrace she might have found herself sprawled on the ground as the gig tilted crazily in the ditch. However, once the vehicle had stopped its sideways motion, and the horse had ceased its panicked whinnies, she simply remained where she was, gazing into the gray eyes that were so unnervingly close to hers.

She should have disengaged herself at once, of course, but she was aware only of the shattering rightness of the feel of his arms about her, and, with her heart thudding in her throat, she lifted her mouth for his kiss. Then she was conscious only of the warmth of his lips and of the slow fire that swept through her.

His arms tightened, and she pressed against him as though she might absorb his very essence. She had never dreamed a kiss could be so pleasurable—so deeply satisfying, yet creating such an urgent wanting. His hands moved on her body, stroking her hair, then her back, creating frissons of sensation along her spine. When his mouth lifted from hers for a moment, she felt instantly bereft, but the soft, quick kisses he pressed on her temple and her cheek caused her to gasp with delight. Her own arms had by now wrapped about him to draw him even closer, and her fingers wound themselves in the dark silk of his hair where it lay on the back of his neck.

As his mouth returned to hers, she felt herself slipping further into the wonder of his nearness. Somewhere in the recesses of her brain, she knew this was madness, but it was only with the rattle of harness and the sound of hooves heralding an approaching vehicle that she drew back. Jem, too, pulled abruptly away, and for a moment they gazed at each other, breathless and dazed.

"I—" he began, and lifted a hand to her. Then, casting a glance at the carriage that lumbered toward them, he shook his head and leaped from the gig. In a few moments, he was able to right the vehicle and to lead horse and equipage back to the road. He mounted the gig once more and turned to Claudia. Her eyes were still wide and distraught.

"It seems I must apologize again." His voice was unsteady. "I do not generally find myself so susceptible to feminine witchery. In fact, I have no excuse for what just happened, except for the—the unusual circumstances, and . . . "

"Your apology is accepted, my lord." Claudia found she was having a great deal of difficulty with her own voice. "We have both been under a great deal of strain today. However, it shall not happen again. And now," she continued, gathering to her every ounce of control she possessed, "perhaps we had better be on our way."

Jem stared at her for several seconds before replying. "No, it will not happen again." He slapped the reins, and the gig moved off at a brisk pace.

It was nearly eleven by the time they reached Ravencroft, though the summer sky still held enough daylight to show them the way through the stone entrance gates. Their conversation during the remainder of the journey had been light and inconsequential, and Claudia felt utterly exhausted by the effort it had taken her to maintain her part.

Lucas hurried forward as they drove toward the carriage house and assisted in her descent from the gig.

"Thank you, January," she said clearly. "I am going to retire immediately, but I shall see you early tomorrow morning to discuss the day's activities."

Jem bowed and gathered up the parcels containing Claudia's purchases and followed her into the house at a respectful distance, promising Lucas to return immediately to help settle the horse down for the night.

When she reached her room, Claudia sank down on her bed, fully clothed, and lay staring at the ceiling. What in God's name was the matter with her? Why did she turn into a puddle of molten sensation at that wretched man's very touch? She was not a smitten schoolgirl, for Lord's sake, she was an experienced woman. Well, perhaps not precisely experienced, but she was not an innocent maid, at any rate. She knew very well what it was that men wanted from women, and she had no intention of pandering to my lord's baser instincts. Or her own, for that matter. If Lord Glenraven thought he had purchased a mistress as well as a stable manager, he was very much mistaken.

She prayed that he was giving some thought to matrimony, for when he brought a bride to Ravencroft, his interests would surely not stray beyond the marriage bed. When he had a wife to cater to his needs and provide him with an heir, he would no longer seek out his stable mistress for stolen kisses. This thought did not provide her with nearly the satisfaction she had expected, and in some irritation, she rose from the bed to disrobe. Donning her night rail, she prepared to settle beneath her covers, but was stayed by an odd sound from across the room. The next moment, her door opened, and, raising her candle, she was astonished to observe Fletcher Botsford enter the room.

"Mr. Botsford!" she gasped. "What on earth . . . " She set the candle down with a thump.

"Oh!" said Fletcher, obviously startled. "I thought you would be asleep. That is, I mean . . . " He started toward her, and Claudia grabbed the first thing that came to her hand, a hairbrush. Brandishing it threateningly, she thrust her covers aside, sprang from her bed and advanced on her unwelcome visitor.

"Fletcher Botsford," she growled. "I don't know what you think you're doing here, but the next sound I hear had better be the door closing on your back."

Fletcher swallowed convulsively, but he continued moving into the room.

"Now, now, my dear, I only want to talk to you. You do not know how hard it is to get you alone, after all."

"Yes, I do know, Fletcher, because I have done everything in my power to keep from being in your presence at all, never mind being alone with you." Claudia was by now so angry that it seemed to the hapless Botsford that her eyes were taking on the quality of molten metal. As she raised the hairbrush again, he quailed, but pressed on regardless.

He stood before her, and at that point seemed uncertain as to how to proceed. He laid a tentative hand on her shoulder.

"Ow!" he squeaked as Claudia rapped his knuckles sharply with the hairbrush. "My dear . . . "

"I am not your dear, Mr. Botsford, and if you do not turn around this instant, I . . . "

A knock sounded at the door. Fletcher turned around slowly, an expression of sly anticipation on his face that died suddenly as he beheld the angular form of Miss Augusta Melksham standing in the doorway. Claudia sagged in relief.

"Aunt Gussie! I'm so glad you're here. Will you please assist me in removing Mr. Botsford from my room?"

"Indeed, my child," said the old lady austerely. "I heard someone creeping past my door and rose to investigate. Just what were you up to, Mr. Botsford?"

"Up to?" Fletcher goggled. "Why-why nothing at all. I merely—that is—"

"My God!" exclaimed a rumbling voice, and Claudia whirled to find Thomas, resplendent in a Turkish silk dressing gown, looming in the doorway. "What's going on here?" Thomas spoke in a tone of appalled astonishment, and Claudia realized at once that his appearance on the scene was not at all by happenstance. Her suspicions were confirmed when Rose tottered into the room a few seconds later.

"I was awakened by all the commotion, and—oh, my gracious!" Her eyes widened in an assumption of incredulity. "Mr. Botsford! Whatever are you doing here?"

At this moment, Aunt Augusta, who had been half hidden behind Claudia's bed hangings moved into full view, and Claudia nearly laughed aloud at the ludicrous expressions of chagrin that appeared on the faces of Thomas and his wife.

"Mr. Botsford seems to have stumbled into the wrong room," she said calmly. "Fortunately, Aunt Augusta heard him pass her chambers and came to investigate. She entered almost on Mr. Botsworth's heels."

"Oh," said Thomas and Rose, almost in unison. "However," continued Thomas, shouldering his way into the room, "Botsford's being in your room in the middle of the night is, nonetheless, highly compromising. I believe you had better rethink your earlier refusal of his suit, young lady."

"Nonsense," snapped Claudia. "I just told you that Aunt—"

"But not," he interrupted in a significant tone, "before Botsford had been here for—for an undetermined length of time."

"Good heavens, Thomas." Claudia experienced a rising exasperation. "No one besides you and Rose and Aunt Gussie are aware of Fletcher's faux pas."

Thomas smiled knowingly. "You may be assured, my dear, that the news will be all over the servants' quarters by morning. The lower orders, you know, have a way of sniffing out the slightest hint of scandal. Speaking of which, what time did you come home tonight? I understand you traveled all the way to Gloucester today—with only your butler for company. I am shocked, Claudia, at your lack of discretion. More food for scandal."

"Scandal! My lack of . . . Oh, Thomas, *really*—"

"In fact," continued her brother-in-law as though she had not spoken, "I think it would be advisable for you to arrange tomorrow for the posting of banns."

Rose had maintained a steady twittering throughout this exchange, but at Thomas's words, she uttered an incredulous gasp, and once again Claudia caught a flash of indignation before it was quickly shuttered. Miss Melksham snorted and opened her mouth as though she would have remonstrated, but Claudia was ahead of her. With narrowed eyes, she stepped to within a foot of Thomas. Her eyes glittered with anger, and her voice, when she spoke, rang with the clash of sabers.

"Thomas, if you and every servant in the house—as well as the vicar himself—had walked in here and found Fletcher Botsford and me stark naked between the sheets, I still would not consider marrying him. Do I make myself very clear on that point? Now, let me discuss another. I believe you and Rose and your ill-disciplined children and Mr. Botsford have overstayed your welcome. I shall instruct the servants that you will be making your departure in the morning."

Her statement was greeted with a gusty chuckle from Aunt Augusta and a squeak from Rose. Fletcher Botsford, who had heretofore said nothing, uttered a weak, "Now see here . . ."

but from Thomas, there was silence. When he spoke at last, his voice was soft and silky.

"You are distraught, my dear sister. We will leave you now and discuss this tomorrow, when you are more yourself. As for your nonsensical talk of our leaving, I know it is merely the result of your overstrained sensibilities. I could, of course, not consider abandoning you in your present state of emotional turmoil. You are my wife's nearest relative, and as such I have a responsibility to see to your well-being."

Claudia gaped at him in consternation and a growing rage.

"How *dare* you—" she began, but was caught up short by Miss Melksham, who strode to her and put a hand on her arm.

"Never mind, Claudia," she said, giving her niece a meaningful glance. "We can straighten all this out in the morning. In the meantime, perhaps you'd better get some rest. We have a busy day ahead of us tomorrow."

Such was Claudia's state of mind, that it took a full minute for the significance of her aunt's words to sink in. Of course! Tomorrow, Jem would announce his identity, and she would be willing to wager Thomas would be out on his ear inside of an hour. She swallowed hard and relaxed the fists she had clenched when Thomas entered the room. She forced her breathing to slow, and turning to her brother-in-law she said in a steely voice, "Yes, we will straighten this all out tomorrow, but for now, you will leave my room—both of you." She shot a glance at Rose, who cast her eyes to the floor. "And," she continued, transferring her gaze to Fletcher Botsford, "take your puppet with you!"

Thomas opened his mouth as though he would say more, but, apparently feeling he had come out of the encounter the victor, contented himself with a smug smile. He propelled Rose and Botsford from the room and closed the door behind him with a satisfied click.

Claudia sank down upon her bed, and Miss Melksham sat down beside her. She placed her hand over that of the young woman.

"Oh, my dear. I never thought I would be grateful for the fact that Lord Glenraven has returned to take up residence here, but I must confess that I look forward to his confrontation with Thomas on the morrow."

Claudia allowed a small smile to curve her lips. "So do I, Aunt. So do I."

"I shall see to the master suite first thing. I am sure his lordship will wish to waste no time in moving out of the butler's quarters. Oh dear," she added as an afterthought. "What a shame—January was such an exemplary butler. Now we shall have to hire a new one."

Claudia uttered a little gasp and then began to chuckle. After a moment, Miss Melksham joined her, and soon the two were clutching each other as laughter erupted from them in bursts of release. Some time later, when they had regained their composure, Aunt Augusta bade her niece a staid good night and left the room, her skirts sighing a soft amen.

Later, Claudia lay in her blessedly silent bedchamber, staring once more at the ceiling. Yes, tomorrow would be a momentous day in all their lives. Was Lord Glenraven still awake, she wondered, in his humble quarters? Was he, too, considering the changes that were about to inundate him?

Three floors below, Jem lay staring into the darkness. This would probably be his last night in Morgan's old chambers, for tomorrow his new life would begin. The erstwhile street urchin known as Jem January would die an unmourned death, and Jeremy Standish, Lord Glenraven would begin anew as master of Ravencroft.

What place in his new life would Claudia hold, he wondered for what seemed like the hundredth time since that timeless, magical kiss this afternoon. He permitted himself a small, sour chuckle. He already knew the answer to that, and he might as well stiffen his resolve right now. He must not let a like occurrence ever happen again. Make up your mind to it, Jemmie, me lad, in the future she must be nothing more than a valued employee. He wished now that he had not offered her the run of the house. He hoped to God she hadn't been led to believe that he'd had more than a moment's dalliance in mind back there in the gig. He had no desire to further the relationship, after all. A woman would only complicate his life—which was already about as complicated as it could hold right now, and it could only end in one or both of them getting hurt. He would take pains from now on to remain on friendly but distant terms with Claudia Carstairs.

He slept at last, a slumber disturbed by dreams of butterscotch eyes laughing into his and of golden hair, silky as thistledown beneath his fingers. He sighed in his sleep at the memory of a soft mouth pressed against his with a warmth and sweetness he had never known.

"Ye're never sayin' so, lad—my lord!"

Jonah gaped at Jem, grooming brush in hand. He had been brushing Trusty, but at the young man's startling words, he had emerged from the gelding's stall. "She gave Ravencroft over to ye? Without a struggle?"

At Jem's confirming nod, he rubbed the back of the brush against his bristly chin. "That don't sound like 'er."

"I told you she would not have the stomach for a fight in court. Not that she didn't take her pound of flesh. You will still be taking orders from Mrs. Carstairs, Jonah, for I have hired her to manage my stables."

The brush dropped from Jonah's nerveless fingers. "Ye never! A female t' run an operation like we has here?"

"She's been doing it for two years now," replied Jem patiently.

"Yes, but, they was 'er own, then. It'll be different now."

"Yes, it will be different. She will need your help more than ever, Jonah, for she feels her loss deeply. I want her to know she still belongs, and that I have entrusted her with complete authority over the stables."

"Have ye now?" Jonah's voice rasped in astonishment.

"The only change I will suggest is that she hire more hands. In fact, you might draw up a list of young men to be found locally who might be acceptable. For," said Jem with a grin, "I am turning in my papers. It wouldn't look at all the thing, after all, for callers to be directed to the stables to find the lord of the manor mucking out the stalls."

Jonah's laughter emerged soundlessly from behind his wrinkles, and Jem left, with a jaunty wave of his hand.

Back in the house, he was greeted by a flustered housemaid who informed him breathlessly that he was wanted upstairs, "imeedgit and to onc't." Surmising what was afoot, he hastened up the wide main staircase, following his ears to where a loud altercation ensued in the direction of the master's chambers.

Rounding a corner, he strode toward the group gathered in the corridor. At its center stood Claudia, her hair catching the light of a single candle still flickering in a wall sconce. Near her, like a bony bulwark stood Miss Melksham, and ranged about them were Thomas, Rose, and a dismayed Fletcher Botsford.

"All I want," Thomas was intoning belligerently, "is a simple explanation. I awoke this morning and rang for tea, and no one responded. I had Crumshaw ring for hot water, and no one was about to bring it up. Now I find you and the greater part of the household staff bustling about a set of rooms that has been unused for donkey's years, and I want to know what is the meaning of it?" Thomas was fairly stamping his foot in irritation, exacerbated perhaps by the fact that Claudia did not quail before his wrath, but smiled calmly up at him.

"My dear Thomas," she began. "I told you, I shall explain—oh!" she broke off, catching sight of Jem. "My lo—I mean, Jan—um . . . " She concluded by simply extending her hand to him.

"*Now* what?" exclaimed Thomas, as Jem strode forward to grasp her fingers in a light salute. "What is your butler doing here?" His gaze flicked suspiciously from Claudia to Jem, dressed in his sober servant's garb, and his eyes widened in horrified accusation. "Claudia!" Her words spilled ponderously from tightly pursed lips. "I am seriously beginning to believe that there is something going on here. Have you developed a *tendre for* your own butler, for God's sake?"

Jem turned and smiled pleasantly at Thomas. "Of course she hasn't. Not that it is any business of yours if she had."

For an instant, Claudia thought Thomas would simply go off in an apoplectic stroke. His complexion, she noted interestedly, exactly matched the purple shawl arranged with precision about Aunt Gussie's shoulders.

Rose squeaked agitatedly and plucked at Thomas's coat, while Fletcher provided a background accompaniment of faint "Here, I say's" and "Upon my word's".

"The impertinence!" roared Thomas, when he was at last able to recover his voice. "My good man, you may consider yourself discharged at once—without a character. And you may feel yourself fortunate that I don't kick you down the stairs."

Jem stepped forward, only to be grasped firmly by Claudia.

"Thomas, that will do," she said icily. "You seem to believe yourself in a position of some authority here, but you are very much mistaken—more so now than ever." She looked for a moment at Jem, her brows lifted in silent query. At his nod, she turned back to her brother-in-law and continued. "I fear you have been laboring under a slight misunderstanding. Allow me to present you to Jeremy Standish, Lord Glenraven—and current master of Ravencroft.

Chapter Fourteen

A profound silence greeted Claudia's statement. For several moments Thomas stared at her, uncomprehending, while Rose stood, mouth agape. Aunt Augusta folded her arms, smiling grimly.

"Wh—wha'?" asked Thomas at last, swiveling to stare at Jem as though he had just been introduced to a being from the netherworld. Jem smiled sunnily and extended his hand. Thomas simply stared at it. Abruptly he came to himself and swung again to Claudia.

"What did you just say?"

"I said, this gentleman is Lord Glenraven, and he has returned home to live here permanently."

"But—but this is nonsense!" Thomas had swelled until there seemed the very real possibility of a horrible explosion. "Emanuel Carstairs was the owner of Ravencroft, and he left it to you. You are the owner now!"

"Ah, I had rather thought you'd forgotten that fact, Thomas. You are right, of course, but I learned recently that Emanuel acquired the estate by, er, highly illegal means. Lord Glenraven is the rightful owner, so I have transferred the title to him."

"You cannot be serious! Do you mean to tell me that you have given away our—your home to this—this"—he waved wildly at Jem—"this jumped up jackanapes merely because he says it rightfully belongs to him?" By now, Thomas had gone as pale as he had been empurpled before. His wife seemed unable to understand what was taking place and gazed from one to the other of the combatants in bewilderment. Fletcher Botsford remained apparently stunned and speechless.

"I suggest," said Jem smoothly, "that we repair to the emerald saloon. We seem to have acquired an audience."

Indeed, every maid and footman in the house appeared to have found some urgent business requiring his or her presence in the upstairs hallway, and the group gathered there found themselves the target of several pairs of curious eyes. Thomas opened and closed his mouth several times, but with a great effort refrained from comment, merely stalking off in the direction of the staircase.

Several moments later, however, when all concerned had assembled in the emerald saloon, he experienced little difficulty in finding his voice again.

"I cannot have heard you right, Claudia. Not even you would do such a buffle-headed thing as—"

Claudia held up her hand.

"I will say this once more, Thomas. Lord Glenraven has offered proof of what I had long suspected, that Emanuel virtually stole Ravencroft. He tricked his lordship's father and then murdered him. Being convinced of this, I could do no other than to return Ravencroft to him."

"I never heard such nonsense in my life!" roared her brother-in-law. "Of course you can do something other than turn the place over to him." He whirled on Jem. "I see what it is. You're a scheming scoundrel who crept in here under pretense of being a butler and cozened an innocent, gullible female. Well, it won't work, you thieving rascal. You're not dealing with a helpless widow, now. No, indeed. Now you have Thomas Reddinger to deal with, and if you think for one minute that I will allow this poor child to be turned out of her own home—"

Again Claudia interrupted. "Thomas, once and for all. You have nothing to say about any of this. I accompanied Lord Glenraven to Gloucester yesterday, and we signed the papers. The deal is done. Ravencroft is his."

Once again Thomas was bereft of speech. Rose, apparently realizing at last what was transpiring, began to moan softly.

"You signed papers?" Thomas gasped incredulously.

"Yes, she did, old fellow." Jem chimed in. "Her signature was notarized by William Scudder of Scudder, Widdicombe and Phillips, and he is now clearing up whatever formalities remain to complete the transaction."

Thomas's eyes widened at the mention of one of the most esteemed attorneys in the county, and he drew a hand across his mouth.

Rose collapsed into an emerald-striped armchair, a shaking hand pressed to her bosom. "I am having palpitations," she quavered. No one so much as glanced at her.

"I see." It was quite obvious Thomas did not see at all, but remained undeterred by that fact. "Nonetheless—old fellow—I do not choose to recognize whatever proof you have managed to concoct." His small eyes fairly glittered with rage.

"What you do or do not choose to recognize," said Jem in the kindest of tones, "is immaterial to me. As is the case, if I am not mistaken, with Mrs. Carstairs." Claudia nodded vigorously in agreement. Thomas bent his attention on her.

"I can still scarcely comprehend all this. It is beyond my understanding that you would let this confidence trickster gull you so completely. Look at him! Lord Glenraven, indeed."

"Indeed," murmured Claudia. "Mr. Scudder had no difficulty in recognizing him."

Again, Thomas's eyes widened, and his expression as he gazed at Jem was unreadable.

"Be that as it may," he blustered. "The man has no claim to Ravencroft. I demand to see whatever papers he provided in evidence."

Jem unfolded his length from the settee upon which he had been sitting very much at his ease. He moved to stand before Thomas.

"Reddinger," he said softly. "You grow tedious. What you think or recognize or demand is of absolutely no consequence. As Mrs. Carstairs has told you, Ravencroft is mine."

Thomas rose also and gazed up into the gray eyes that met his with a maddeningly indifferent but somehow menacing coolness. He took a step backwards. He attempted a return to his blustering self-consequence, but his voice was high and unsteady. "We'll see about that!" he shrieked. "I can gather attorneys about me, as well, you know."

"Go right ahead," returned Jem in a bored tone. "But be so kind as to do it elsewhere. You have overstayed your welcome, Reddinger, as you've done, if I am not mistaken, from the moment you set foot here. Please gather up your stricken wife and your fatuous friend and your detestable children, and remove yourselves from the premises with all possible speed."

Thomas's neck swelled like that of a striking cobra. "What! Now see here, you can't—"

"With all possible speed, Reddinger," repeated Jem. He had not raised his voice, but Thomas, starting forward with clenched fists, halted suddenly and once again stepped back.

"And what if I refuse," he snarled.

"I don't think that would be wise." Jem's voice held nothing but friendly concern, but there was that in his tone that caused Thomas to hesitate. Swinging about, he barked at his wife. "Come, Rose." To Mr. Botsford, he said nothing, but that gentleman perspicaciously chose to follow him silently toward the door.

As he made to leave the room, Thomas turned back once more. He pointed a finger at Claudia. "And you needn't think you'll be coming with us, my girl. You've made your bed"—here an ugly, suggestive grin spread across his face—"and you can lie in it."

"Oh, but Thomas," cried Rose protestingly. "She is my sister. We cannot just let her starve in a gutter."

"Never mind, Rose," interjected Claudia, and in a few brief words, she described the arrangement she had come to with Jem.

Rose screamed faintly. "You cannot! You cannot remain here, virtually under this man's roof. At least—under what he claims . . . " she trailed off unhappily.

Thomas grasped her arm. "Let her do whatever she damn well pleases," he snapped. "I wash my hands of her."

He stormed out of the room, a sobbing Rose at his heels, and Fletcher bringing up the rear.

"Would that were so," said Claudia, dropping into an armchair. She glanced at Jem. "Well, I think we brushed through that fairly well, don't you?"

"Mmm. I suppose so. Though I seriously doubt we have heard the last of—" He was interrupted by a scream coming from the hallway outside the emerald saloon. Jem rushed through the door, with Claudia and Miss Melksham in his wake. In the corridor, they found Rose, her voice still rising in piercing screeches. Before her stood Nanny Grample, wringing her hands in her apron.

"Oh, mum!. It's true! The young master has killed hisself!"

At this, Rose, with a loud moan, fell to the floor. Fletcher fell to his knees beside her, but Thomas grasped Nanny Grample by the arm, shaking her until her spectacles were in danger of sliding from her nose.

"What do you mean?" he bellowed. "Stop that infernal sniveling and tell me what happened."

"The childern were in the nursery," blubbered the nurse, throwing her apron up to her face. "They was doing some schoolwork. I turned me back for the merest instant—going into the next room to—to find my mending, when all on a sudden I heard a dreadful crash." She was once more taken by a spasm of weeping strongly reminiscent of the braying of an army mule. "I rushed to see what had happened," she continued, "and found that the little dev—the little dear had been climbing up the wall."

"Climbing up the what?" queried Thomas and Rose in unison. Rose had by now recovered from her swoon and was sitting on the floor, listening in horrified fascination to Nanny Grample's tale.

"Oh yus, mum. He had bet Miss Horatia that he could go around the room without touching the floor, and he had begun by clambering up one of the bookcases—and he'd reached a window. He was walking along the valance, when it gave way."

Rose moaned again, faintly.

"Well, where is he now?" This from Thomas, who was still barking like an enraged mastiff.

"I left him with Kettering, the upstairs maid," wailed the nurse. "He's hollerin' fit to lift the roof."

"I thought you said he was— Never mind," concluded Thomas angrily, shouldering past Rose and the nurse, who, with Fletcher Botsford, followed in some disarray. Claudia, Jem, and Miss Melksham, after a startled exchange of glances, hurried after the group.

The sounds of Master George's distress could be heard long before the party reached the nursery floor. Kettering's distracted sobs and Horatia's gusty bellows added to the cacophony, but it was seen at once that Master George lay far from death's door. Red-faced and screaming, he clutched wildly at his foot, which was bent at an unnatural angle.

Jem at once beckoned a footman attracted by the commotion, and bade him go for the doctor, while Claudia, sharply adjuring both the maid and Nanny Grample to cease their lamentations, sank to her knees beside the boy. Thomas, for once appeared to be at a loss, and stood aside, ineffectually attempting to silence his wife.

Claudia gathered the terrified boy in her arms.

"George, I have something to tell you." She spoke in a whisper, whereupon the child ceased his wild sobbing, turning to her in attention. "I know your foot must hurt horribly," she continued soothingly, "and I just want to tell you I find it amazing that you can be so strong about it. You have cried a little, but I can see that you are ready to stop. I don't know when I have ever seen such a brave young man."

To the surprise of all, George promptly closed his mouth and, gritting his teeth, assured her that though it did indeed hurt something awful, he wasn't a crybaby, after all.

"I can see you are not," replied Claudia admiringly. She gestured to the remaining two footmen, and together, they lifted George in their arms and carried the boy to his room.

Rose followed with arms outstretched, her voice still raised in unceasing lamentation. Thomas followed, and Fletcher Botsford, after standing uncertainly for several minutes in the center of the hallway, followed. By mutual consent, the remainder of the little group, Jem, Claudia, and Miss Melksham tiptoed away.

Much later, the three sat in Claudia's former study, their faces set in gloomy reflection.

Miss Melksham commented acidly, "If I didn't think it were pretty much impossible, I would suspect Thomas of concocting this whole episode to prevent his leaving Ravencroft."

"Indeed," said Jem. "I could hardly order the family to leave with Master George brandishing a broken ankle—much as I was tempted to do so."

"I suppose it could have been worse," added Claudia. "The

doctor said that within two weeks the healing process should have gone forward enough so that he can travel home in a carriage. In the meantime," she sighed, "you will have to put up with Thomas and Rose."

"For two weeks, a man can hang by his thumbs," Jem said with a smile, "or so I've heard. At least, we have been relieved of Mr. Botsford's presence."

Claudia chuckled. "Not without protest, however. I've never heard a man offer so many excuses for staying put—everything from not having transportation to the need of the family for his support to feeling terribly unwell himself as a result of all the uproar."

"All in all," added Jem, "I feel the loan of a horse to get him on his way was a small price to pay for his departure."

Claudia's smile faded as she replied. "What a good thing you sent a boy along with him to bring the animal back, else I do not think you would have seen it again."

Miss Melksham cleared her throat, and spoke tentatively. "In the meantime, my—er, my lord, I believe you have other things with which to occupy your mind."

Jem swung toward her with a warm smile. "The first of which, my dear Miss Melksham, must be an apology to you for the deception I perpetrated. Please believe me, when I say that I felt I had no alternative."

Miss Melksham lifted mittened hands. "Oh—as to that . . . "

"And I hope you are in full agreement with the arrangement your niece and I have come to. You have performed miracles here at Ravencroft, and I'm sure I do not know how I would muddle along without you now." His gray eyes crinkled engagingly, and to Claudia's astonishment, Miss Melksham blushed rosily for a moment, before once again assuming her usual mien of austere propriety.

"As to that, my lord," she said in severe tones. "I cannot say I approve of the situation, but I am convinced that were it not for you, Claudia and I would be in sad straits. You heard Thomas. Nor do I believe William—Claudia's father—would be any more amenable. Besides," she added with a swift look at her niece, "returning to her parents' home would be almost as bad as starving in a ditch."

"You are being generous, Miss Melksham, for I am much

aware that it is I who have put you in sad straits. However"—Jem rose and went to seat himself next to the older woman—"please believe that I will do everything in my power to assure the comfort of you and your niece, while you remain here."

Miss Melksham murmured an inarticulate rejoinder and, rising, cleared her throat once more. "Perhaps, my lord, you would like to announce your, er, change in status to the staff. I have taken the liberty of arranging to have everyone brought together in the kitchen in fifteen minutes time."

"Excellent, Miss Melksham. Then, perhaps you and I might sit down to discuss the improvements that need to be made here. To start with, I thought we might hire more staff."

Claudia noted with amusement her aunt's start of pleasure. Lord Glenraven, she reflected rather sourly, certainly knew how to get what he wanted. Flattery and cajolery from the old ladies, and tender kisses for the young ones. What else did he have in his bag of tricks, she wondered. Not that she need worry. He had already got what he wanted from her, and if he had anything else in mind . . . Her heart jumped uncomfortably, but her thoughts marched on along a purposeful path. If he had anything else in mind, she told herself firmly, she had her defenses firmly in place.

The rest of the day passed in a blur of chaotic activity. The news of Jem's sudden rise in fortune and the coming increase in staff was greeted by the servants with gratifying expressions of surprise, pleasure, and not a little surmise.

Lucas was sent forth to London with messages of instruction to persons there regarding the forwarding of money, clothing, and other personal possessions. Miss Melksham put plans in motion for a dinner party to which the neighboring gentry would be invited for their first look at the new master of Ravencroft.

Jem saw little of Claudia during the remainder of the day, and knew her to be readying the estate accounts for his perusal. As the dinner hour approached, he made for the master's bedchamber, his belongings having been moved there by unseen hands. In an ancient oak cupboard, he found, lying in isolated splendor, the one gentleman's ensemble he had brought with him. One of the maids had declared herself more than willing to rescue the garments from the parcel in which they'd been carefully folded and tied with string, but she made it clear that she considered such an activity to be much above her station. When, she had asked diffidently, would his lordship's valet be arriving?

Jem chuckled as he donned pantaloons and a coat of Bath superfine. They were perhaps not suitable for evening wear, but they were fashionable and well made. Fortunately they had been tailored to fit his form so that he could don them without help. He mused on the time he had spent performing the services of a valet for Chad Lockridge, and the weeks he had toiled some years earlier as dogsbody in a tailoring establishment. Certainly, he could act as his own valet, except possibly for the laundering and pressing end of the operation.

He whistled softly as he tied his cravat, affixing to it a small emerald pin that had belonged to his father. It had been one of the few pieces of jewelry taken from Ravencroft by his mother, and he had stubbornly refused to sell it during his years of penury.

He bowed to his reflection in the mirror, and waving a hand in jaunty salute, he departed his chambers.

Downstairs, Claudia entered the emerald saloon, and was relieved to find herself alone there. The Reddingers had not appeared at luncheon, having sent for trays in their respective rooms, but they would almost certainly be down for dinner.

Claudia sighed. The days ahead would be difficult enough for Glenraven—and herself—without the depressing presence of Rose and Thomas. Not that she hadn't every confidence in Jem's ability to handle the offensive pair. At the thought of the task that lay before her, her heart gave a panicky lurch, though there should be nothing in the prospect of managing his lordship's stables to disturb her. She would only be continuing what she had been doing successfully for almost two years. In any event, she would probably be gone before long.

The thought startled her. When she had first demanded that Glenraven hire her as stable manager, she had considered the position as a sort of sinecure. Her love for Ravencroft was still a driving force in her life, and she wished to stay there forever—as an employee if not as its chatelaine.

But now . . . The thought of her continued proximity to Glenraven made her nervous, and for some reason the thought of the inevitable arrival on the scene of his yet-to-be-chosen bride filled her with an urgent desire to be elsewhere. Yes, she would save carefully from the handsome stipend she had wrung from his lordship, and at the first opportunity she would set up her own stables—far from Gloucestershire and Ravencroft. Surely, somewhere in England there must be a place as beautiful, as welcoming, and as satisfying as Ravencroft.

To her dismay, she felt tears rising behind her eyes, and she dashed them away in irritation. At a small sound behind her, she whirled about, only to feel her heart leap in her breast.

There, poised with a careless elegance on the threshold, stood the handsomest man Claudia had ever seen!

Chapter Fifteen

If Jem January was compelling in a stable hand's work clothes, thought Claudia dazedly, or in a butler's sober garb, he was absolutely magnificent in pantaloons that fit smoothly over muscled thighs and a superbly tailored coat that emphasized the compact elegance of his form. He crossed the room to her and pressed a light kiss on her fingertips.

"Good evening, Mrs. Carstairs," he said in the demurest of tones. His mist-colored eyes, however, sparkled in obvious anticipation as he turned about for her inspection. "What do you think of the transformation?"

Claudia laughed aloud. "Nothing short of spectacular, my lord. You make us all look shabby."

He surveyed her, his gaze traveling over her lutestring gown of celestial blue, trimmed with ribbons of a darker hue of the same color. Her décolletage, while not precisely daring, was more revealing than any of her other gowns, and earlier she had pondered at some length before throwing caution to the winds and slipping it over her head.

"Shabby is not the word that comes to mind, Mrs. Carstairs."

Claudia felt the heat rise to her cheeks as his glance paused for just a moment on the place where the lace of her bosom met what she now felt was an appalling spread of mounded flesh. She opened her mouth to speak, but was stayed by the entrance of Thomas and Rose.

They trooped into the green saloon together, obviously geared for battle. Thomas moved to stand before Jem, and Claudia could not help but note the contrast between the two men. Lord Glenraven's quiet elegance made Thomas look showy and overdressed in his florid waistcoat.

Rose bobbed a nervous curtsy, but Thomas surveyed Jem with a marked sneer.

"Fine feathers, indeed—my lord," he drawled, somehow turning Jem's title into an insult.

"Why, thank you, Reddinger." Jem's smile was wide and guileless, but the glance he turned on Claudia held a sardonic glint.

It was with some relief that she turned to greet Aunt Augusta, who entered the room just behind the Reddingers. It had taken much persuasion on Jem's part to convince her to eat with the family, since she now considered herself a servant, and he turned to usher her to a seat. From that point on, conversation was desultory at best, and to Claudia the time before they were ushered in to the dining room by a nervous footman dragged for an eternity.

As might have been expected, dinner was an unpleasant ordeal. Cook, in honor of the occasion had outdone herself with a rack of lamb and an assortment of vegetables in season with appropriate sauces, ending with raspberry tarts, accompanied by a syllabub and custards and fruits. And all of it, concluded Claudia in rising irritation, might have been concocted from straw and ashes for all the enjoyment anyone took from it. Except for Lord Glenraven, of course, who made a very good repast indeed, apparently oblivious to the slurs and thinly veiled insults offered during the course of the meal by Thomas. Thomas imbibed heavily through every course, demanding constant refills of his wineglass, and when at last the group rose to depart, he could hardly stand.

"Rose," said Claudia with distaste. "Perhaps you would be good enough to see your husband to his rooms. Aunt Augusta and I have promised Lord Glenraven our attention for the remainder of the evening, for there is much to be discussed."

Without waiting for an answer, she turned to Jem and Miss Melksham with a regal nod. Jem said nothing, but offered an arm to each of the ladies and proceeded from the chamber without so much as glancing at Thomas, who still stood swaying by his chair, glaring malevolently after the departing group.

Miss Melksham had already held an exhaustive session with Jem earlier in the day, so upon reaching the small study, now dotted with small crates containing Claudia's personal possessions, conversation was almost solely between Jem and Claudia. Miss Melksham settled in a nearby chair, watching the two with an expression that was benign, yet shrewdly watchful.

Claudia sat at the Sheraton desk, account books spread before her. It had been decided that she would show the books to Jem on the morrow, so she merely indicated them with a wave of her hand.

"I think you will find everything in order, my lord. You will observe that things are vastly different from what they were in—in the old days. Our standards are considerably lower, I fear, although—"

"Since I was but a boy 'in the old days,' " interrupted Jem, "I am pretty much unaware of precisely what standards were in effect then. What I do observe is that when you took over the reins at Ravencroft, things were in a sad state of affairs, and you have done wonders."

Claudia flushed, quite adorably to Jem's mind, but spoke purposefully. "I suppose you have noticed that there are many items missing—other than the books. I sold them. I'm terribly sorry to have done so, but there was no other way."

"I understand that," replied Jem quietly. "I would have done the same in your position." He smiled, and Claudia felt her heart lighten. "I daresay we shall muddle through without the suits of armor and the tapestries. We may even get them back someday."

"Claudia kept meticulous records, my lord," interposed Miss Melksham. "And many of the items were sold to persons living in Gloucester—although some went to dealers in that city, as well as in London."

Claudia sighed. "I'm afraid getting all the things back will be like trying to get all the troubles of the world back into Pandora's box."

"Let us hope we shall be more successful than Pandora and her friend—what was his name? Epimetheus, I think."

Claudia glanced up, startled. When had a streetwise urchin found his way to tales from Greek mythology? As though reading her thoughts, Jem grinned. "I worked in a bookshop for a few months when I was about seventeen. I did some unauthorized borrowing from time to time."

"I might have known," said Claudia repressively.

Conversation continued amiably among the three until Miss Melksham, exclaiming over the lateness of the hour, proclaimed herself ready to seek her bed and took her leave.

"Perhaps you would care for a game of piquet before retiring, Mrs. Carstairs?" suggested Jem.

This offer Claudia firmly declined, the vision only too clear before her eyes of herself sitting across a small table from the newly refurbished and terrifyingly attractive Lord Glenraven while candles flickered and died, leaving them in an intimate pool of light.

She yawned ostentatiously. "Thank you, my lord, but I am extremely fatigued myself. I shall bid you good night," she concluded, scurrying after Aunt Augusta, who had disappeared into the dimness of the corridor.

At the top of the stairs, she waved her aunt a cheerful good night, and made her way to her own chamber. Truth to tell, she was very tired, indeed. It had been a momentous day, and she felt in dire need not only of a night's rest, but of some solitude in which she could sort out the day's events.

Entering her room, she moved to set her candle on the small table that stood just inside the sitting room door, but to her surprise, the table was not there. Looking around the room, her mouth opened in surprise. The little table now rested across the room, near the fireplace, and the two chairs that had always stood near the fireplace had been moved to the window. One or two other small pieces of furniture had also apparently sprouted wings, for they rested in spaces formerly occupied by something else.

One of the housemaids must have been seized with an excess of housewifely zeal, Claudia surmised, moving items in order to clean behind them and then forgetting where they belonged. She would see about it in the morning, she concluded wearily. Right now, she was for bed.

She had promised herself an analytical review of the day's events, but no sooner had her head snuggled into her pillow than she sank into a dreamless sleep, unbroken until the sun's rays called her to another day.

She stood uncertainly before her wardrobe. Ordinarily, she would have slipped into her working garb of shirt and breeches for a brisk morning ride. Exercising the horses was the most pleasant of her chores, and although Jonah would not allow her to mount any of the big geldings or either of their two stallions, there were several young mares that suited her well.

But today was promised to Glenraven, although, she reflected, he would certainly not require her presence before breakfast. The matter decided to her satisfaction, she strode, breeched and coated, into the kitchen some minutes later, only to be confronted by Aunt Augusta. That lady, who had long since given up pointing out to her niece the error of her ways in dressing in such a scandalous fashion, merely pursed her lips in disapproval.

"I suppose you're going out on horseback," she murmured stiffly, and at Claudia's unrepentant nod, she sniffed. "I thought you were to be occupied with his lordship this morning."

"Yes, but not until later. I thought—"

"Good morning, ladies." Claudia whirled at the sound of a voice from the doorway. It was Jem, of course, dressed in his familiar stable garb. Catching Claudia's glance, he glanced down at himself and smiled ruefully. "I feel a little like Cinderella, sent back to the cinder heap."

"But of course, my lord," said Miss Melksham with some asperity. "You have naturally not had time to acquire a wardrobe suitable for your station. You will no doubt be going into Gloucester at your earliest opportunity to remedy this situation."

"Actually, I have a portmanteau full of clothing"—he sent Miss Melksham a mischievous look—"suitable for my situation. It should be arriving with Lucas in a few days. In the meantime, I don't imagine we will be receiving many visitors. Nor do I plan on making any duty calls," he added.

"The news will spread quickly, I should imagine," Miss Melksham replied. "I would not be surprised if the vicar will be calling today—or tomorrow at the latest. He is always hot on the scent of the latest gossip, using his duty as an excuse to nose out its trail."

Jem sighed. He had known that becoming master of Ravencroft would involve more than just running the estate. In his father's day, when things had been going well, there had been much coming and going between the other houses in the area. He could hardly remember their names now, but he was aware that he would be obliged to renew acquaintance with his neighbors.

Claudia, observing him, felt she could almost read his thoughts. It would not be long before he took his place as a leader in the county. And even before that, the matchmaking mamas would be at him. Claudia could think of at least three eligible misses living in the immediate vicinity. A coldness settled in her stomach, which she tried unsuccessfully to relieve by picturing herself far from Ravencroft, mistress once again of her own modest estate.

"What?" she asked blankly, aware that Jem was speaking to her.

"If we are to go riding, we'd best be on our way."

"Riding!" exclaimed Claudia, "But, I thought you did not—"

"I said it's been a long time since I've been on a horse. When I was a child, I rode constantly, however, and I am hoping that it's one of those things that once learned, are never forgotten." Placing a hand under her arm, he propelled Claudia toward the door, and, though she knew this was not a good idea, she allowed herself to be swept along, unresisting. At the door, she turned to Miss Melksham.

"I almost forgot, Aunt. Would you speak to one of the housemaids for me?" She described the unexplained liveliness of her furniture, and though she raised her eyebrows, Miss Melksham said only, "How very odd, to be sure," and agreed to look into the matter.

Jem's theory on learned activities proved to be correct. Claudia watched with trepidation and some amusement as he climbed awkwardly aboard a mount chosen for him by Jonah, but after a few cautious turns about the stable yard, he seemed to come to terms with the spirited gelding and motioned Claudia to lead the way along a worn path leading toward the fields of the home farm.

Claudia pointed to fields of ripening grain, rippling like a golden sea in the breeze. "We anticipate a good crop this year," she said.

Jem nodded abstractedly. "And the tenants? With so much of the land sold off, do you have enough laborers for the harvest?"

"Oh yes. Most of the land I sold to Squire Foster was pasture. I was forced to let some of the arable land go, but no, you will find that most of the tenant families who served your father are still working Ravencroft land."

Jem smiled. "That's good news. I daresay I won't know any of the families, but—wait, then. I wonder if Will Putnam is still about?"

"Why, yes. His wife just had a baby not two months ago. It was their fifth. Will must be—what, five years older than you?"

"Mm—just about. He was kind to me when I was a boy. He knew all the best fishing spots and all the most promising coverts. It was much beneath his dignity, of course, he being in his teens when I was just a grubby brat, but he knew I had no one my own age to be with, so he was patient."

Claudia laughed. "I can well imagine. He's a wonderful husband and father."

Jem glanced at her curiously. "Are you so well acquainted with all the tenants then?"

"Oh yes. I visit frequently and always enjoy a good chat. I have learned a great deal about estate management from them."

"Have you, indeed?" Jem was silent for a moment. "I guess Father did, too, come to think of it. I have missed a great deal in being away."

Unthinking, Claudia drew her mount near and placed her hand on his arm. "Yes, you did, Jem, and I wish with all my heart that Emanuel Carstairs had never entered the lives of your family. I—I hope he is burning in hell even as we speak."

At once ashamed at the vehemence of her speech and the intimacy of the contact she had just instituted, she drew her hand away abruptly and cantered ahead, up along a slight rise. When Jem caught up, she gestured to the distant pastures, visible from their vantage point.

"Most of what you see still belongs to you, but beyond that ridge of oaks—all that now belongs to Squire Foster."

"Yes, that's what I gathered from what Jonah said. I see you have sheep grazing there now."

"Only about half the number there should be, I'm afraid. I have spent most of the estate profits in the horse business, you see." She looked at him anxiously. "I felt I had a chance of success there, with Jonah to advise me."

Jem twisted in his saddle to look at her straightly. "I hope that was not said as an apology," he said, his tone serious. "For you have nothing whatsoever to apologize for."

She stiffened. "I know that, but—"

"It may be that not every one of your decisions was wise, but who among us can say we always choose rightly. Whatever goal you elected to pursue was chosen with care and intelligence, Claudia, and a love for this land. For that, I shall always be grateful to you, and I shall never second-guess what you have done."

Once more Claudia felt the sting of tears behind her eyes, and she nodded a wordless thank you. Swinging about, she pointed out in the most prosaic tone of voice she could manage that it was time they returned home.

"But we have been out for less than an hour," said Jem. "I had hoped to look at the tenants' cottages."

Claudia, however, felt she had spent quite enough time alone in his lordship's company for the moment. It was not so much that she did not trust Jem, she concluded in some irritation. It was her own emotions that were proving traitorous.

"We have much to do today, my lord," she said stiffly, and turned her mount toward the manor house.

"That's another thing," said Jem. "If you are to complete every sentence with 'my lord,' you are going to drive me into a megrim. I am unused to being called anything but Jem. Could you not manage that?" His smile was warm and winning, and it wreaked havoc with her interior.

"I think not, my lord," she said stiffly. "That is how you should be addressed, and you must become used to it."

"But, I refuse to become used to it," Jem replied in a tone of utmost reason. "You have already called me Jem once or twice."

"That was wrong of me. I was not thinking."

He grinned. "Just as I thought—you do entirely too much thinking." When the expected smile at this sally did not appear, he continued. "When we are alone, I do not see why we cannot call each other Jem and Claudia."

"But we shall be spending little time alone with each other," pointed out Claudia in a chill little voice.

At this, Jem looked somewhat taken aback, and stared at her for several seconds before replying.

"Yes, that's true," he said detachedly, and abruptly wheeled his mount about. Claudia gazed after him for a moment, feeling oddly forlorn, before moving to follow him.

Upon returning to the stable yard, Claudia dismounted quickly.

"My lo—sir, shall I wait upon you in the study after breakfast?"

"That would be agreeable, Mrs. Carstairs." Jem bowed stiffly. "I shall see you in the breakfast parlor."

Claudia hesitated. "I was not planning to eat there, my—sir. It is not appropriate that I take my meals with you any longer. I am your employee, after all."

Jem sighed gustily. "Am I to have the same difficulty I had with your aunt?" He drew breath to continue, but observing the mulish set of her mouth, he capitulated with suspicious good grace. "Very well, I will accept your argument—for the time being. But, you are not my employee yet. Today you are still my guest, who is about to turn over the reins of Ravencroft—but has not yet done so."

Claudia opened her mouth.

"That being the case," continued Jem in somewhat of a rush, "it is entirely proper for you to breakfast with me, since if I am not mistaken, your aunt will be joining us."

Claudia closed her mouth. She inclined her head, feeling remarkably foolish as she did so, and swept off toward the house with as much dignity as her trousers and slouch hat could afford.

On reaching her room, she found a housemaid there, industriously polishing the windows. Glancing about, she saw that her furniture had been restored to its proper arrangement.

"Thank you, Pritchert," she said, smiling. "I find I am such a creature of habit that I do not function well unless everything in my chamber is as it should be."

The little maid bobbed a curtsy, but stared blankly at her.

"The tables and chairs." At Pritchert's continued puzzlement, she continued. "Thank you for putting them back where they belonged."

Pritchert shifted her stare to the items indicated, then back to Claudia. "Put them back, mum? I—I didn't do nothing to them. They was in place when I come in. Did you want them moved?"

"That's just it, they weren't in place," replied Claudia, beginning to feel somewhat awkward. "They had been moved, but now they are back where they should be. I assumed it was you who did it—moved them, that is, and that you had now . . ." She stopped in the face of the growing bewilderment on the girl's face. "Never mind, Pritchert. If you've finished here, you may go now."

The maid, with a single backward glance of puzzlement, whisked herself from the room. Claudia sat herself in a chair and looked about her. "How very odd," she said, echoing her aunt's words earlier. She pondered the matter for some moments before deciding the explanation was quite simple, really. One of the other maids must have rearranged the furniture and, realizing her mistake—or having been told about it by Aunt Gussie—had crept in earlier to make things right.

Still, she felt oddly unsettled as she shed her work clothes. Shrugging, she put the matter from her mind and bent her thoughts to choosing a morning gown. She told herself that the fact that she would be dining with Lord Glenraven had nothing to do with her choice of a daffodil cambric that she had been told matched her hair. It was trimmed with lace and a silk ribbon of a light amber, that her mirror told her matched her eyes. Threading a ribbon of like color through curls teased into an artful curve, she hurried from the room, giving no more thought to her wandering furniture.

She found Lord Glenraven already at breakfast with her aunt. Pouring herself a cup of coffee from the urn on the buffet, she selected toast and jam before joining them at a small table that overlooked the east garden.

Miss Melksham beamed at her niece. "His lordship was just—" she began, but Jem held up his hand.

"I really think I must get this my lord and your lordship settled. Since both of you seem so adamant against using my Christian name—which, I must say I always thought extremely, er, acceptable—I propose that you call me Glenraven. That still sounds a bit toplofty to me, but it's better than the other. Agreed?"

Two pairs of eyes stared unwinking at him for several moments before turning to each other. Miss Melksham raised her brows in silent question, and Claudia finally nodded in unspoken agreement.

"Very well then." Miss Melksham began again. "Glenraven was just asking what I thought it might take to bring the garden back." She gestured to the scene outside, which, though its former beauty could be discerned, had dwindled to a few dispirited rosebushes, fighting a losing battle with the weeds that grew sturdier every year.

"Why," responded Claudia coolly, "if several men were set to work now, I think you might see a vast improvement by next season. Do you have the means for this?" Her aunt gasped, and she knew her question had been embarrassingly farouche, but her curiosity about Lord Glenraven's vague promises to restore Ravencroft had been of great concern to her.

"Yes," replied Jem with an appreciative grin. "I think my funds might stretch to a few gardeners—and a clutch of housemaids and footmen, too. In fact, after we have had our discussion, I shall see about hiring additional hands in the stables, and for farming, as well. And we must not forget the sheep. The flock, as you say, needs rebuilding."

Claudia strove to maintain an air of dubious approval, but the gaze she turned on him fairly glowed. "That sounds wonderful, my—Glenraven."

Looking at her, Jem was as dazzled as though he had looked full into the sun. Lord, he berated himself a moment later. What a susceptible looby he was turning into, to be turned inside out by a single glance. He returned to his eggs and toast and, for the rest of the meal, maintained a flow of determinedly colorless conversation with both ladies.

At length, the three rose from the table, and Miss Melksham left to go about her duties. Claudia and Jem made their way to the study, but had just settled in for an examination of the estate books, when Aunt Augusta entered unexpectedly.

"I'm sorry to disturb you," she said in apology, "but Mr. Scudder has just arrived."

"Scudder!" exclaimed Jem. "But he was not supposed to come for several days."

"That's what he said," replied Miss Melksham, "and he begs your pardon, but he said something has come up. He seemed quite disturbed," she added apprehensively.

Chapter Sixteen

When Claudia and Jem arrived in the emerald saloon, they found Mr. Scudder treading an agitated path before the fireplace. He swung around as they entered the room, and hurried toward them.

"My lord!" he exclaimed. "And Mrs. Carstairs—I am glad you are here, too. I do apologize for coming without warning, but—"

"Not at all," said Jem in a soothing voice. "Pray be seated, sir." Settling the older man into a chair, he poured some wine from the decanter resting on a small sofa table and handed it to him. He gestured Claudia to a nearby settee and sat down next to her.

The wine seemed to have a beneficial effect on Mr. Scudder, for when he spoke again, his voice, though still anxious, was calm.

"I'm afraid I am the bearer of bad news, my lord," he began. "It has come to my attention that Mrs. Carstairs's brother-in-law—Thomas Reddinger?"—he raised his brows questioningly at Claudia, and she nodded grimly—"has retained an attorney for the express purpose of preventing the transfer of Ravencroft from her possession to yours."

"What?" Claudia stared for a moment. "But, he cannot do that—can he? I have already signed the papers."

"That's just it," said Mr. Scudder, taking a large handkerchief from his coat pocket to wipe his brow. "He is apparently trying to have you declared mentally incompetent, or at least acting under undue influence. If he is successful—the documents you signed will be null and void."

"But that's absurd," Jem exclaimed incredulously. "There's nothing wrong with Cl—Mrs. Carstairs's mind."

"N-no," responded Mr. Scudder, his mouth turned down in a dubious curve. Claudia and Jem exchanged glances, and observing this, Mr. Scudder continued. "Mr. Reddinger has hired the firm of Morland, Welker and Pennyfine to—"

"But Cornelius Welker was Emanuel's man of affairs!" interjected Claudia.

"Precisely." Mr. Scudder pulled at his lip. "I should not be saying this, but Welker is a disgrace to the profession. He has already sent around to my office for copies of the documents you offered as proof of Carstairs's misdeeds. He has no right to see them, of course, and I told him as much, but if he is successful in proving undue influence—or mental instability, Reddinger will no doubt be made your ward, and will then be granted access to them."

"But—" began Claudia hotly, and Mr. Scudder sighed deeply.

"Welker has already begun with his despicable campaign. He mentions your 'scandalous preference' for dressing in men's clothes for example."

Jem grinned. "At the most, her preference in dress could be called an eccentricity—or an abysmally poor fashion sense." Claudia shot him an indignant glance, but said nothing.

Mr. Scudder pulled a long face. "If she were very wealthy and protected by the existence of several male relatives, perhaps. As it is, there is no getting away from the fact that Mrs. Carstairs has got herself talked about among the area tabbies, who are more than happy to add another spoonful of spite to make the pot boil. There is, for example, the story that you cavort about the house wearing a teakettle on your head."

This time it was Jem who stared. Claudia, too, seemed at a loss for a moment, then her face cleared. "Oh, how perfectly ridiculous," she said with a laugh. She turned to Jem. "One day I was in the stables, and just as I started to return to the house, it began pouring a perfect torrent of rain. Someone had set an enormous empty kettle on a table near the doorway, and upending it over my head, I made a dash for the kitchen door. Cook and the others in the kitchen were quite convulsed at my appearance, and said I must surprise Aunt Gussie with my 'new hat.' I pranced into the emerald saloon, still wearing it, and there was not only my aunt, but Lady Goodall, Mrs.

Squeers, and Mrs. Rumbolton, who had come to call. You should have seen the expression on their faces! Particularly," she added with another gurgle of laughter, "since I had also thrown an old horse blanket over my shoulders, as well."

Jem chuckled, but Mr. Scudder did not join in their amusement. "I'm afraid some of your neighbors did not see the incident in that light. Tell me, Mrs. Carstairs," he continued, "when was the last time you saw Squire Foster?"

"Squire Foster? Two or three weeks ago, I think. I met with him to discuss grazing my sheep on his land." Claudia directed a questioning stare at Mr. Scudder.

"Apparently," said that gentleman dryly, "Foster is not foremost among your well-wishers. He has for some time been very busy behind your back, speaking of your unwomanly absorption in animal husbandry and describing you as almost demented in your greedy obsession with 'making a showplace' of Ravencroft."

Claudia went pale. "He is saying that?" she asked in a whisper. She rose from the settee to stand before Mr. Scudder. "I knew he did not approve of my running the estate myself, but I had no idea he was so—so virulent in his opposition."

"Mmm." Mr. Scudder pursed his lips. "I think Foster has a vested interest in discrediting you, for he wishes to retain the land he purchased from you. He only agreed to sell it back to you—at an exorbitant price—because he assumed you would never be able to buy it. There is no doubt that Welker has been in contact with Foster, and Foster is more than willing to propagate this fancy of your being unbalanced. He has already said that when he refused to allow your sheep to graze on his land, you became so incensed he thought you were going to attack him."

"This is monstrous!" exclaimed Jem, who had also risen to stand beside Claudia.

"Yes," agreed Mr. Scudder distastefully. "But that is not the worst—at least as far as you are personally concerned. If Reddinger and Welker are successful, and Mrs. Carstairs's transfer of Ravencroft to you is invalidated, you will have a thin time convincing the court of your legal right to the place, based on the documents you showed me."

"My God," said Jem, slowly. He sank back again on the settee, pulling Claudia down with him.

"I cannot believe this," added Claudia dazedly, trying to sort out the implications of this turn of events. Her thoughts flew to the creased sheets of paper hidden in her dressing table. She had retained them as a sort of insurance—well, a form of extortion, really, if she were honest. It was only Jem's realization that he might lose a battle in court that had enabled her to negotiate employment for her and Aunt Gussie. But now . . . If she were rendered powerless by Thomas and his machinations, Jem would be drawn into the battle after all. And she would be ruined, forced to live in Thomas Reddinger's thrall for the rest of her life. She felt sick at the thought, and cold with dread.

Mr. Scudder reached to pat her hand. "Perhaps I have stated the case too strongly. Welker is a long way from accomplishing his goal. While there are no doubt some of your acquaintances hereabouts who will be only too glad to see you brought down—such is always the case with beautiful young women—you have many staunch friends in the area who will do their utmost to support you. The vicar, for example, is most definitely your friend, and I'm sure there are others. I need only to seek them out."

"Of course." Jem smiled. "I'm sure we are taking much too dim a view of things."

Mr. Scudder rose. "I shall mount a counterstrategy to Welker's nefarious activities, but in the meantime . . ." He stared earnestly at Claudia. "Do be careful, Mrs. Carstairs. Reddinger will be watching you—with witnesses to corroborate anything you might do or say that could possibly be interpreted as—unstable behavior."

"I think not," interjected Jem, tight-lipped. "While I am forced to house Reddinger's wife and his progeny, I see no reason why Thomas Reddinger should stay one more night under my roof. He can move to the Three Swans in Little Marshdean if he does not choose to go home."

Mr. Scudder held up an admonishing hand. "Your sentiments are most understandable, my lord, but such a course of action might be unwise. No, no, hear me out," he added hastily, as Jem opened his mouth to expostulate. "It would create a great deal of talk if Mrs. Reddinger and the children remained at Ravencroft, while her husband was forced to reside elsewhere. And, the Three Swans would merely serve as a stage for Mr. Reddinger to air his supposed grievances."

"Mr. Scudder is right," said Claudia to Jem. "I'm afraid you must put up with Thomas. Honestly, I could strangle the man. And Rose, too, for that matter. If she weren't such an utter ninnyhammer, I'd ask her to try to talk some sense into her husband. I'll tell you what we can do, though," she added after a moment's thought. "The east wing has been closed for years, but there is no reason why we could not transfer the entire family there for the duration of their stay. They could even take their meals there."

"Excellent idea," said Mr. Scudder, before Jem had a chance to answer. "I must be on my way now, but—"

"Oh!" interrupted Claudia. "What about that other phrase you used—undue influence? What is meant by that?"

The attorney exchanged a glance with Jem, who drew his brows together. Mr. Scudder cleared his throat. "As to that . . . Well, Lord Glenraven is young and certainly personable. You, Mrs. Carstairs are young and inexperienced in the ways of the world, and you are a widow, and, ah, as such must be considered susceptible to the, er, blandishments of—"

"Oh, for heaven's sake!" cried Claudia in exasperation. "Are you saying that just because I live without the protection and counsel of some omnipotent male relative that I would be such a wigeon as to succumb to the wiles of a—a handsome butler claiming to be what he is not?"

Mr. Scudder was by now perspiring profusely and once more drew his handkerchief across a streaming forehead.

"No, no," he said vehemently. "Lord Glenraven's credentials cannot be considered suspect. It is his claim to the estate that will come under minute scrutiny. As I have already told you, the documentary evidence his lordship has provided is rather slender, and there are those who will wonder at your unwarranted capitulation to his demands."

"And as I have already told you," she replied tightly, "I had suspected for some time that Emanuel never had any real right to the place."

"I understand, my dear lady, but—"

Jem intervened at this point, holding up his hand for silence. He spoke quietly, but with a calm authority.

"I think we are agreed that the suggestion of undue influence is as ludicrous as one of mental instability. I am sure, Mr. Scudder, that you will spare no effort to counter these charges, and I have complete confidence in your ability to do so."

Mr. Scudder expelled a sigh of palpable relief. "To be sure, my lord. Mr. Reddinger and his attorney must ultimately fail in their wicked scheme."

With further expressions of reassurance, the attorney shortly made his departure, leaving Jem and Claudia to stare at each other in dismay.

Jem was the first to speak. "My God, Claudia," he said harshly, drawing her down on the settee beside him. "Not only have I caused you to lose the home you love, but now on my account, you have become the target of an unbelievably vicious plot."

She felt lost in his gaze, as though she had stepped into a warm, enveloping mist that filled her senses. He was seated so close to her that she could feel the caress of his breath on her cheek. Clenching her fingers in her lap, she drew a deep breath.

"You are not responsible for Thomas's greed," she replied, struggling to maintain her composure. She rose abruptly. "I have a great deal to do today, my lord—I must see to my removal from the manor house, so perhaps we could go over the estate accounts now?"

Jem looked at her strangely. "Very well, Mrs. Carstairs. I am at your disposal." Unfolding his length from the settee with fluid grace, he followed her as she left the room.

To Claudia's relief, Jem kept the conversation brief and businesslike as she spread account books, property lists, and figures on livestock and crop production over the desk for his perusal. She had left the door to the study wide open, and several times during the course of the afternoon called in passing servants to issue a number of trivial orders.

As the last sheet of figures was explained, and Claudia finally straightened her aching back, she spied a housemaid hurrying by with a dust clout in her hand.

"Fimber!" she called. The maid scurried into the room and

bobbed a swift curtsy. "When you return belowstairs, will you ask Cook to serve raspberry sauce with the custard she is planning for this evening?"

As the maid bobbed again and left the room, Claudia looked up to find Jem eyeing her quizzically. "Apparently, you are right, Mrs. Carstairs."

"I beg your pardon?"

"By my count, we have not been alone for more than five minutes at a stretch throughout this very long afternoon."

Claudia stiffened, but after a moment, gave an unwilling laugh. "Yes, I suppose I have been rather transparent. I must admit that I took Mr. Scudder's words to heart—about the undue influence thing. I wish to avoid the slightest hint of impropriety in our dealings." She looked at him straightly, but could not control the rush of heat that surged into her cheeks.

"Of course," replied Jem in a colorless voice, "I quite understand. I shall see you and your aunt at dinner, then." Inclining his head, he turned away and moved down the corridor, leaving Claudia to stare after him.

In his chambers, Jem slumped in a chair covered in worn brocade and gave himself up to thought. Good Lord, what had he done to Claudia Carstairs? He recalled the exultation that had swept over him just a few days ago—the pleasure that had grown in him ever since at the plans he was putting into motion. My God, how could he have foreseen that his return might result in the ruin of an innocent woman? He had already snatched away her home; now, she was liable to lose her reputation and, yes, her freedom as well.

His lips curved in a sour smile. After their conference this afternoon, he had thought of asking her to accompany him on a stroll about the manor grounds before dinner. He was surprised at his anticipation of an hour spent listening to her rich laughter and watching the play of sunlight on that glorious golden mane. He realized, with a jolt of dismay, that he was becoming entirely too fond of the bewitching widow's company.

On the other hand, what was wrong with that? There was nothing wrong with a strictly platonic relationship, surely. Had he not as much right as the next man to enjoy good conversation and the companionship of a pretty woman? Well, no, pretty was not precisely the right word, was it? More like lovely. No—radiantly lovely, perhaps. The kind of loveliness that comes from an inner beauty, he rather thought. Which brought him back to her charming laughter.

He sighed. With Claudia's pernicious brother-in-law at her throat, her laughter, charming or otherwise, would rarely be heard in the days to come. And with her newfound sense of propriety in effect, she would be available for precious little in the way of conversation, either. He'd be lucky if she so much as asked him to pass the peas at dinnertime.

Was it, he wondered suddenly, Thomas's threat that had caused her to withdraw from his company? Had he been wrong in thinking she enjoyed their conversation as much as he? And not just the conversation, he thought abruptly, his thoughts flashing inadvertently to that moment in the gig when he had covered her soft, warm mouth with his own. She had responded. There was no doubt of that, and if they had been in a more secluded spot, God knows how the embrace would have ended.

He drew a deep, somewhat shaky breath. Damn! In talking to himself just now, he had been speaking with a fool. Platonic friendship indeed! If he were to be perfectly honest, he would be forced to admit that his interest in Mrs. Carstairs went far beyond simple companionship. Somehow, while he wasn't looking, she had crept into the center of his being.

He stood, and began to pace the carpet. This was very bad. How had he not seen that he would be drawn so inevitably into her net? Not that she had exerted any wiles to capture him. No, it was the woman herself who had become so essential to him. She was warm and giving and open. And intelligent and witty. All the things that drew him to her shone in those topaz eyes that gazed at the world with such clear honesty.

The emotion that swept through him left him dazed and shaken. It was a feeling with which he was unfamiliar, and he found it profoundly unsettling. What frightened him the most was the need for her that surged within him. When he wasn't with her, it seemed as though some critical part of him was missing. The thought that she might someday leave Ravencroft left him cold and empty.

He knew a moment of panic. This would not do, he told

himself fiercely. He must maintain his self-sufficiency or he would be lost. Opening himself to another would make him vulnerable once again to the heartache and disillusionment he had vowed he would never experience again.

He ceased his pacing and stood still upon the carpet. Claudia Carstairs had the right of it. Distance must be kept, and a proper relationship maintained. He would seek a suitable bride at the earliest opportunity—an amenable young woman who would bring him that much-needed dowry. A woman whom he could like and respect without a singing of the blood or the lifting of the spirit whenever he saw her. Then, Claudia Carstairs would have no place in his life—or his heart.

He nodded abruptly, satisfied, he told himself, at his decision. He moved slowly to his wardrobe to begin preparations for dinner, wondering why he felt so inutterably weary.

In another area of the house, Claudia sat in her own chambers, staring before her. In her hands, she clutched the sheets of paper she had removed from their hiding place when she had entered the room. Here, she thought dully, lay the solution to Lord Glenraven's problems. And to hers, as well—at least the ones involving her wretched brother-in-law.

All she had to do was to give Emanuel's incriminating list to Mr. Scudder. He in turn would show it to Cornelius Welker, who would then inform Thomas that Jem's claim to Ravencroft was airtight. Thomas, realizing that he now had no hope of beating Jem in court, would no doubt cease in his effort to have her declared mentally unstable.

In the end, Jem would have his home, and he would know that she had duped him. Would he understand that it had only been her desperate need for a bargaining chip that had led her to withhold the papers from him?

These thoughts, Claudia found, were doing nothing to relieve the self-revulsion that was beginning to fill her. She could at least have given him Emanuel's list as soon as he had signed her contract of employment. Why had she felt it so important that he continue to think well of her? Why had *he* become so important to her? He was a man, after all, and therefore of a species for which she had little use. There was not the slightest doubt in her mind that without the bargain she had been able to negotiate with the master of Ravencroft, she and Aunt Gussie would have found themselves tossed out on their respective derrieres without a character.

Despite herself, a tendril of doubt twisted its way into her self-congratulatory mood. She was finding it hard to maintain the certainty that Lord Glenraven was the sort of person who thought only of his own needs. He had been everything that was kind and honorable in his dealings with her. He had promised her a handsome settlement, even before she had come forward with her proposal to him, and he was providing her with a handsome salary.

He seemed truly fond of her, didn't he? Could a man who had kissed her in such a manner that she still blushed to think of it treat her with anything but consideration? Hmph, a sly voice muttered in the back of her mind, Emanuel's kisses were hot and demanding, but that didn't stop him from trying to bully you.

She shrugged. The deed was done. She had kept the knowledge of the list from Jem, and must now pay the consequences. Or, perhaps not precisely now. She would wait to see how Thomas's campaign went, and if things began to look really black, then would be time enough to reveal her dishonesty to him.

She dressed dispiritedly for dinner, her thoughts turning to her immediate problem. How could Thomas treat a relative in such a manner? She had not seen him or Rose since Mr. Scudder's revelations, and dreaded the moment when she must do so. This would probably not come until the morrow, at least—for surely the Reddingers would keep to themselves tonight—so she might as well try to enjoy dinner with Jem and Aunt Augusta. It would probably be the last meal they would partake of together, since by tomorrow night, she and Aunt Gussie would be ensconced in Hill Cottage.

Completely gowned, her hair arranged to her satisfaction, she drew a simple strand of pearls from her jewelry box. Her mouth curved in a grim smile as she gazed at the necklace. In what was supposed to have been a symbol of sisterly closeness, the pearls had been a gift from her mother and father on her sixteenth birthday, an identical set having been given to Rose on her own sixteenth birthday. Clasping them about her neck, Claudia laughed shortly. Tossing a zephyr scarf about her shoulders, she made her way hurriedly from the room. As she entered the emerald saloon, she was shocked to behold the last persons in the world she expected to see.

"Rose!" she exclaimed. "Thomas!"

Chapter Seventeen

Thomas approached his sister-in-law, eyeing her warily. "Evening, Claudia," he said, with an effort at heartiness. Rose echoed his words in an agitated whisper.

Claudia struggled with the effort it took not to fly at him with fingers curled into talons.

"What are you two doing here?" she rasped, her eyes narrowed to slits pouring golden fire. "How can you possibly have the nerve to show your faces after what you have done?"

For a moment, Thomas's features assumed an expression of feigned innocence, but after a moment, he shrugged his shoulders heavily.

"I suppose you're referring to the litigation I've instituted," he said at last.

"Liti—is that what you call it?" Claudia fairly shrieked. "Litigation? To make a byword of my name? To make a laughingstock of your wife's sister? I knew you were a greedy bastard, but I would not have thought even you would go this far!"

"Claudia!" squealed Rose. "Language! Try to remember you are a lady!"

Claudia swung on her sister. "Oh no, Rose. Not a lady. I am a poor, demented nitwit, who would allow herself to be gulled by the first handsome fellow to come down the pike with sweet words in his mouth and larceny in his heart."

"A mixed compliment, if ever was," a voice drawled lazily from the doorway. "I believe I'll pretend I heard just the first part." Claudia did not turn, but remained glaring at Thomas and Rose. Jem sauntered into the room to stand beside her. Thomas took a swaggering step forward, but halted as Jem's contemptuous gaze swept over him.

"One must certainly give you credit for effrontery," continued Jem softly, "but I fail to see why Mrs. Carstairs should be expected to put up with your presence."

"Now see here, Glenraven." Thomas blustered. "No need to take that attitude. I am simply looking out for Claudia's best interest. Any man would do the same."

After a long, amazed silence, Claudia said, "I cannot believe you just said that. Are you trying to tell me that your efforts to make me appear a candidate for Bedlam are for my benefit?"

"Cut line, Reddinger," growled Jem. "You're a grasping muck worm, and your tactics to gain control of Ravencroft for yourself, are pitifully obvious—as well as being doomed to failure."

Thomas assumed an expression of outraged virtue.

"You wrong me, sirrah. Look at it from my point of view. You claim that Ravencroft was stolen from you, which may very well be true. But nothing is proven, and from what my attorney has been able to uncover, your case is more than somewhat lacking. My sister-in-law in her innocence has agreed to simply turn over the place to you. Well, you know what women are—gems beyond price, in their place, but quite incapable of dealing with anything beyond their little domestic affairs."

Claudia bristled, and Jem laid a hand on her arm to still the words that seemed to boil visibly on her lips.

Thomas's features arranged themselves into an assumption of pious concern. "I'm not saying I would not have acted as you did," he said. "One can understand that you would do anything to get your old home back. However, I could not in all conscience stand by and allow my wife's sister to be so duped." He pursed his lips judiciously. "You might consider my action as plain good business sense. Nothing personal at all."

At this, Jem was forced to laugh. "You are an original, Reddinger. I'm not sure whether you have an infinite capacity for self-delusion, or you are simply totally lacking in scruples. In either case, you are persona most definitely non grata here. I may be forced to house you, but I'll be damned if I feel compelled to look at you." Briefly, he outlined Claudia's plan for the Reddinger's removal to the fastness of the east wing.

"Sister!" wailed Rose weakly. "I cannot credit this of you. That you would treat your nearest and dearest in such a way! Think of poor little George wrenched from his bed of pain and thrust into heaven only knows what wretched accommodations. I simply cannot—"

"Rose, be quiet," replied Claudia, her eyes glittering dangerously. "You may be my nearest, but you are far from being my dearest. As for little George and his bed of pain, he will be as comfortable in the room assigned him as he is at present. More so, perhaps, since his new bedchamber will overlook the exercise paddock. He will be able to watch the horses while he is still unable to run about."

Rose subsided in a series of unintelligible squeaks and mutterings, while Thomas stood silently, rigid with indignation.

At that moment, Miss Melksham bustled into the room, but stopped short on observing the Reddingers.

"My goodness!" she exclaimed, "what are you two doing here?"

"Why does everyone keep asking us that?" replied Thomas in some irritation. "We are guests here, and we must eat, after all."

"Perhaps," said Miss Melksham balefully, as though unwilling to accept this premise, "but I had given instructions that you would take dinner in your new quarters. I sent word to you of this a good two hours ago. The maid said she had spoken to you personally."

Thomas flushed, and Rose twittered anew. "I could only assume," said Thomas, drawing what remained of his dignity to him like a battered shield, "that the silly chit was mistaken in your message. How could I dream that we would be treated so shabbily?"

"How could you dream that you would be treated any other way?" murmured Jem, and turning his back on Thomas, he led Miss Melksham to a comfortable chair.

Swelling with umbrage, and turning quite purple with rage, Thomas stepped farther into the room. Gone was his semblance of propitiating cordiality. "Have it your way, Glenraven," he snarled. "We'll soon see how far your high and mighty ways will get you in a court of law. You may be master of Ravencroft now, but when I am through with you, all that will remain will be your precious title, for you will have neither pillar nor post on which to lay your head—my lord." He uttered this last with sneering contempt, and waited for Jem's response. When the young man did not so much as lift his head from his conversation with Miss Melksham, Thomas turned on his heel, and grasping Rose's arm, strode from the room.

Claudia sank down upon a nearby confidante, white and shaken. Jem shot her a quick glance, and placing himself next to Miss Melksham, said in a cheerful voice, "Well, I think we brushed through that rather well, don't you?"

"I feel sick," was Claudia's leaden response. "I have never been comfortable with Rose, and I have disliked Thomas since our first meeting, but I never thought he would serve me so ill. Or that Rose would stand by his side while he did so."

"Rose does not have the gumption of a sick rabbit," sniffed Miss Melksham. "She takes after her mother. Thank goodness you took after *my* mother. Now, there was a woman with enough gumption for twelve people."

Claudia smiled unwillingly.

"There, that's better," said Jem. He rose and moved to her chair, pulling her to her feet. "And now, my butler's instinct tells me that dinner is served. Shall we?"

Tucking one of the ladies' arms in each of his, he exited the emerald saloon with a flourish.

Somewhat to Claudia's surprise, dinner turned out to be a pleasant experience. In the absence of the Reddingers, conversation flourished, at first among all three of the particicpants, but later mainly between Jem and Claudia, as Miss Melksham sat back and watched benignly. Jem told the ladies more of his experiences as a boy growing up in London. His descriptions of the characters he had encountered during his growing-up time were vivid, so that Claudia could plainly see the "gentleman" who had taught him the art of picking pockets and the gambler from whom he had learned the knack of estimating odds.

Of the time when he had been with his mother and his sisters, he said nothing, and Claudia forbore to ask. She was aware that memories could soothe and create their own world of enjoyment, but they could also slash like knives cunningly positioned in the back of one's brain.

When they rose at last from the table, Jem declared his intention of forgoing a solitary session with the port decanter.

"I have always thought it rather ludicrous for a man to be obliged to sit alone for a specified period of time, while pleasant company awaits in another room."

"Oh," said Claudia uncertainly. She glanced at her aunt. "As to that, I had planned to retire to my rooms immediately after dinner. I have not even begun my packing, and Aunt Gussie and I had formed the intention of moving into Hill Cottage tomorrow."

Jem opened his mouth, but closed it again immediately, an unreadable expression crossing his features. "Of course," he said, his voice smooth and courteous. "I should go out to visit the stables. Jonah hired a few hands at my direction today, and I must see how they're getting on."

"Oh." Claudia's fingertips flew to her face in a guilty gesture. "I have not been out there all day. I did not know that you had spoken to Jonah—"

"For just this one day, I think we can acquit you of failing in your duties. As for the other, I apologize for hiring men without consulting you first, but with neither of us available to help out, I thought you would not mind if I set a few things in motion."

Claudia flushed. "Of course not. It was very considerate of you—it was something I should have thought of myself."

"Nonsense. You have quite enough on your mind for the present." He bowed to the two ladies. "Until the morrow, then."

The next moment, he was gone, leaving Miss Melksham to stare at her niece in surprise.

"Well! Did we say something to upset him?"

"Oh, I'm sure not," replied Claudia hastily. "He simply understood that—um—if you will excuse me, Aunt, I shall go upstairs to begin some packing. I'll see you in the morning."

She nearly ran from the room in a craven rush, and did not stop until she had reached her chambers. Once there, she dropped the zephyr shawl on her dressing table, stripped the pearls from her neck, and remained frozen before her dressing table for some minutes in a brown study. She came to herself with a jerk only when she realized that her thoughts were occupied not with her immediate task, but with the tall, loose-limbed aristocrat she had left moments before.

Really, she chastised herself, aimlessly opening drawers and cupboards, she was behaving like a green schoolgirl in the throes of a crush. Of course she liked Jem Standish (though she certainly would not let him know she called him that in her thoughts) and she enjoyed his company, but to find herself falling into silly daydreams about him when she was not actively thinking about something else was the outside of enough.

What was there about him, she wondered irritatedly, that drew her thoughts? Of course, there was the fact that the two of them were engaged in a life-and-death struggle with a common adversary—that sort of thing tended to create a bond between people. On the other hand, she and Aunt Augusta had been allies against the world for some time, and she seldom found herself dreaming of that lady's warm laughter or her compelling eyes.

Many of her illicit thoughts, she was ashamed to admit, centered on the two occasions when Jem had kissed her. Her fingers trailed across her lips as they curved in a slow smile. The next moment, she caught sight of herself in the mirror and stiffened.

She might be looking at the picture of a woman in love! But that was ridiculous. Love was a delusion, created by the authors of vapid romance fiction. In real life, there was no such thing as a happy ending for two people who might find themselves drawn to each other by a common goal. A woman would be stupid beyond words to lose her heart to a man who seemed different from all others, a man whose raven hair and silver eyes filled her dreams.

"You fool!" she said baldly to her reflection, and whirled to the stack of empty pasteboard boxes that had been placed in a pile earlier at her direction. Swiftly, she packed the contents of her wardrobe before starting in on the cupboards. It was fully dark when she finished, and, gazing at her belongings—seemingly the sum and total of her life at Ravencroft—she was overcome by a sudden weariness. Pausing only to remove her gown and make the briefest of ablutions at the pitcher and basin that stood on a nearby commode, she climbed into bed, blew out her candle, and was soon asleep.

At some time during the night, she opened her eyes, awakened by she knew not what. For a moment, she received the impression that she was not alone in the room, but when no sound reached her ears, her lids drooped again, and in another moment she was asleep.

When she awoke early the next morning, she was startled for a moment at the sight of the boxes, looming like intruders in the gray, early light. As memory returned, tears thickened in her throat. Lord, she was really leaving. Ravencroft was no longer her home. The words she had said so often in the past few days struck her anew with the force of a blow, and she knew an insane desire to dive beneath the covers and whimper like a stricken child.

She was forced to smile at the absurdity of her thoughts. Sliding from her bed, she strode to the windows and flung them open. With the same vigorous stride, she moved into the small sitting room that adjoined her bedchamber and promptly found herself "end over tail" as Jonah would have said, landing in a surprised heap on the floor.

"What in the world . . . ?" she gasped, and looked about her. Unbelieving, she plucked at one of the small objects scattered near her on the carpet. Pearls! And there, next to her dressing table, the broken string and clasp that had held them.

On hands and knees she retrieved the little globes and deposited them in a small dish on her dressing table. Picking up the string, she examined it closely. It showed clearly where it had frayed through, allowing the opalescent bubbles to slide to the floor.

How odd. There had been nothing wrong with the string last night. In fact, she had examined the strand not a week ago, as she did periodically, and it was in good condition.

Claudia dressed swiftly and made her way to the lower part of the house. On the stairway, she met Fimber, the housemaid, ascending to accomplish her morning duties.

"Your necklace, ma'am?" she replied blankly in response to Claudia's question. "I'm sorry to hear it's broke. What is it you want me to do?"

"I want to know," said Claudia patiently, "who was in my room earlier this morning. The pearls must have been dropped—or perhaps they caught on something when they were moved. Although, why anyone should come into my room at daybreak to tidy my dressing table—"

She stopped, aware that Fimber was gazing at her with a most peculiar expression, as though she were being confronted by a madwoman.

"No one has been upstairs at all this morning, ma'am. Me and Becky were just setting out." The maid gestured to a young woman who was approaching them from the bottom of the stairs, carrying an assortment of hot-water cans.

"But—" Claudia bit her lip. Nothing could be accomplished by questioning the girl further. She forced a smile. "Never mind, Fimber." She turned to accompany the maids upstairs. "Since I have run into you both, let me show you the things I need taken to Hill Cottage this morning. Most everything is packed, but I shall be taking a few other things as well."

As she spoke, she led the young women back to her room. "All the ornaments on the mantelpiece will go, as well as—what is it, Fimber?"

The maid was staring ahead of her, her finger pointing in the direction of the dressing table, and as Claudia followed her gaze, a small sound of surprise escaped her. There, coiled carelessly over the dish that had a moment before contained loose pearls, was an unbroken strand, gleaming in the first rays of sunlight that streamed into the room.

"I don't understand," said Claudia, crossing the room swiftly. Lifting the pearls in her fingers, she examined them closely, tugging gently and turning them carefully. She raised her eyes and intercepted a glance between Fimber and Becky. "I don't understand," she repeated. "They were broken—lying all over the carpet . . ." Observing their uncomfortable stares, she abruptly thrust the pearls into her jewel box. "Well, never mind that now." She gestured to a shelf full of figurines above her bed. "I shall be taking those as well." She indicated a few more items of a personal nature, and hurried the maids from the room.

She stood in the center of the room, her brow furrowed. No matter what the thoughts of her servants, she knew what she had seen. The pearls had been broken. Now they were not. What possible answer could there be to the puzzle? The pearls could not have been repaired in the few minutes that had elapsed between the time she left her room and when she had brought the maids back. In any case, why would someone steal into her room for the express purpose of destroying her property, and how . . . ?

She shook her head. Perhaps she was being foolish, devoting too much attention to what was really an unimportant occurrence. On the other hand, she hated unsolved mysteries, no matter how trivial. And she seemed to be coming in for more than her share, of late. First, there was her wandering furniture, and now suicidal jewelry. Very strange.

She shook herself. She really had not the time for this nonsense, she thought irritably as she left the room. Still, the incident was very much on her mind when she met Jem some minutes later in the stables. Since her employer's announcement last night concerning the hiring of new hands, she had made it her first order of business this morning to see what miracles had been wrought with the extra help.

She found Jem there before her, and as always, the sight of him, bursting upon her unexpectedly, caused her heart to jump in a most disconcerting manner. For an instant, his eyes became luminescent as they rested on her, but the next moment, they were shuttered.

"Have you come to inspect the fruits of our new laborers?" he asked, when their good mornings had been said.

Claudia laughed. "It seems strange to come out here dressed in muslins instead of a shirt and breeches, but I must admit . . ." She gestured to a young man just emerging from one of the buildings, propelling a wheelbarrow full of straw and manure. ". . . I shan't miss that particular chore."

Jem grinned. "Come, let's go look at Goblin. He's grown amazingly in two weeks."

Two weeks! thought Claudia, startled. Goblin had been born on the night after Jem's arrival, but it seemed that Jem had been a part of her life for much longer than two weeks. Really, it seemed that there was hardly a time in her life when she had not known him.

She glanced at him surreptitiously as they made their way to the stable that housed Jenny and her foal. Please God, let him find his prosperous parti soon. The thought of his marrying some simpering debutante was more painful than she would have thought possible, but at least it would put him firmly out of her reach.

"What?" she asked blankly, aware that he was speaking to her.

"You are looking uncommonly pensive, this morning. Has some new disaster occurred to enliven our dull little doings?"

"Oh. No, of course not. That is—" She turned to him impulsively. "Yes, there is. Have you a moment, my lord?"

Concern sprang to his eyes. "Of course." He led her to the stable office and settled her in a comfortable old chair before taking one himself. "What is it?"

She laughed self-consciously. "It is nothing, really, yet—well, I hope you won't think I have gone 'round the bend when I tell you my tale." Briefly she recounted the history of her misplaced tables and chairs, and the broken pearls that were not really broken after all.

When she had finished, she was surprised to see his jaw harden in anger.

"Why, it is perfectly obvious, my dear, who is at the bottom of your little mystery. You have no further to look that the little group ensconced in our east wing."

Chapter Eighteen

"Thomas?" squeaked Claudia in utter astonishment. Then, as comprehension spread across her features, her eyes darkened ominously. "Of course! How could I have been so stupid?"

"Possibly," responded Jem dryly, "because you are unaccustomed to being the target of a malicious campaign on the part of what others might call your loved ones. Reddinger will apparently stop at nothing to make the world think you've gone loony. He no doubt plans to bring in the two maids you spoke of as witnesses against you."

Claudia's thoughts raced. "After our confrontation with him the other night—he was quite foxed, you know—he must have made his way upstairs immediately to disarrange my furniture. Then—good heavens, he must have risen before first cockcrow and waited, concealed somewhere in the corridor. When he saw me leave my room, he simply nipped inside and put everything back where it belonged."

"Yes," said Jem musingly. "I can see where he could have accomplished that. But what about the broken pearls? I mean, breaking them would be easy—but repairing them in two or three minutes . . . ?"

"Well," said Claudia slowly, considering. "Ugh! He must have crept into my dressing room while I was asleep! For I woke once in the night, thinking there was someone about."

Intent on her reconstruction of the event, she did not notice Jem's hands clench into fists.

"As for repairing them . . ." She slapped her hand in her lap as realization struck. "Rose has an identical set of pearls! It would be the easiest thing in the world for Thomas to hide himself again outside my door, slipping in when I left. He could have scooped up the loose pearls in a twinkling and replaced them with the whole strand."

"I think I must have another chat with your esteemed relative," said Jem harshly. "This is becoming intolerable. I don't care if it does look strange, that man will leave the house today. He can go home to his own residence, for God's sake."

"I agree with you," said Claudia after a moment. "I have had quite a surfeit of my brother-in-law. Rose will not be nearly so intolerable without Thomas to pull her strings, and the children aren't such bad little creatures when they are not forever brangling with each other."

Jem moved to her, and without thinking, lifted a hand to brush a golden tendril from her cheek. "I must apologize again," he said roughly, "for embroiling you in such a coil."

For a moment, she stared into his eyes, her own wide and vulnerable. Then, she thrust herself backward and said briskly. "Nonsense. I have told you repeatedly, it is Thomas who is responsible for my present difficulty. And, as you have told me, he will not succeed."

"No, he will not." His lips curved downward. "However, I think I shall resume my search for the list described to me by Giles Daventry. It might very well prove to be the one piece of evidence that will see me home—literally."

Claudia found herself unable to respond. Fighting to conceal the tremor that shook her, she nodded wordlessly.

Jem bowed, and smiled the smile that never failed to turn her knees to jelly. "I shall leave you now to seek out your wretched brother-in-law. Shall I see you at luncheon?"

Claudia swallowed. "No. No—I shall be at Hill Cottage by then. Aunt Augusta began removing her things from the manor house yesterday, and most of mine will be gone later this morning."

The smile disappeared suddenly, and Jem's face grew closed. "Of course, but—"

"Aunt Gussie wishes to speak to you, however. She has drawn up a list of those in the neighborhood with whom you will shortly become acquainted—or reacquainted."

"Yes," said Jem musingly. "I suppose many of the families I knew are still in the area."

"And you must meet the Misses Flowers, and Sir Wilfred

Perrey's daughter. They are all eligible young ladies with extremely respectable dowries."

The surprise evident on Jem's face at this statement was nothing to what Claudia felt. She prayed devoutly for the ground to open up beneath her, but it remained dismayingly solid. What had possessed her to say such a thing? She knew her cheeks must be flooded with crimson, and she searched frantically in her mind for something to say that might relieve the situation.

Nothing.

Jem's mouth curved in what might have been a smile. "I shall certainly keep that in mind," he said softly before turning away.

Claudia watched as he closed the door behind him, then collapsed into a chair. Dear Lord, she thought. He must think her a complete wigeon, to say nothing of the effrontery of advising him on his affairs.

Why had she committed such an unpardonable solecism? After a few moments reflection, the answer became obvious. If Ravencroft were to prosper, its master must marry well. He had, after all, stated his intention of marrying for advantage, and the proper wife, besides bringing him a handsome dowry, would insure his comfort. She merely wanted to see this accomplished as soon as possible. To be perfectly honest, of course, she wanted also to see him removed as a target for her misplaced romantic yearnings.

The silence in the room roared about her as she turned these thoughts about in her head, rearranging and repatterning them in an effort to make them ring true. All at once, bursting from the chaos, a realization struck her like a thunderclap. She had spoken those words to Jem in order to hear him deny them! She had fairly ached for him to turn aside her suggestion that he marry.

But why? Had she not decided that a bride for Jem would solve all her problems? Well, yes, but . . . She lifted her head as though listening to an unseen speaker, and her eyes widened in horrified disbelief.

Dear God, she had indeed been stupid, for there was no longer any denying that what she felt for Jem was not a brief, aberrant infatuation. She loved him! While she had been prattling on to herself about lust and the necessity of keeping her distance from him, he had somehow become the cornerstone of her existence.

Was this a punishment? she wondered miserably. She had perpetrated a wicked deception on Jeremy Standish, and now she had come to love him—with a passion she had never thought to feel for any man.

What was she going to do?

She stared sightlessly for some minutes toward the window, through which morning sun streamed in uncaring radiance, and rising at last, she straightened her shoulders and moved to her dressing table. There was at least one thing she must do right away.

"I don't know what you're talking about." Thomas's voice rose in an indignant whine. "What would I know of moving furniture or broken pearls? I think you must have rats in your attic, Glenraven."

Jem faced Thomas Reddinger in the sitting room that had been allotted to them as part of their quarters in the east wing. Rose had entered the room a few minutes ago, having just seen to breakfast for George and Horatia. She perched on the edge of a straw satin wing chair in anxious attention.

Jem gripped his patience and his temper. "Then perhaps," he responded smoothly, "you would not mind producing your wife's pearls. The string she received from her parents on her sixteenth birthday."

"My pearls!" cried Rose faintly. "Whatever do you need my pearls for?"

Jem related again the attempts to create an impression of madness on Claudia's part. Rose gasped.

"Are you saying you believe Thomas responsible for such an iniquity? Really, my lord, you go too far." She sprang from her chair. "If you will but wait a moment, I shall show you my pearls."

"Rose!" Thomas's voice roared a warning. Hesitating only a instant, he continued. "I have no intention of dignifying this ridiculous charge with an answer. Claudia has obviously become completely unbalanced. We need prove nothing."

Rose eyed her husband for a long moment. Then, bowing her head, she left the room.

Thomas turned to Jem. "Now, my lord, if you will be good enough to leave us in peace—"

"You deserve to be left in pieces, Reddinger," retorted Jem. "It is, however, you who will do the leaving. Your wife and children may stay as long as they like, but I expect you to be gone by this afternoon."

"What?" Thomas had once again gone purple. "If this isn't the outside of enough! Not content with snatching my sister-in-law's home from her, you now intend to throw me out as well?"

"You may feel yourself fortunate that I do not accomplish the process bodily, you contemptible swine. When I think of you creeping into that innocent girl's bedroom in the dead of night—"

Thomas opened his mouth in preparation for a bellow of protest, but observing Jem's fingers curved into purposeful fists, contented himself with a reproachful, "You wrong me, sirrah!"

"I have not described the half," Jem grunted. He turned toward the door. "You will be out of this house by lunchtime."

"Now see here—" began Thomas, with a return to his usual bombast but he was interrupted by the whirlwind entrance of Rose, whose flushed face was contorted with distress. Her hands were clenched, and, advancing on a startled Thomas, she opened one of them to reveal a cluster of loose pearls, which she astonished him further by flinging in his face.

"How could you?" she screamed. "Thomas Reddinger, I have put up with a great deal from you. I have listened silently to your pompous pronouncements, and I have stood by and watched you ride roughshod over anyone who stands between you and what you want. I have been a good wife—and an obedient one. But this"—she thrust out her arm in a sweeping gesture to indicate the pearls scattered about the carpet—"this is the last straw!"

"Rose!" If his wife had sprouted wings and flown about the room, his expression could not have contained more baffled amazement.

"Don't you 'Rose' me!" she cried, her voice ascending in an

ominous crescendo. "I know you think me a spiritless nod-cock. You've told me so, often enough—and worse—but I could not believe my ears when I heard you plotting with that wretched Welker to destroy my sister. I was not overly concerned at the time because I didn't see how you could possibly accomplish your purpose. I never dreamed you would actually stoop to fabricating vicious lies out of whole cloth."

Thomas, not to put too fine a point on it, goggled. He opened and closed his mouth several times during this diatribe, but either through his stunned disbelief that it was taking place at all, or merely through lack of opportunity to make himself heard, he said nothing. Rose advanced and, raising her hand, thrust her finger into his chest to emphasize her words.

"Now, you listen to me, Thomas Reddinger. You will contact Cornelius Welker, and you will tell him to drop this whole, miserable action."

Thomas recoiled, as though he feared his wife might bite him. Still immobilized by her unexpected onslaught, he gasped weakly. "But, Rose—just think. We will lose any chance at—that is, I cannot allow Claudia to be so deprived." As he spoke, he managed to regain some of his former bluster. "I don't know what's got into you, Rose, but I won't have it. You will cease this ridiculous—"

But this time Rose was not cowed.

"If you do not do as I say," she said with conviction, "I shall appear as a witness for Glenraven's attorney. I shall testify as to Claudia's soundness of mind, and I shall reveal the ugly strategems to which you were reduced." Once more, she waved her hand over the pearls.

Thomas turned ashen. "Rose," he quavered. "I—I cannot believe this of you!"

"Believe it," she replied simply, in a voice of steel. "Claudia and I were never close, and I disapprove of much of what she does, but she is my sister."

As though that disposed of the matter, she reseated herself in the chair she had vacated earlier. Picking up her embroidery, she bowed her head in her usual pose of submission and resumed her stitching.

Thomas gaped at her, and Jem, who had remained silent during this entire exchange, stifled the smile that sprang to his lips at the man's expression of stupefied frustration. Feeling that further intervention on his part was unnecessary, he turned and tiptoed from the room, unobserved by the still reeling Thomas.

Shaking his head in wonderment at the unexpected depths displayed by the woman he had previously considered a veritable cipher, Jem went to find Claudia. He discovered her in his study, where she had evidently come in search of him.

She stood at his desk, very pale, with a queer, blind expression in her eyes.

"Are you all right?" he asked in quick concern.

She smiled. "Yes, of course. I—I've been looking for you. I must—"

"And I for you," said Jem with a grin. "You'd best sit down, for the news I have to impart will—"

Claudia drew a hasty breath. "No, Jem, this cannot wait. I have something I must tell you."

Struck by the sound of his first name on her lips, he grasped both her hands and led her to a small settee.

She glanced down at the papers just visible in her clenched hands. She felt weighted down with the pain of what was to come, but she drew a deep breath and looked straight at Jem.

She spoke clearly and calmly as she told him of her discovery of the charred papers tucked in the spine of Milton's volume of rural poetry. With scarcely a quiver in her voice, she explained how she had reached her decision not to reveal their existence to him. Her recital was brief, and as she reached its conclusion, she held out her open hands to him so that he could receive the list.

He said nothing as he took them from her, but looked at her disbelievingly before lowering his gaze to the grimy little pages. He perused them with great care, while Claudia sat rigidly on the settee, her hands clasped in her lap. With her eyes, she traced the line of his cheek and the strength of his jaw. With her heart, she bade him farewell, and felt herself die inside.

He lifted his head at last.

"This certainly assures the acceptance of my claim to Ravencroft," he said, his gaze remote and questioning. "You have had it in your possession all this time?"

Unable to speak, she nodded.

"I do not understand. You say you felt you had to negotiate your position?" He said the words slowly and awkwardly, as though he were speaking a foreign language.

"Yes." She whispered the word.

"I don't understand," he repeated. "You evidently feel that Ravencroft is mine by right, but you were unwilling to provide the one piece of evidence that would assure my ownership. You thought it necessary to manipulate me." His eyes had by now taken on the color of a winter sea, and she could no longer meet his gaze.

"I had nowhere to go," she said, quietly and without self-pity. "My back was virtually against the wall. I had to provide for myself and Aunt Gussie, and this was the only thing I could think of. I understand that you will no longer want me here, and I shall, of course, relieve you of your commitment. You may consider our contract null and void, and I shall be gone by week's end."

She rose from the settee, and would have fled the room, but Jem grasped her wrist.

"One moment, if you please. I am somewhat dismayed at your reading of my character, Mrs. Carstairs. Do you really think me such a monster that I would throw you and your aunt out into the world, alone and unprotected?"

She looked at him blankly. "No, of course I do not think you a monster. On the other hand, you had no reason to accede to my request for employment. You mentioned a settlement, but I could not, of course, place any credence in that."

Jem had by now grown very rigid. "Why 'of course'?" he asked softly.

Claudia turned to him, her eyes very wide. "Because it was not to your advantage. Why should you throw away perfectly good money on a stranger for no good reason?"

" 'For no good reason'!" He ran slender fingers through his hair. "I was about to eject you from a place you called home—a place you had come to love. Do you not think that would weigh with me? And afterward—I rather thought we had become—friends—" Again, he seemed to be having trouble with his words.

"Yes," she said in a rush. "This is what made the whole

thing so increasingly difficult for me. I truly did intend to give you the list if it began to look as though Thomas would be about to ruin everything."

"Did you?" He stared at her as though at a stranger. "I thought I knew you, Claudia, but—" He lifted his hands in a baffled gesture. "Why," he asked after a moment, "are you giving me the list now?"

She gazed again at the hands clenched tightly in her lap. "I—I could no longer keep them from you. Things had come to such a pass—"

"Indeed," Jem interrupted. "They had reached the point, had they not, where your own status was in jeopardy. How uncomfortable for you to run the risk of such public humiliation. Pilloried as a lunatic!" His laughter came in an ugly rasp. "To think that I believed you to be warm and open and giving. You may congratulate yourself, Widow Carstairs. You performed magnificently, even though," he added cryptically, "your efforts were all so unnecessary, as it turns out." He made as though to stride from the room, but halted suddenly and whirled on her.

"And no," he said harshly. "I shall not tear up our contract. I, for one, signed it in good faith. You are still my employee. What an edifying ring that has, don't you think? It quite clarifies our positions. Particularly since you so wisely chose to live under another roof. With any luck at all, we shan't have to spend more than an hour or two a week in each other's company, which, I assure you, is about all I'll be able to stomach."

He left the room, closing the door quietly behind him. Claudia remained motionless, at last allowing the tears that had gathered in an aching lump at the back of her throat to spill down her cheeks. Unable to stand, she sank to her knees, rocking back and forth and sobbing in her anguish like an abandoned child.

Claudia was not apprised of Thomas's capitulation until late that afternoon.

"I cannot believe that Glenraven did not come to you immediately with the news," said Miss Melksham. "He told me hours ago." The two ladies stood in the parlor of Hill Cottage, surveying the small mountain of boxes that surrounded them.

It was a small, comfortable house that had been furnished with care two generations before for the use of an admired artist who took up residence for some months on the Glenraven estate. Claudia had claimed a large, sunny loft on the top floor for her bedchamber, while Miss Melksham happily took a spacious, yet cozy room on the floor below.

"The whole thing," continued the older lady, "quite put me in a humdudgeon. I had not known of Thomas's sneaking into your rooms, of course, though I wondered when you said your furniture had been moved."

For some minutes after her aunt's recital, Claudia started at her in amazement. "Rose said all that?" she said at last. "Rose did that for me? I can scarcely credit it." She fell again into a wondering silence before speaking again. "I don't understand it at all. I would never in my life have dreamed that she could act so." She lifted her eyes to her aunt. "And Thomas gave in? He agreed to stop his litigation?"

"Well, I understand he did not actually promise—at the time, but according to Glenraven, he just sagged in on himself like a pricked balloon. Glenraven believes, since there can be no doubt Rose will carry out her threat, we can regard Thomas Reddinger as a spent force."

Claudia felt dizzy with relief and gratitude toward her sister. To think that the woman she had viewed from childhood with such contempt could stand up to the person she no doubt feared the most in the world! She must go to Rose and thank her as soon as possible.

Later, however, as she put her belongings away in cupboards and wardrobes scattered about the sunny loft, her happiness fell away from her abruptly. It must have been Thomas's removal as a threat to which Jem had referred when he spoke of her "unnecessary" revelation of Emanuel's list to him. He believed, thought Claudia with a pang, that the only reason she had given them up to him was her concern for her own difficulties.

And how could she blame him? He no doubt thought her a grasping harpy, willing to stoop to extortion to gain her own ends. He was very nearly right, after all.

On the other hand, how could she have known that he would be so different from every other man she had ever known? Her instinct had told her to trust him; it was her mind, with only the logic of experience to guide her, that told her men were the enemy. Men used women like convenient tools for their own designs, without thought to the damage and heartbreak they caused, and a woman must be ferocious and unyielding in her defenses.

Well, she had defended herself right into a broken heart. Jem had trusted her, and she had betrayed that trust. She had only herself to blame that he felt nothing for her now but contempt.

On the other hand, perhaps this was all a blessing in disguise. Her love for Jeremy Standish was a golden dream, and like all such fantasies, would eventually become corroded and hurtful when exposed to the cold light of reality. If they had remained on friendly terms, the seed of hope would be a constant, disturbing presence in her dealings with him. He had kissed her—twice—with a warmth and passion that had stirred her to her core, but two kisses did not a romance make. Jem obviously had nothing more permanent in mind than an occasional pleasant interlude. No, he had made it clear that he must seek a bride for profit, not for love. She took a deep breath. Now, at least, she would see little of him. There would be no laughter between them—no banter, or warm, casual conversation. He would be cold and correct during their infrequent meetings. As would she.

This line of thought, not unexpectedly, brought her little satisfaction, and tears rose once more behind her eyes. Raising a hand, she dashed them away. She had cried once for her doomed love. She would not do so again.

Chapter Nineteen

The ensuing days followed one another in a dreary sameness. Claudia saw little of Jem. She kept to the stables, hurrying back and forth between her duties there and the little cottage that she attempted to call home. She caught only brief glimpses of Jem as he slipped into one or another of the stable buildings for a visit with Jonah. He had apparently decided to confine his interest in the Ravencroft horse-breeding endeavor to these infrequent conferences.

From Aunt Augusta, she discovered that the bulk of Jem's days were spent in inspecting his estate. He had met with his tenants and examined their cottages, promising much-needed repairs, and he walked over his fields, discussing the methods of crop improvement he planned to put into effect. Did he have the funds to put all this into effect? she wondered. Aunt Gussie mentioned tentative visits to a few of the neighboring families, as well as callers received. She wondered if Lord Glenraven might be considering her ill-advised suggestion regarding the Misses Flowers and Miss Perrey.

Or perhaps he would look higher. He might travel to London for the Season next spring, where he would have the pick of a whole bevy of wealthy maidens. In this arena, surely Jem's title and lineage and plans for the future would outweigh the present scantiness of his funds.

As for herself, she would begin making plans for her departure from Ravencroft. All her pleasure in the thought of remaining on the estate was gone, replaced with a gnawing sadness that she knew would be with her for all her days here. With careful budgeting, she could save nearly all she was earning as Jem's stable manager, and within a year, she might look about her for a small place of her own.

The one bright spot in all this, she reflected with a lightening of her heart, was her reconciliation with Rose. Her sister had replied to her thanks with a surprising response of her own.

"I should imagine you were astonished," she said with what could only be described as an impish grin that made her look years younger. "Well, no more so than I was. If Thomas had not been nearby—if I had been obliged to contain my outrage for a long period of time, waiting for him to come home from the hunt or his club, or whatever, I would never have summoned up the courage to face him. I would simply have swallowed my anger and my pride as I have done so many times in the past, and bowed before his masculine assurance that he must always know what's best."

"Oh, Rose, I know how hard it must have been for you to—"

Rose raised her hand and smiled ruefully. "Not as hard as it should have been. I never had much difficulty submitting to his judgment—as I had always done to Papa's." She laid a hand on Claudia's arm. "You know, I always used to envy you your independence."

Claudia's mouth opened in astonishment. "I always thought you disapproved of me!"

"I did—most of the time. At least, I tried to convince myself that I did. That way, I could make myself believe that my own lack of spirit was a virtue."

"Oh, Rose." Her mouth curved in a warm smile. "Sometimes I used to get so furious with you, but on many an occasion, I knew deep inside that your sense of propriety was to be envied." She gave a watery chuckle. "Perhaps if Mama and Papa had produced only one daughter, she would have been a happy combination of conventionality and individualism. And perhaps she would have been happier in the long run."

Startlingly, a mischievous twinkle appeared in Rose's eyes. "As it happens, sister, I consider myself a great deal happier than I was a few days ago. When Thomas left for home, his attitude to me bore more respect than I would ever have thought to receive from him." She continued earnestly. "He is not a bad man, you know, despite the trick he tried to pull on you. You believe him to have acted out of pure greed, but I am sure he did not covet Ravencroft for himself. I think he simply could not bear to see a woman in control of such potential wealth. He could not bear to see a woman in such control of her own life, for that matter, and he felt that you would do ever so much better under his guidance, if you only had the sense to see it."

Claudia laughed. "You may be right. Thomas does seem to have a wide managerial streak in him." She lowered her gaze to her hands, searching for a subject with which to turn the conversation. "How is George doing? When I saw him yesterday, he was doing his very best to outwit Nanny Grample's efforts to keep him in bed."

At this, Rose laughed as well. "Indeed, we are at our wits' end. I told him he might have Rumple—his puppy, you know—in the room with him, but I'm not sure that was wise. The dog creates as much chaos as does George, and when Horatia joins the fray, the noise level rises beyond what is bearable." She flicked a glance at her sister. "Never fear, we shall be away from Ravencroft in a few days."

"Oh! I didn't mean—"

"No, it's all right," said Rose with a shrug of her shoulders. "Perhaps the next time we see each other, the awkwardness will have subsided. Although, I do regret leaving you here in such a compromising situation."

"I beg your pardon?"

"I fear you will find it most uncomfortable when it becomes known that you are living in such close quarters to Lord Glenraven."

Claudia felt her temper rise. Apparently Rose's admiration for an independence of spirit did not extend to present circumstances.

"I am not living under the same roof," she snapped, "and I believe that Aunt Gussie's presence will deter any unpleasant gossip."

Rose delivered herself of a small, superior smile, but said nothing further.

I suppose, reflected Claudia later in the privacy of her room at Hill Cottage, it is too much to expect a lifetime of animosity to be dissolved away in one conversation. Still, she felt a sort of understanding had been reached with Rose, and a sense of better things to come between them.

She sighed wearily, her thoughts turning again to Jem—as they seemed to do with a dismal frequency. Her relationship with him had not improved, and she was having little success in convincing herself that this was a situation to be desired.

"Goodness," Miss Melksham had said only this morning at breakfast. "The man never rests from morning till night. He traveled all the way to Cotterborough yesterday just to talk to old Mr. Chilfer about sheep."

"Oh yes," Claudia replied thoughtfully. "He raises that new breed of sheep we've been hearing about. Merinos, they're called. Does Glenraven think to replace our—his Gloucesters, I wonder?"

"As to that, I cannot say." Her aunt surveyed her closely. "Has he not talked to you of all this?"

"No, of course not," Claudia answered in some irritation. "Why should he? I am only the hired help, after all. It would not be seemly for him to discuss estate matters with me, other than the horse operation."

"Mm," said Miss Melksham noncommittally. "I suppose that's true." Her eyes sharpened as she gazed at her niece. "You have not had a falling out with his lordship, have you?"

Claudia assayed an airy laugh that fell far short of success. "Really, Aunt, my relationship with Glenraven is purely professional, which is much the way I prefer to keep it."

"I see," Miss Melksham had replied thoughtfully. She had left almost immediately, her skirts rustling crisply.

Now, as she sat in the stable office, trying to keep her mind on her accounts, Claudia recalled the conversation and sighed. Her aunt was far too sharp-eyed for comfort. An attempt to resume a cordial relationship with Jem was, of course, impossible. An aching sadness spread within her. No, she could not bear to contemplate the look of contempt that would surely blaze from those gray eyes were she to approach him.

In another of the stable buildings, Jem sat on a barrel facing Jonah, who leaned against a stall door. Jem had formed the habit of visiting the old man at least once a day, for he found him a comforting source of honest wisdom and a certain astringent kindness.

"And not only is Henry Samuels still in residence at Northbridge Hall," said Jem, "but his son Robert is home for a visit with his new bride. Lovely girl."

"I s'pose some of the other nobs has been t'see you, as well," said Jonah in a ruminative tone.

"A few. I met a Mr. Winstead a couple of days ago, and Mrs. Fletcher and her two daughters and a son called this morning."

"Squire Foster ain't been about yet?"

"No—and I am rather looking forward to meeting him. We have much to discuss."

"How about Squire Perrey? I hear that daughter o' his is a lively little filly. Make somebody a good wife."

Jem flushed. "There is plenty of time for me to consider my nuptials. Tell me," he continued brusquely, "how does that yearling come on? The one we have earmarked for the Earl of Litchfield."

"Ah, Miz Carstairs is right on top o' that sich'ation. She posted a note to the earl this very day, setting a date for him to come fer a look-over. Didn't she tell ye?"

There was a small silence. "No," replied Jem at last. "I—I have not seen Mrs. Carstairs for a few days."

"Well, mebbe ye should. She ain't lookin' good a-tall."

Jem stiffened in concern. "Is she ill?"

"I don't think she's sickenin'—just lookin' a mite peaked."

"Oh."

Another, long silence fell in the stable, and once again Jem felt his insides clench at the thought of Claudia Carstairs and her perfidy. He might have known, he thought bitterly, what the results would be if he let his guard down. It was almost laughable, really. One would think that at the age of twenty-four he would have learned his lesson. Indeed, he thought he had learned it well—that to give oneself wholly to another was to court disillusion and heartbreak. Some men, he was given to understand, loved happily—found wives or mistresses to bring joy and laughter to their lives and good friends to bring pleasure to lonely hours. He very much doubted this concept—it had certainly proven false in his case. His beloved father had brought tragedy upon himself and his family through his weakness. The aunt and uncle to whom he had transferred his childish devotion, had turned his family out without a qualm when it became inconvenient to have them in their home. Others for whom he had come to feel affection, such as Burt Finch, the pickpocket, had betrayed him.

How could he have been such a fool as to forget all this over a pair of amber eyes and an understanding smile? He had let her become a part of his life—a part of his very soul, it seemed. He felt complete with her at his side and empty when she was not. Thank God he had been unable to tell her that he loved her. What a fool he had almost made of himself.

He recalled his disbelieving anguish as he had read Emanuel's wretched list. She had deceived him—manipulated him with consummate skill, and he, self-proclaimed master of the confidence game, had fallen into her trap like the veriest greenling. He had believed her response to his kisses was genuine—a warm, innocent giving of herself. A hot current of rage and pain twisted through him at the memory of that soft mouth, her scented breath against his throat.

"Leastways, I hope there's nothin' wrong with her."

Jem jerked himself back to the present as Jonah spoke.

"She's a real nice leddie," continued the old man.

Jem laughed shortly, and at Jonah's expression of concerned puzzlement, found himself disclosing Claudia's perfidy, the words spilling from him like poison released from a sore.

At the conclusion of Jem's tale, Jonah said nothing for a long moment, pulling on the pipe he had lit moments before. At last he said consideringly, "It don't seem t'me the leddy did you any real harm."

"No harm!" responded Jem indignantly. "But she—"

"She quit Ravencroft and signed it over t'ye, didn't she?"

"Yes, but—"

"She needn't have done so, did she? I mean, knowin' yer case was weak without Mr. Carstairs papers, she could've just sat on 'em and took her chances in court. And her chances was pretty good, by what you've told me."

"That's true, but she—" He stopped abruptly as the stable door opened and Claudia stepped into the building.

"Oh!" she said, her eyes wide in startlement. "I came to see—that is, I thought you alone, Jonah." She backed away. "I shall return when—"

"Never mind, Mrs. Carstairs," said Jem harshly. "I was just leaving."

He rose from his seat on the barrel and made his way past her, jerking his arm as though burned when it brushed hers accidentally. He had a hand on the door latch when he turned to face Claudia.

"Jonah tells me you have written to the Earl of Litchfield concerning that yearling."

His tone was prosaic, but when Claudia lifted her eyes to his she felt the icy contempt in his gaze like a physical assault.

"Yes," she replied quietly.

"Will you let me know when he is due to arrive?"

"Of course. Would—would you care to handle the transaction yourself?"

A slow sneer spread over Jem's features. "No, I merely wish to meet him. His father and mine were friends. I have every confidence in your ability to wring the last possible farthing from him. You are so very good at that sort of thing, after all."

Claudia whitened as he returned her gaze with a bleak stare of his own. The next moment he was gone.

It was some moments before Claudia was able to turn to Jonah. She wanted nothing more than to find a dark corner in which to weep away her hurt, but with a supreme effort she controlled her voice.

"I came to speak to you about Morrison, Jonah—one of the new men. He—" She choked, and to her horror felt tears welling in her eyes. Despite her best efforts, they spilled over almost immediately, rolling hotly down her cheeks.

"Oh, my goodness," she gasped, dashing her hand against her face. "I'm so sorry. I don't know what—"

"Na, na then, lass." Jonah laid an awkward hand on her arm. "I know somethin's been troublin' ye. Don't be afeared to cry it out."

The next moment, Claudia found herself enclosed in a comforting embrace, smelling of hay and horse, and throwing propriety to the winds, sobbed her heartache out against the rough fabric of Jonah's shirt.

Jem slammed the kitchen door behind him and strode along the corridor leading to the great hall. Damn! The vision of

Claudia's stricken face rose up before him. After what she had done to him, why had he felt an almost overpowering urge to gather her in his arms and assure her that he hadn't meant a word he'd said?

He moved through the hall, intent on reaching the sanctuary of his study, but expelled a sigh of irritation on discovering Miss Melksham in his path.

"Ah, Glenraven," she said briskly. "I have been looking for you." She waved a piece of paper for his attention. "I have been jotting down a preliminary list for the dinner party."

"What dinner party?" asked Jem blankly.

"Why the one you will be giving shortly." Her voice rose in surprise. "We discussed it some time ago."

"I have no recollection of such a conversation, and I really do not wish—"

"But it is expected," she said in a tone that brooked no dispute. "You have been wanting to meet Squire Foster, and this will be a good opportunity. And you must meet Sir Wilfred Perrey. His daughter—"

"Is extremely eligible," finished Jem wearily. "I have been hearing a great deal lately about the charming and enticingly wealthy Miss Perrey."

Miss Melksham did not respond to this, but said in a tentative voice, "It will also be a good opportunity to show the neighbors that you and Claudia are on good terms."

Jem said nothing, ignoring the unpleasant quiver her words produced in his belly.

"*Are* you on terms? Yes, I know I'm being presumptuous," she added in a rush, her pewter-colored curls quivering agitatedly, "but—" She paused and drew in a long breath. "Glenraven, have you a moment? I would speak with you on a matter of some delicacy."

Jem groaned inwardly. Was he about to receive yet another lecture from one of Claudia's well-wishers? There was really nothing anyone could say to sway him. Jonah could say all he wanted, as could Miss Melksham—Claudia had deceived him. He did not hold it against her. He had merely made a mistake in not recalling that what one treasured the most was what would inevitably be lost. In a moment of idiocy, he had come to treasure Claudia Carstairs beyond anything or anyone he had ever known. And now he was paying for it. The only way he could cope with the desolation he now felt was simply to have nothing more to do with her. He wanted no more interference in his resolution.

"I was on my way—" he began, but Miss Melksham, grasping his arm, led him out of the hall and into his own study, where she virtually pushed him into a chair before seating herself in one near him. Jem found himself in unwilling admiration of her masterful tactics.

"This won't take a moment." She gazed into her lap for some moments before continuing. "I was wondering—you and she were spending a great deal of time together—sorting out the estate affairs—did she ever speak to you of herself?"

"Herself? Why, I suppose she must have—that is, no," he said in some surprise. "Actually, beyond telling me something of her husband, she divulged little of her background." Despite himself, he leaned forward in his chair. "I take it she was a somewhat unusual girl."

Miss Melksham permitted herself an affectionate smile. "Yes, she was. In a world full of peahens, she was a young eaglet. Wild and independent to a fault, and loving and giving and vital. How she came to be born to a pair like Walter and Eliza, I cannot imagine. They certainly did everything within their power to press her into the same mold into which they'd fitted Rose so nicely. Walter, in particular, found her behavior inexplicable and utterly unacceptable. She had few children to play with near her home, but when she joined the village children in their games, her father forbade it. She loved to roam the fields and forests near her home, but when Walter discovered her habit of disappearing for hours with a fishing pole in hand, he decreed that she should not stray beyond the garden wall by herself.

"Rose was sent into Gloucester to a young ladies' seminary, and Claudia looked forward to the time when she would go. I think it was not so much her desire to become more accomplished in embroidery and singing that prompted her eagerness, as an ardent desire to escape Walter's smothering environment. It was not to be, however, for her father decided that, in view of her hoydenish behavior in the past, it would be better if she were kept at home until she was of a marriageable age."

"I suppose," said Jem quietly, "that she did not accept her confinement easily."

"Heavens, no! The battles that used to rage in their home were positively Homeric. Claudia did not win one of them, but that did not stop her from protesting the next ukase to come down from on high. For a while," continued the old lady reflectively, "she sought refuge in books. My, how that child loved to read. There was little to stimulate her mind in her father's library, but the vicar opened his to her, and soon she was absorbing all kinds of dangerous notions. When Walter discovered this, he shut Claudia in her room for two weeks, with nothing to occupy her except the mending of household linen."

"Two weeks!" exclaimed Jem, appalled. Miss Melksham nodded. "But did no one come to her aid? Surely her mother—"

"Tchah! Eliza's only action on her daughter's behalf was to murmur, 'There, there, dear, I'm sure it's all for the best.' "

"And her father culminated his career as a father by marrying Claudia to Emanuel Carstairs." Jem's voice was a rasping whisper.

"Yes. Of course, none of us knew at that time what he was really like, but he was thirty years older than Claudia, and she was afraid of him without quite knowing why. When her father confronted her with the completed fact of her betrothal to Carstairs, it was as though he had struck her a mortal blow. I was visiting in their home at the time, and I saw her emerge from Walter's study, a look of such blind misery on her face that my heart went out to her. She did not plead or rage this time—she knew the futility by now of such an action. It was I who interceded for her with Walter, and was ordered from the house for my pains."

Miss Melksham rose and went to stand before one of the long windows that overlooked the south lawn. "Her years with Carstairs were pure, unmitigated hell."

"Thank God there were not many of them," said Jem in a low voice.

"Yes," she replied with some asperity. "One would think that she had finally escaped the prison her life had been up to that point, but she had no sooner buried Emanuel than Thomas Reddinger strode onto the scene. He had always been a thorn in her side, of course, but now she saw him as merely the next man in a progression of males whose only use for her was to serve their needs, and who were determined to wring every ounce of spirit from her because it interfered with their comfort."

Miss Melksham returned to her chair and folded her hands in her lap. She cast a level glance at Jem.

"She was, however, no longer the green girl who had been forced to do her father's bidding and then her husband's. Ravencroft had been picked bare, but she was fierce in her determination to make a success of the horse-breeding operation. Never, she declared, would she be at the mercy of any man ever again."

She rose again. "That is all I have to say, Glenraven. She does not know that I planned to speak to you. She would not want me to do so, but I felt you should know." Silently, she left the room, leaving Jem to take up her position at the window.

So, he mused in a chastened mood, it was not only he who bore the scars of bitter experience. He gazed unseeing at the green beauty spread before him. Claudia had deceived him, but her reasons had been compelling, he reflected sadly.

His mouth curved in a bitter smile. His rage at Claudia's perfidy may have dissipated in the cool light of understanding, but the ache of her betrayal still remained, creating a grinding sense of desolation that seemed to have settled in the center of his being.

With a sound that was almost a groan, he moved to his desk to bury himself in the mound of paperwork that waited there.

Chapter Twenty

"Oh, Jonah, I'm so sorry!" Claudia mopped her cheeks with the conveniently deep ruffle bordering her sleeve. "I don't know what got into me, turning into such a watering pot."

Jonah patted her shoulder awkwardly. "Don't give it another thought, ma'am. I disremember the number o' times I've had t'offer a shoulder to some weepin' female. Curse o' the sex, this weepin' business. And if ye don't mind me sayin' so, ye hadn't orter take on so. His lordship's in a rare takin', but it don't seem t'me he has the right to rag at ye the way he did."

"You're a good friend Jonah," she replied through a shuddering hiccup. "And you know, I think you may be right." She recalled the ugly words Jem had spoken to her, and the chill contempt of his expression. She had felt as though she had been physically struck. How could he have deliberately caused her such pain?

Had what she done really been so wrong? She had not acted with the intent to deprive him of his rightful home. In convincing him to hire her to manage the stable operation, she had done him no harm. In fact, her assumption of that position was to his benefit, releasing him to attend to the other pressing matters of the estate. Really, the way he was acting, one would think he had caught her slipping hemlock into his soup.

For the first time since she had turned over Emanuel's incriminating lists to him with such disastrous results, a small coil of anger began to twist inside her.

She looked up at Jonah. "Yes," she repeated in a whisper, "I think you may be right."

She bethought herself then of the reason she had come to Jonah. "I want to speak to you about Morrison. This morning I told him to apply a compress to Prince's foreleg—he's been suffering from stone bruises, you know, but when I—"

Once again, she was interrupted, this time by the sound of shrill barking taking place outside the stables. Claudia and Jonah, hastening to fling open the door, observed Rumple, young George's dog, engaged in a frenzy of high-pitched yapping at an object unseen around the corner of the building. Some distance away, from a second-floor window of the manor house, George could be seen at the window, waving furiously at his pet and shouting encouragement.

"Great God," said Jonah, breaking into a run. "I jist told Lucas to bring Warlock out of his stall inta the paddock." As he spoke, Rumple vanished from sight in pursuit of his quarry.

Gathering up her skirts, Claudia hastened to follow. They rounded the end of the building just in time to observe the little dog racing toward Warlock, who was being led by Lucas through a narrow corridor leading to the paddock outside.

As she watched in horror, Warlock reared suddenly, tossing an unprepared Lucas into a heap at one side of the corridor. Jonah made a grab for the stallion's leading rein, but missed, and in another moment, Warlock had plunged through the open half door at the end of the corridor. Rumple followed as fast as his short legs would carry him, still barking furiously.

Claudia raced in pursuit, together with Jonah and a somewhat groggy Lucas. Outside, they discovered that Warlock, rather than running to the paddock, had turned and was heading toward the closed gate that led to the carriage house. Claudia screamed as the sound of splintering wood reached her ears, accompanied by that of a piercing neigh, filled with pain and panic.

Out of a corner of her eye, Claudia caught sight of a figure running toward the scene from the direction of the house, and turned to behold a white-faced Jem sprinting to intercept Warlock. His course brought him into the stallion's path just as Warlock reached a small courtyard that gave entry to the coach house.

"Get behind him, so he can't retreat!" shouted Jem to Claudia and the men behind her. "I'll try to drive him into the corner!" He gestured toward an angle formed by the stone courtyard wall and the building that housed the carriages.

As Warlock plunged farther into the courtyard area, Jem ran headlong at him, forcing him into the prescribed area. The horse, apparently further frightened as he saw his escape routes being cut off, reared on his hind legs. Once again, the air was filled with frenzied whinnies as his eyes rolled wildly and his forelegs pawed the air. On one of these, an ugly wound could be seen from which blood oozed in an increasing stream.

Jem approached cautiously, calling words of reassurance, but the stallion was beyond soothing. Abruptly, he turned on Jem and, with murder in his eye, bore down on him. He struck Jem broadside, throwing him against the side of the stone building from whence he slid into a motionless heap.

To Claudia's unbelieving horror, the stallion reared above him, hooves pawing in an arc that came perilously close to Jem's head.

Without volition, she plunged toward the stallion, her whole being focused on preventing Warlock's assault on the man who lay helpless beneath him. She was aware that Jem had begun to stir, and, unthinking, she raised her arms and flung herself against the huge animal. Not surprisingly, her action had no effect except to send her reeling backward. Dimly, she heard voices raised behind her, but she was consumed by her need to get between the horse and the man. Gathering her strength, she hurled herself once more at the stallion, and this time, the horse, momentarily distracted, stumbled and lurched sideways. Claudia found herself embracing the animal as he strove to regain himself.

The next moment, Warlock had bunched his muscles beneath him once again, preparatory to making a bolt for freedom, and Claudia's world was filled with the smell of blood and the sight of flared nostrils and bared teeth and huge, wild eyes that seemed to envelop her in their panic.

The next instant, she was lifted bodily into a strong grasp that swung her out of harm's way. She raised her head to meet Jem's glittering gray gaze fixed not two inches from her own. With a sob of relief, she buried herself in Jem's embrace. The next instant, she found herself being shaken unmercifully.

"What the bloody hell did you think you were doing just then?" Jem roared, his voice rising until it cracked.

"I was tr—trying—" Claudia's teeth were chattering so that

she could hardly speak. "That is—I—I thought you w—were going to be k—killed!" Her own voice shook with remembered terror.

"And what did you think you were going to do?" Jem's face was very close to hers. "Just scamper up and fling a fifteen-hundred-pound beast out of the way? My God, it was you who were almost killed!"

A mindless fury took possession of Claudia, and she wrenched herself free of Jem's grasp. She stepped back a pace and raised clenched fists. "You stupid oaf! I was trying to save your wretched life! I wish I hadn't! I wish you'd been squashed like a gr—a gr—" She broke off, wholly overcome by the shuddering sobs that shook her body. She turned to run from him, but was once again caught in his arms as he pulled her roughly to him.

"I'm sorry, Claudia. Please—I—" But he was interrupted by a breathless Jonah, who hurried up to them at that moment.

"My lord!" he wheezed. "Miz Carstairs! Be ye all right?"

For an instant, Claudia held Jem's stricken gaze before turning to Jonah. For the first time, she was aware of the other men present, who were now ministering to Warlock. She drew a deep, shaking breath.

"I'm fine, Jonah, but Warlock—how is—? Good lord, he's hurt!"

She pointed in dismay at the ragged gash that ran from the stallion's shoulder down the length of his foreleg.

"Yeah," Jonah replied tersely. "He's hurt bad. Musta caught some splintered wood when he went through the gate. Tore him up some, but ain't nothin' broken, praise God." Having satisfied himself that she and Jem were indeed undamaged, he hobbled back to give instructions that sent the men scattering in all directions.

"Lucas! Do you find some fresh manure. It's got t' be still steamin'. Fred, go int'the tack room, and you'll find vinegar and a measure o' chalk in the med'cine cupboard. Seth, run ask Miss Melksham for a length of linen. Hold it up t' the fire till it's scorched."

"Manure?" asked Jem faintly.

"Best thing there is fer a tear wound. Make up a compress of it with the vinegar and the chalk and wrap it in burnt cloth, and the hoss'll be right as a trivet in no time. That is," he amended, balefully eyeing Rumple who still squirmed in the grasp of yet another stable hand, "if nothin' don't set him off again."

He stumped off to murmur gently to Warlock, who had at last ceased his efforts to escape his captors and stood trembling and heaving.

Casting a single, fiery glance at Jem, Claudia swung on her heel and, still gulping as small, shattering aftershocks swept over her, marched in the direction of the stable office. She had proceeded for perhaps two feet, when Jem once more caught her arm.

"Allow me to accompany you back into the house," he said brusquely. "Your aunt will want to—make you some tea—or something."

"I do not need any tea," Claudia snapped. "I merely wish to be left alone."

"Nonetheless, you will return to the house with me until you have recovered yourself."

"I am fine, and I do not need—" but Jem was propelling her firmly toward the gate to the kitchen garden. They had no sooner entered the garden, when the figure of Rose bore down upon them. She was moving purposefully toward the stables, and in her face could be read a mixture of trepidation and outrage.

"There you are!" she cried. "What have you done to George's little dog? I saw that filthy stable person scoop him up like a common pig. I want to know—"

"Considering," replied Claudia hotly, "that he almost caused us to lose our prize stallion, the little beast will be fortunate if he does not fall to the fate of the average swine."

"Oh!" gasped Rose. "George said the puppy was merely romping about. Oh, dear! I really don't . . . That is . . ."

She left her sentence unfinished, and ducking her head, hurried past them. Claudia stared after her until recalled by the pressure of Jem's hand on her arm as he pulled her toward the house.

"Really, my lord," she said through clenched teeth. "I am quite well. I do not need tea and comfort."

He did not reply, but tightened his fingers, bringing to Claudia an unwilling but intense awareness of his nearness. He changed direction abruptly, taking her along a path that led to an overgrown bower in which was placed a small bench.

"Let us sit here for a moment," said Jem harshly. "I wish to talk to you."

"But I do not wish to talk to you." Claudia's eyes were molten gold, and she gasped with indignation as Jem pushed her firmly onto the bench and sat beside her.

"I'm sorry I was so—abrupt back there." He looked at her unhappily. With her hair tumbling down in disorder, with smudges on her chin and a bruise spreading across her cheek, she was still heart wrenchingly beautiful, and his whole body clenched with the effort it took not to gather her in his arms.

"I was frightened for you," he concluded awkwardly, cursing himself for the ineptitude of his words.

Claudia stared back at him. She wished he were not so close. Lord, how could she possibly be ready to do him murder and still wonder if the rigid line of his mouth would soften if she were to press her lips against it. His hair had fallen over his forehead, like a drift of night cloud, and her hand twitched to reach up and smooth it back.

"That is very good of you," she sniffed, and prepared to rise. She immediately wished she had not, for Jem placed his hands on both of her shoulders to prevent her from doing so.

He took a deep breath. "I also wish to apologize for the things I said—earlier. It was unjust of me."

Claudia said nothing, but her eyes widened.

After a moment, Jem continued quietly. "I was so caught up in my own righteous indignation, that I did not consider your feelings."

Claudia uttered a sound that might have been interpreted as a snort.

Jem dropped his hands and pushed himself away from her. "I still believe I had every right to be angry," he continued stiffly. "You did deceive me. However, I should have taken into consideration your motives in doing so. You no doubt—"

"Oh!" Claudia jumped up from her seat and whirled to face him. Her fists were clenched, and her eyes ablaze. "How very condescending of you my lord, to forgive me for my transgression. After I nearly ruined your life by agreeing to give Ravencroft over to you and to act as your stable manager, thus providing you with additional income with which to refurbish the estate!"

Jem, too, sprang to his feet. "Why, you little termagant! Of all the—"

"And if we are to talk of deception, what about you? Did you or did you not creep into Ravencroft under false pretences? From the moment you strolled into the stable, looking as though butter wouldn't melt in your mouth, you were planning to take Ravencroft from me."

"I didn't take Ravencroft from you," shouted Jem. "It was always mine—you admitted as much."

"Then why"—stepping up so that she stood almost nose to nose with her adversary—"could you not have come up to the front door and explained your position like a gentleman instead of skulking around pretending to be what you are not?"

"Because I thought you would turn me out and fight my efforts to—"

"And I thought you would do the same thing to me. Admit it, you betrayed me just as cruelly, if not more so, as I did you!"

Jem found himself completely taken aback. He had never given consideration to his own actions in retrieving his home. But, surely, she could see that what he had done differed greatly from her own reprehensible behavior. He would never have deceived her if he had known . . . His confused mental ramblings ground to an abrupt halt as a single thought flashed through his mind. He had been so caught up in his own turmoil that one supremely important fact had escaped him. Claudia had nearly got herself killed for his benefit! The thought echoed in his brain like a thunderclap. She had—*risked her life*—to save him.

He felt as though he had been stripped naked and plunged into an icy stream, all his notions and conceptions ripped from him in one burst of revelation.

After a long moment, he brought his hands up to encircle her shoulders once more. "But don't you see?" he said brokenly, "I wasn't in love with you then."

The stillness of the little bower surrounded them, shutting out the rest of the world as completely as though they stood alone on a remote mountaintop. To Claudia, it seemed as though the silence was filled with the thundering of her heart, and lifting her eyes wonderingly to his, she raised her arms in an involuntary gesture.

"Then," she said softly and a little breathlessly, "I rest my case."

For an instant, Jem stared at her uncomprehendingly before his eyes lit with a blazing warmth.

"What do you—Are you saying—?" He spoke huskily, and bent toward her, grasping her uplifted hands in his.

Joy rose suddenly within Claudia, to escape at last in a gasp of delighted laughter. "Why, that I love you, too, of course."

"Claudia," he murmured dazedly. His hands tightened on her, and the next moment, he swept her into his embrace. "Claudia," he said again, pressing kisses against her forehead, temple, and cheeks. "Dear God, I've been so wretched and—and I love you so."

"Jem," she responded, almost unable to breathe for the intoxicating gladness that surged through her. Words became impossible then, as his mouth came down on hers, warm and tender and urgent.

For some time they remained thus, lost to the present until Claudia emerged from Jem's embrace, breathless and laughing.

"I think we had better go into the house, before I find my reputation compromised beyond redemption," she said, her eyes sparkling mischievously.

"Not," Jem replied, keeping her firmly in his grasp, "until you promise to marry me at the earliest opportunity."

At this, Claudia sat up very straight. "Oh! I had forgot for a moment." She continued haltingly. "You must marry for—"

"Advantage? Yes, well that's perfectly true, but I have been considering. If I can cozen you into marrying me, I shan't have to pay your wages anymore. With the money I'll save, I should be able to bring Ravencroft back to solvency in no time.'

"Jem, be serious." Her face had paled. "All the things you want to do for the estate—"

"Can wait," Jem interrupted again roughly. "I might restore Ravencroft to rival Blenheim Palace, but what good would it do me if you are not at my side? No, my love . . ." He stopped to avail himself of her willing lips once more and did not speak again for many moments. "It may take a little longer, but we will work together to make our home all that we want it to be. It's already a wonderful place to raise children, after all."

"That's true," she said softly, fingering the top button of Jem's waistcoat. Silence reigned in the little bower for another extended period of time before the two turned at last to make their way through the kitchen garden, arms entwined about each other's waists.

"Aunt Gussie will be pleased, but I wonder," said Claudia, her voice brimming with laughter, "what Thomas will have to say about this?"

"Ah," replied her beloved. "He will no doubt be somewhat taken aback at first, but when reason prevails—as far as it ever does with him—I rather fancy he will be enormously set up at your socially advantageous marriage. To say nothing of the fact that you will be again under the judicious guidance of a wise male. No more mucking out the stables in man's garb for you, my girl."

At the sound of her indrawn breath, Jem turned to her. "Unless, of course," he said, his eyes serious behind the lightness of his tone, "you have truly found fulfillment and pleasure in this task."

"Would you allow it, Jem? Truly?" Claudia held her breath waiting for his answer.

"Claudia, my very dearest love," he said slowly. "It is not for me to allow or not to allow. You are an intelligent woman. You love me and I love you, and our actions will, I hope, be governed by a consideration for each other's feelings, but in the end, you are responsible for your own actions, as am I, and accountable only to your own standards."

For an instant, Claudia went weak from the dizzying sense of wonder that swept over her, and with infinite tenderness, she traced his jawline with her fingertip.

"You know, my darling," she said in a voice so soft he strained to hear it, "I must have done something quite wonderful in the past to have found someone like you."

"I hate to disillusion you, my love," he replied with a shaky laugh, "but fellows like me are a ha'penny a hundred. Not," he added, "that I have any intention of disputing you."

She laughed again, and turning to face him, she placed her hands on either side of his face and pulled him to her for one more kiss, that was neither urgent nor demanding, but achingly sweet in its warmth. She had been engaged in this pleasurable activity for some moments when she became aware of someone calling her name.

She turned, and still in Jem's embrace, she observed Rose hurrying back toward them, her face working in agitation. In her arms, she clutched Rumple, who protested vociferously in outrage.

"Claudia!" she fairly shrieked. "What do you think you are doing?"

"I should think that would be perfectly obvious," Claudia replied calmly. She turned to smile at Jem. "I am kissing Jeremy Standish."

"I can see that," retorted Rose, very much out of patience and out of sorts. "What I want to know, is what is the meaning of it?" She sputtered incoherently for a moment. "Have you no regard for the proprieties?" she queried her sister in a tone of horrified outrage.

"You know I have not, Rose. However, you may wish us happy. Lord Glenraven and I are to be married."

"M-ma—" If anything, Rose became even more agitated. "Married! But what will Thomas say?"

"Oddly enough"—Jem laughed—"we were just discussing your husband's reaction."

"And we came to the conclusion," finished Claudia, "that it does not matter much what Thomas says."

"But," she quavered, "he will be furious!" She opened her mouth to say more, but abruptly closed it as her lips began to curve upward. "He will be absolutely livid," she continued in a unsteady voice. Suddenly, her shoulders quivered, and a small sound escaped her. Rumple slipped to the ground unnoticed, where he stood with Jem and Claudia watching his mistress in some astonishment as she clutched her sides in laughter. At length, she wiped her eyes and moved forward to embrace her sister.

"Indeed," she said, "I do wish you happy." Claudia flung

her arms out, and the two stood in mute closeness until Rose turned with a smile and a nod to continue on her way. Rumple followed, his plump little body bouncing and his tail awag.

Claudia returned to the encirclement of Jem's arms.

"Well," he murmured, pressing a kiss on her hair. "This continues to be a day of surprises. You know," he continued meditatively, "I rather begin to look forward to this dinner party."

Claudia tilted her head up to glance at him in some surprise.

"It will be the perfect opportunity to announce our betrothal, don't you think? I believe"—his face lit with a wicked grin—"I shall prevail upon Rose to keep our little secret until then. I would very much like to see Thomas's face when he receives the glad news."

Claudia chuckled. "I should imagine his expression will be somewhat similar to that of Squire Foster. I wonder," she continued innocently, "how the other neighbors will feel—Sir Wilfred Perrey, for example."

"Ah yes." The grin grew wider and more wicked. "He of the beauteous, wealthy daughter. I wonder if I am not making a mistake here." He fingered his chin thoughtfully.

She leaned back in his arms and favored him with a raised eyebrow. "I should be very careful if I were you, my good man," she said throatily. "I don't think you'll be wanting to trifle with Granny's curse." She waggled her fingers suggestively under his nose.

"Ah," Jem responded, unfazed. "I fancy I shall be much too busy trifling with Granny's granddaughter to worry about the curse."

Her ensuing laughter ended in a gasp of delight as Jem silenced his love with one more lingering kiss before leading her into the manor house.